Stolen Hearts

Books by Jane Tesh

The Madeline Maclin Series
A Case of Imagination
A Hard Bargain
A Little Learning

The Grace Street Mysteries
Stolen Hearts

Stolen Hearts

A Grace Street Mystery

Jane Tesh

Poisoned Pen Press

First Edition 2011

10 9 8 7 6 5 4 3 2 1

Library of Congress Catalog Card Number: 2011926965
ISBN: 9781590589373   Hardcover
         9781590589397   Trade Paperback

Poisoned Pen Press
6962 E. First Ave., Ste. 103
Scottsdale, AZ 85251
www.poisonedpenpress.com
info@poisonedpenpress.com

Printed in the United States of America

This book is dedicated in memory of my father,
Clyde E. Tesh, and in honor of our favorite band,
The New Black Eagles Jazz Band (www.blackeagles.com),
whose music continues to delight and inspire me.

Acknowledgments

Sometimes you feel your work is perfect just the way it is. That's when you need people to convince you change is possible. I would like to gratefully acknowledge Barbara Peters for placing me with Annette Rogers, whose suggestions made this story so much better (even though I didn't believe her at first! You were right, Annette. Thank you!). A special thanks to Ellen Larson for her continued belief in these characters, and to my family, my friends, and everyone at Poisoned Pen Press for their support and encouragement.

Chapter One

"I've Found a New Baby"

I didn't expect a murder to happen right down the street from my second wife's house, but then, I didn't expect a lot of things, including sleeping in my car. Admittedly, there's plenty of room in the back seat of a '67 Plymouth Fury, but October in Parkland, North Carolina, can be pretty steamy, even at dawn, so I was awake when the sirens and flashing lights came by.

My first wife, Barbara, and I parted ways two years ago. I really thought Anita and I might make it to our second anniversary—aluminum foil, I believe it is—but now that was another date I could scratch off the calendar. I'd parked outside my former home telling myself it was because Anita might relent and let me back in, but the real reason was I had nowhere else to go.

When I first heard the sirens, I was in that odd state of not quite awake not quite asleep, and my heart jumped, thinking I was back on that hillside twelve years ago searching for Lindsey through clouds of black smoke, not realizing my world was about to end. I shook myself as blue and red lights bounced off the interior of the Fury and zigzagged through the neighborhood like some crazed lightning. The eerie blue light made the trees look like they'd risen from some alien swamp and gave a zombie glow to the few curious neighbors who'd ventured from their houses. Car doors slammed. Shadowy figures ran and called to each other.

Lindsey! My God, where was she?

I shook myself fully awake. Get up! I told myself. This wasn't the wreck. This was something else, maybe something that needed my help. I wanted in on what was happening down the street.

When I arrived at the scene, my friend Jordan Finley, one of Parkland's homicide detectives, scowled at me.

"I saw that car of yours. What are you doing here?"

"I live down the street," I said. "Well, I used to."

Jordan spared me a brief look of sympathy. We'd worked together on several cases. Maybe "worked together" isn't the right term. When there's something like a dead body, I definitely call him, but there have been times when I fudged a little and kept clues to myself. Jordan likes to claim all the credit for solving a crime. I can't blame him. I like to claim all the credit, too. He's built like a refrigerator topped with a stiff brush of black hair and wary blue eyes. Right now, he was a refrigerator about to freeze over so you couldn't get the door open.

"And you just happened to be dressed and awake?"

"Anita threw me out, but never mind that." A body was brought out of the house on a stretcher, an elderly man in his pajamas. The bloodstains on his head looked black in the jarring patterns of blue and red light. "What happened here?"

"Albert Bennett was found murdered in his home. Did you know Mr. Bennett?"

I couldn't remember ever seeing anyone at this house. "No."

"Did you see or hear anything unusual last night?"

Besides my recurring nightmare? "No."

"Then you can move along."

Another policeman came up to Jordan and showed him a notebook. "Found this on the lawn. Doesn't appear to be anything else missing from the house."

The notebook had been mangled, and a few pages fell out. I managed to pick them up and have a look before Jordan grabbed them out of my hand. My brief glance had shown me what looked like music.

Jordan glared. "Do you mind?" He gave the pages back to the policeman. "What's inside?"

"Just some music notes and weird scribbling. Looks like code."

"Check it out."

The policeman left, and Jordan turned to me. "Heard you left Morton's."

"Yeah. I've got to go by and pick up a few things, but I'm done."

"Packing it in? Giving up being a detective?"

I wasn't sure what else I could do. "Morton's is a dead-end agency. I thought I'd give it a shot on my own, which is why I'd like in on this case."

Jordan signaled another policeman to move around to the other side of the house. "Doesn't look like much of a case. Someone broke in, possibly surprised Bennett, knocked him over the head and killed him, possibly by accident. Alarm goes off, they cut and run."

"Why would they be after a notebook?"

"That's what my team is going to find out."

"Does Mr. Bennett have any family?"

"That's something the police department will find out." Jordan gave me another look. "So, you got a place to stay?"

"Not at the moment."

"See if Cam's got a room."

"Yeah. Maybe."

I had one more friend left in the world, but did I really want to call him? He'd let me stay in his house. Camden lets anybody stay in his house. I called his goofball tenants the Sponge and Leech Club because, as far as I could tell, no one contributed a penny. The last time I was there, he was sheltering some old codger named Fred plus two factory workers who argued all the time and chased each other around the kitchen with a baseball bat and a water gun because one of them left the ice trays out. That was two years ago, when Anita and I were on the outs about something. I stayed for a week until I got tired of all the nonsense.

Until you got tired of avoiding Camden and his all-knowing stares, I reminded myself. I'm an only child and like to think of Camden as the brother I never had, but he's psychic, which sounds like a lot of fun, but most of the time it's damned annoying. He knew what my problem was. I knew what my problem was, too, and I didn't want to talk about it, or have Camden delve into my brain for the answers. In fact, I hadn't seen him in a long time. I kept telling myself it was because I was too busy.

It started to rain, and the inside of the Fury steamed up like a rain forest. I cranked up the air, and as soon as the windows were clear, I headed toward the nearest Motel 6. It takes about twenty minutes to navigate the one-way streets in town, crossing Smith and Elm to get to Regent, which is the main street going back out of the city. Plenty of time to rethink my life.

My life. What there was left of it. My life went off the rails when Lindsey died. Instead of clinging to each other, Barbara and I grew apart. We both blamed me for the accident. I bounced over to Anita. I don't know what I was thinking. It was vastly unfair to her, and to her credit, she figured out she couldn't fix me. I was useless.

But I wasn't going to be useless forever. I headed back to Albert Bennett's, hoping the crime scene team had finished and maybe I could look around, but no luck. The police cars were still there, the lights still shuddering through the neighborhood. I'd establish a base camp and come back later. I'd been jarred awake, not only from sleep, but from the dullness of my daily routine tracking deadbeat dads and cheating spouses. I wanted to solve this puzzling crime, a wealthy man with plenty of possessions, apparently murdered over a damn notebook. If I couldn't make Lindsey's life right, I sure as hell could avenge someone else's.

The situation called for a little mood music. At the next red light, I slid a CD into the player. I like traditional jazz, a preference from my early days when Dad played his favorite records during dinner and on into the evening. He liked The Dukes of Dixieland, a bunch of cheerful-looking guys in red and white striped jackets who tore into every tune so vigorously, it was impossible to sit still when the Dukes were rolling. Later, Dad and I progressed to the New Black Eagle Jazz Band, and that's what I had on now, specifically a zippy little number called "I've Found a New Baby." It helps me think. A burst of jazz makes my brain perk up, putting thoughts together like a run of notes along a staff.

But at the moment, my brain wasn't too perky. I pulled into the parking lot of the Motel 6 and looked at the drab building with its rows of dingy white doors, the empty beer cans, and plastic cups piled on the curb. I caught a strong whiff of rotten garbage from the overflowing Dumpster. The spluttering neon sign said "No Vacancy." I slumped in the car, trying not to see my life as a long row of large doors slamming in my face. There were hundreds of motels in Parkland. I'd keep sleeping in the Fury if I had to. Either way, it was clear that I needed refreshments.

The nearest convenience store was a little shop called Joe's Market just across the street. I found several packs of the fluorescent orange peanut butter crackers I like and was heading to the back for the beer when to my disbelief, Camden came up the aisle carrying a six-pack of Bud.

"Thought you might need this," he said.

As usual, he looked like he'd slept in his clothes. His pale hair was in his eyes, and his shirt was buttoned crooked. He had on baggy white trousers and a black vest decorated with iridescent hummingbirds, probably pulled from the depths of some Goodwill bag. Like me, he's fast approaching the big three-oh, but he looks years younger, because he's not very tall and has features women call "cute," and big blue eyes. Anita once told me women go for expressive eyes and that Camden's were "beautiful." She told me mine were nice, too, but that was an afterthought. Mine are brown and I can see out of them. That's all I care about.

And I wasn't really sure what I was seeing out of my brown eyes. I guess I shouldn't have been surprised. "You frequent Joe's Market this time of day?"

"Sometimes. What's up?"

You tell me, I wanted to say. I knew he wasn't buying beer for himself. He has absolutely no tolerance for alcohol. A couple of sips and he's up on a table entertaining the troops, which is what he was doing when we met. There's something about sharing massive hangovers that creates a lifelong bond.

A bond that was scary right now.

"I've been pretty busy," I said. "Tracking down people, finding things. Anita decided she'd had enough of me, so I'm checking into a motel for the night."

He gave me the full force of those eerie blue eyes. "Well, I'm glad I ran into you. I need a ride home."

He said this with complete innocence. I knew he didn't drive. Too many signals coming in, he says.

"Yeah, sure."

I paid for my crackers, and Camden paid for the beer. We got into the Fury and I steered the car back toward the south side of town. After passing the community college and the coliseum, I turned back on Old Parkland Road, also known as "Food Row." Every town has one of these streets lined with fast food restaurants, but our Food Row has a median filled with magnolia trees, and when those trees are in bloom, the heavy flower scent mixed with the smell of burgers and fries is a heady combination. Then up three streets, and it's as if you've entered an entirely different city: calm, quiet, and green. It used to be the wealthy part of town, before all the rich folks moved to the suburbs, leaving their massive old homes hidden beneath ancient trees.

Camden's house is on Grace Street, number 302. It's a big three-storied house painted light yellow with white trim. It must have been quite a showplace in its day, but now, like all the houses in the neighborhood, it's sliding gracefully into old age. Because it's surrounded by even older trees, even when the sun is at its brightest, the house is still sunk in shade. There's a wide porch that goes around three sides complete with rocking chairs and a porch swing. When Camden came to Parkland, he lived there and helped the man who owned the house remodel it, making four bedrooms, each with its own bathroom, on the second floor, and another bedroom and bath out of the large attic. They worked out some sort of deal that if Camden kept up the house, he could live there. When the man moved on to other projects, he sold Camden the house. In order to keep it, Camden has to take in boarders, but, as I said, they usually aren't very helpful.

I parked the Fury in the dirt driveway. "Here you go."

"Thanks," he said. "Why don't you come in and have one of your beers?"

I was tired and thirsty and not ready to continue my motel hunt. "I guess I could do that. Just for a little while, though."

We walked up the wide stone steps. Camden opened the screen door, and we went in.

"Have a seat, Randall. I'll be right back."

I had to admit it was a relief to come into the house. Everything looked the same as it did two years ago. The smell was the same, too, a pleasant mixture of old wood and cinnamon. The living room sprawled over most of the first floor, windows reaching from floor to ceiling. I walked around to the left and sat down in my favorite spot, a faded blue armchair beside a green corduroy sofa parked on brightly colored throw rugs. This area was referred to as "the island," a kind of relaxing place where you could leave your book open and no one would turn a page, or leave your drink by your chair and no one would take a slurp. I pulled off my wet shoes and socks and propped my feet on the low wooden coffee table where a bag of pretzels shared space with stacks of magazines, including *Sky Watchers Monthly* and *UFO Reporter*, a couple of necklaces, and a glass paperweight shaped like a pear holding down a stack of coupons. Beside the wicker rocking chair, red and yellow yarn spilled out of a big basket of needlework. Next to another chair, textbooks and sheet music stood in a sloppy tower, topped by a well-chewed pet toy.

I glanced to my left. The old upright piano still filled the corner of the room, surrounded by music and hymn books on the floor and on the bench. A couple of big plants in tubs guarded the bookshelf crammed with books, knickknacks, and photographs. Toward the back of the room, a large round dining room table and eight matching chairs were still positioned in front of the bay window that displayed a scene of wet green backyard and more huge trees. I knew if I walked around the dining area, I'd find a counter and stools and a kitchen tucked in behind the stairs.

Camden came back carrying a large plastic cup that no doubt held a mixture of the most caffeine-laden sodas on the market. He indicated the bag of pretzels. "Free snacks."

"Thanks." I popped open a beer and took a swig.

He sat cross-legged on the green corduroy sofa. He didn't ask for details about my latest marriage disaster. He didn't have to. He took a drink of his soda. "How are things at Morton's?"

"The same." I loosened my tie. "Going to start my own agency."

"Got someplace in mind?"

"Not yet."

"You need an office? You can use the downstairs parlor there across the foyer."

I started to tell him I needed to find a place more private when a young woman came in. This girl was a knockout. Long corn-silk blonde hair held back by a headband framed a perfect face dominated by big warm brown eyes. Her long elegant legs were in tight jeans, the rest of her excellent figure in a soft yellow sweater. My mouth flopped open, but Camden wasn't fazed by this vision.

"Oh, hello." She gave me such a dazzling smile I checked my beer to make sure it wasn't foaming over. "I'm Kary Ingram."

I was surprised my voice worked. "David Randall."

"Randall will be staying here a few days," Camden said.

Another smile. "Nice to meet you, David. I hope the piano playing won't disturb you."

She could've played the tuba for all I cared. "I love piano music."

Her golden hair swung in a sleek wave as she turned to Camden. "Cam, about what we discussed earlier."

"It has to be your decision."

"Donnie's a wonderful person."

"Seems like a good guy."

"But am I doing this for the right reasons?"

"That's something you'll have to work out."

"That's true. Have you seen my *Elements of Education* textbook?"

"It's on the kitchen counter."

Kary went around to retrieve her book. "Kary's taking classes for her teaching degree at Parkland Community College," Camden said.

That was not the important info. "And who is Donnie?"

"A fellow she met at the college."

Damn. "Are they in a serious relationship?"

"Well, he is."

Kary came back and picked up a book bag propped beside the piano bench. "And if you'll excuse me, I'm on my way to class. Will we see you at dinner, David?"

"Yes, you will." I hadn't planned to stay, but there was no way I was refusing this angel's request. My spirits took a definite upswing. She was so full of life and energy and purpose, everything I wanted to be again. Was it only a few hours ago I stood surrounded by jittery police lights, haunted by death? The harrowing scene faded in the warmth of her smile. But what was the deal with this Donnie character, and how soon could I dispose of him?

When a car drove up and the driver honked the horn, the sound jarred me from my tangled thoughts.

Kary looked out one of the front windows. "There's my ride. See you later."

I stared at Camden, who settled back innocently on the sofa with his drink. "Don't tell me she's living here, too."

"Working her way through school on pageant money."

"You liar. You dirty old man," I said. "Any more like her upstairs?"

"Fred's still here, and Rufus Jackson. You remember him. He's doing construction work on the new stretch of I-85. That leaves a room for you."

"Any of them pay rent?"

This earned me a dark look. "They do what they can to help out."

"In other words, no." I took a drink of beer and reached for the pretzels. "How long has Kary been living here? I would've remembered her."

"Off and on the past year."

"How old is she? Do her parents know she's living here?"

"Kary's got some issues with her parents. That's why she's here. I know she looks young, but she's twenty-four. She has one more year to go at the community college to get her teaching degree. She had some health problems that sidelined her for quite a while. Don't get any ideas."

"Ideas? Who's got any ideas?"

"Well, for starters, you can roll your tongue back in. You're getting drool all over my rug."

I flipped him a friendly finger and took another swig of beer. "How serious is she about Donnie?"

"As I said, he's more serious than she is."

"Are they engaged?"

"Nope."

"Best news I've heard all day." A gray cat slid in from the kitchen and wound its way through the chairs. Then it leaped to the top of the sofa and curled itself around Camden's neck.

"This is Cindy. Another stray." The cat gave him a long green-eyed stare. He patted her head. "Okay, I'll take care of it."

"I'm not going to believe you can read the cat."

He scratched Cindy behind her ears. "Only when she lets me."

Cindy leaped gracefully to the coffee table, sniffed the open bag of pretzels, and gave me an unwavering green stare. Then she jumped down and ran from the room.

Camden grinned. "What did you say to her?"

"What did she say to me is the question."

He gave me one of his power stares. "So how long do you want to stay?"

"I'll stay tonight, thanks, but that's all," I told Camden. "And turn down the high beams, will you? I don't want you in my brain."

"But it's so nice and roomy in there."

"Ha. I see your comedic skills haven't improved."

"'Comedic.' That's good."

"Give credit to my Word-A-Day calendar." I put my feet down and heaved myself out of the chair. "I mean it, Camden. Don't start."

He took another drink. "Okay."

I retrieved my belongings, went up the worn stairs to the second floor, and stopped in the doorway of the bedroom. I remembered this room: a calm shade of green with a big four-poster bed, green bedspread, green curtains, a chunky dresser with an oval mirror, a closet, and a small bathroom, also green. I stepped in and put my suitcase on the bed. The room smelled pleasantly of rain and old wood. I took a look out the wide window at the backyard, more large oak trees and a hedge full of ivy. Rain beat a steady rhythm on the thick leaves of the trees and on the uneven metal gutters. At least it wasn't one of the violent thunderstorms we often had in the summer. That was another thing I'd gotten used to in the south.

Camden couldn't afford air conditioning, but there was a large fan by the window in case the room got too stuffy. Thanks to the rain shower, the room was cool, though, and slightly damp. I thought about unpacking my suitcase, hanging a few clothes in the closet, putting other things in the dresser drawers. I'd have to retrieve the rest of my wardrobe later, when Anita was away. I could probably find it on the lawn right now.

Tomorrow, I'd start looking for an apartment. I wasn't going to stay here.

I peeled off my suit and put on drier clothes. Camden could get away with the refugee poet look. I like a little more class. I combed my hair and decided I didn't look too old for Kary. Six years wasn't that big a gap, was it?

Chapter Two

"All the Fair Ladies"

I went downstairs and found Camden with another good-looking young woman, damn it. This one had short bouncy blonde curls, blue eyes, and a nice figure in a light blue power suit. She looked good, but she had a definite whine in her voice and a glare in her eyes. Whoever she was, she was severely pissed. Camden was still on the sofa, and the blonde was in the blue armchair, leaning forward in an attack position. She'd stopped talking when I came into the living room and cut those blue eyes toward me as if she'd caught my hand where it wasn't supposed to be.

Camden looked relieved by the interruption. "Randall, this is Ellin Belton. Ellie, my friend, David Randall."

She gave me the full force of that killer glare and a slight nod. "Nice to meet you."

I'll stick with Kary, I thought as I walked past them to the kitchen. "Nice to meet you, too. Go right ahead. I want to see what's in the fridge." Their voices carried clearly.

Camden sounded calm, with a slightly steely tone. "I've told you, I'm not interested."

"But this is good news, Cam. I'm on my way to WPKD. We go on the air tomorrow at midnight. It's not an ideal time slot, but it's a start."

Camden used to work for the Psychic Service here in town. I'd heard something about the group recently launching their own cable TV show.

"That's great," Camden said. "I'll be sure to watch."

"I want you to do more than watch. I want you to be a guest."

"I appreciate the offer, but you know I can't."

"Nothing drastic. Just tell about your experiences. I think this would be perfect. Everyone knows how good you are. You could add a lot to the program."

Which meant he could add respectability. Most of the so-called psychics who worked for the service are spacey-looking people, well-trained in the correct responses. Camden's the genuine article, possibly the only one. But the last thing he wants to do is flaunt it.

"Ellie, if I go on TV, I'll be swamped with requests. You know I've retired from the service."

"I know you need money. This house must cost a fortune to keep up, and all these deadbeats don't help."

"No, thanks. I wish you all the success in the world, but I really think you can do the show without me."

She kept her tone sweet. "Of course, but I'd rather do the show with you."

Camden wasn't fooled. He tried to divert her. "Why don't you ask Reg? He's good, and he's a lot more photogenic."

I'd seen Reg Haverson, a sleek preppie type who wouldn't look out of place in a Sears catalog modeling the latest suits.

Ellin refused to be diverted. "Haverson's a media hog. He'd want to take over the whole show."

"I'm really not interested."

"Well, you might be interested in the big PBS special about music that's going to be filmed here. I'm going to get in on it, and you'd be perfect, Cam."

"What, as the Singing Psychic? No, thanks."

"You think about it."

Camden didn't promise anything. Ellin said good-by and hurried out. I came around the corner. "She seems nice."

"If there's an angle, she'll find it." He pushed his hair out of his eyes. "She can be a little intense, but she's the one."

"Really?"

"I'm afraid so."

I gave him a Deep Look of my own.

"I know, I know," he said. "But I've been dreaming about her for years. What can I say?"

"You'll say yes to whatever she wants. I'm heading back to Morton's. He's supposed to have a paycheck for me."

He gave me one of his power gazes that in earlier times would have gotten him condemned as a witch. It felt as if my brain has become a Rolodex, cards flipping as he read my inner thoughts. "I think your luck's about to change."

"You see a wealthy client coming my way?"

"A client. I'm not sure if she's wealthy."

◇◇◇

I drove to Morton's Detective Agency on Coronation Avenue. Coronation Avenue isn't much of an avenue, and Morton's isn't much of an agency. We specialized in finding runaway spouses who don't want to be returned, deadbeat dads who don't want to pay child support—those sorts of fine upstanding citizens. Nothing your average community watch or crime stoppers TV program couldn't solve. I spent most of my time on the computer and on the phone, tracking people through driver's license bureaus, airline reservations, relatives who hated them, and other ridiculously simple sources. The other investigators spent a lot of time camped out in our dingy waiting room drinking coffee, playing poker, placing fantasy bets on sporting events, and wondering why they didn't get a better class of clientele.

Those days are over, I told myself as I got out of my car. I climbed two flights of stairs and pushed open the door. An investigator was sprawled asleep on the cracked leather sofa with a newspaper over his face. Morton's office door was closed. I knocked and went in.

"Got a paycheck for me?"

My soon-to-be ex-boss scowled. Imagine one of those Disney pictures where all the inanimate objects come to life. Gordon Morton would be the cranky but lovable bowling ball. "Gordon Morton"—can you believe it? What were his parents thinking?

"Sit down for a minute, Randall."

I took the metal folding chair opposite the desk. Aside from his P.I. license, which must be written on papyrus, Mort didn't have much in the way of decoration. There was a dead plant on top of the filing cabinet, a stack of faded magazines in the corner, and a football trophy he used to prop up the window.

Randall, I told myself, this is your life. Unless you do something drastic, you're going to end up just like Mort. Get out. Get out now.

Mort screwed up his small features. "You sure you want to do this? Leave the agency? You got a real talent for finding things."

"I'm tired of following people who don't want to be married anymore. Maybe if we'd gotten some real clients with real cases. I think it's time for me to be on my own."

Mort straightened the papers on his desk. 'Well, don't expect me to take you back if you get in over your head and can't finish whatever jobs you might find out there. Paycheck's on your desk. Don't spend it all in one place."

For the last time, I went to my office. My closet, I should say. An industrial gray closet. I had considered hanging out here until I found an apartment, but there was barely room for the desk, a chair for me, a chair for nonexistent clients, and the battered filing cabinet a family of elderly mice were using for a retirement condo. I looked out the small window at the rain falling on the gray street and into the gray trash cans and had a sudden image of the view from Camden's front parlor window, all trees and grass and quiet neighborhood street. I imagined Kary coming home from work, and I'd be right there to meet her. We'd sit on the porch and talk about her day. Then while I cooked dinner, she'd play the piano. We'd watch TV in the island, talk about our dreams and plans and maybe even a family—stop, I told myself. No more fantasy. You had a family. You had the perfect family, and it all went to pieces. You're not going through that again. You can't.

I put the paycheck in my pocket and went back down the stairs to my car. Just as I was unlocking the door, a red Honda pulled into the place next to me, and a woman with long light brown hair called from her window.

"Excuse me. Could you tell me where I could find Morton's Detective Agency?"

"It's on the second floor of this building." On impulse, I added, "But I think they're closed for the day. Maybe I could help you." I dug out my ID. "My name's David Randall, and I'm a licensed private investigator."

She checked my ID and then looked me up and down. Apparently she liked what she saw. "I have kind of an unusual problem."

"Then you don't want Morton's. They're strictly deadbeat dads and cheating spouses."

"Oh, it's nothing like that."

Seize the moment! "I have an office on Grace Street, if you'd like to stop by."

She thought it over. "I might do that."

"302 Grace. You can follow me if you like."

"All right."

I got back into the Fury and gave the woman a little friendly wave. As I started back toward Camden's, I grabbed my cell phone and punched in his number.

"About that parlor," I said. "It needs to look like an office in about twenty minutes."

◇◇◇

I'm not sure what had been in the parlor before, but by the time I got back to Camden's house, he'd managed to make the room look like someone worked there. There was a small but nicely polished desk and swivel chair by the window, a chair for my soon-to-be-the-first client, some papers and pencils. I set my laptop on the desk and went back to hold the screen door for the woman. I gave her a closer inspection as she passed. She had a serene, serious air, as if she were the queen of a small but important country. She wore a long denim skirt and a bulky sweater decorated with farm animals with those little plastic swirly eyes. Slim legs piqued my interest about the rest of her figure. Her face was slender with brown eyes under well-plucked brows, a long nose, and lips that were just full enough.

"Please come in. Have a seat."

"Thank you." She sat down in the chair. "I'm Melanie Gentry."

I sat down in the swivel chair. "How can I help you, Ms. Gentry?"

"I'd like to talk to you about my great-grandmother."

"How long has she been missing?"

"She's been dead for sixty years. But I need help proving she was not a thief."

Great. A sixty-year-old robbery. Bound to be dozens of clues. My expression must have given away this thought.

"I know you're thinking it's ridiculous to try to solve a mystery that's so old, and I suppose I could live with it, except I know the truth, and I know my great-grandmother would've wanted the truth to be known."

"And the truth is?"

She leaned forward, hands clasped in her lap. "My great-grandmother, Laura Gentry, is the one and only author of *Patchwork Melodies*, the definitive collection of folksongs from the Appalachian Mountains. Those songs were stolen from her, and the credit has gone to John Barrows Ashford."

I know nearly as much about folksongs as I do about ballet dancing, but when Melanie Gentry mentioned songs I flashed on the torn pages I'd seen from the murdered Albert Bennett's notebook. The policeman said his notebook contained music notes and weird scribbling. Was it possible there was a connection?

"Do you have any proof the songs were stolen, Ms. Gentry?"

She dug into her shoulder bag. "I have all my great-grandmother's letters." She heaped an untidy pile of paper on my desk.

"She and Ashford were lovers. They agreed to share everything. But he became greedy and wanted the credit. They say she fell into the river, but I think it was no accident. Then he claimed he had written all the songs himself."

I picked up a faded love letter to "Dearest John," signed "Your loving Laura." "Ms. Gentry, if this is true, why have you waited so long to tell anyone?"

"A man named Kendal Robertson is planning a major documentary for PBS on early American music along the lines of Ken Burns' Civil War series," she said. "They'll feature folk songs from this area. Ashford will get all the credit, and I can't bear the thought of that."

"Have you approached John Ashford about this?"

"Oh, he's dead, too, and his great-grandson, Byron, refuses to see me. I tried to get the police involved, but they say I don't have enough real evidence. As far as they're concerned, Laura Gentry drowned in 1929, and that's the end of it."

I pulled a limp songbook from the pile. The cover had faded flowers and a title in white: "Flowering Tree" by John Burrows Ashford and Laura Gentry. "Your great-grandmother's name is on this music."

"That's probably the last copy. There will be new copies of all the songs, only without my great-grandmother's name. Byron Ashford will see to that. He thinks Laura stole from his great-grandfather and caused his death. Right now, it's his word against mine."

"Is there anyone else alive who knew both of them? With a case this old, I'm not sure where to start."

Melanie Gentry came prepared. "I have some names for you." She pulled out another piece of paper. "I work at Charles Park University, and Tate Thomas, a music professor there, could help you, and Harmon Lassiter is a retired folk musician who lives in Oakville, Ashford's hometown. He didn't want to talk to me, but he might be willing to talk to you. And there should be some women at Shady Oaks Retirement Home who knew Laura."

I took the piece of paper. "Okay, I'll see what I can do."

She smiled. "Thank you, Mister Randall."

"One other thing, Ms. Gentry. Did your great-grandmother or Ashford know an Albert Bennett or his family?"

She frowned. "No, I've never heard of Albert Bennett. Do you think he had something to do with this?"

"I'll look into it."

She stood and offered me her hand. "Thanks again. I've been everywhere, and no one wanted to help me. You were my last hope."

When I worked for Morton's, I often joked that he should call his place the Last Resort Detective Agency, because we were last on everyone's list. Now I had assumed that dubious honor.

"Glad to help."

Another dip into the bottomless bag. Melanie Gentry pulled out a wad of bills. "Here's three hundred dollars. I'm not sure it's enough, but it's all I have right now."

Three hundred dollars was more cash than I'd seen in a long time. I carefully straightened the pile of bills. "I'll get right on it."

She gave me another grateful smile. I escorted her out, pleased with the way today was progressing. I had a client and three hundred dollars.

And an office.

I stood in the doorway, wondering if I could make this work. I didn't waste much time soul-searching. Instead, I went through all the Bennetts in the phone book, hoping to find a relative of the murdered man, but every Bennett I called was not related to him. Then I had an idea. The contacts Melanie Gentry had given me might know more about Bennett. I could solve the Bennett case from another angle, beating Jordan at his game and improving my detective credibility.

Tate Thomas' secretary said he was out of the office and wouldn't be back until tomorrow. I made an appointment to speak with him. Harmon Lassiter didn't answer his phone, and the message on Byron Ashford's said he was in the Bahamas and would not be in Parkland until later in the week.

Next, I read Laura Gentry's letters to John Ashford. The first few were chatty and full of endearments. Then "Dearest John" became just "John" as the letters became more and more frantic, begging to see him, questioning his whereabouts, and accusing him of stealing her music. I looked up Ashford and *Patchwork Melodies* on my computer and found a list of his songs and a brief biography. Laura Gentry was mentioned only as his lover who died in a tragic accident. The online *Parkland Herald* account of Albert Bennett's murder included a picture from his notebook. Bennett's handwritten notation looked like worms, little curls and squiggles. Then I called Jordan and asked if he could tell me any more about Albert Bennett.

"I won't be taking any of your glory if you tell me what your people think about the writing in the notebook," I said.

Jordan must have been in a good mood. "We think it's some kind of private or experimental music code."

"Is it worth anything?"

"If it is, nobody's come forward to explain why."

"Nothing else was missing from his house?"

"Yep, a pretty clumsy job. Looks like Bennett surprised the thief. The intruder hits Bennett on the head, takes his notebook, and then drops it in the yard. A house full of antiques, jewelry, paintings, all ignored."

"Anything else you can tell me?"

"Nope." Jordan hung up.

I went looking for Camden to thank him for the quick office makeover and found him in the kitchen, spooning vanilla ice cream into a large bowl.

"Use it as long as you like." He offered me the ice cream carton, but I declined.

"It was great for today, but I need some place a little more private."

"Nobody's here during the day. Fred goes to the park. Rufus goes to work. Kary will be at the college, and I have a part-time salesclerk job at Tamara's Boutique."

"Tamara?" I'd met her before. "Tamara Eldridge? Dynamite brunette?"

"That's right."

"As I recall, she's sweet and kind and nice and doesn't try to push you into doing things you don't want to do."

"That's her. Plus I do carpentry work." He closed the ice cream carton and put it back in the freezer. "Cabinets, shelves, things like that. Every now and then someone hires me to refinish a table or build a TV stand."

"So definitely no more Psychic Service, no matter how many blondes beg and plead."

"That's about it. You can have a room and an office space for a very reasonable rate."

And I'd be in the same house as Kary Ingram.

Camden grinned as if he'd heard that thought, and he probably had. "After my snack, I've got to check on the neighbors' house. I'm bringing in the mail while they're on vacation. Why don't you sit on the porch and think about it?"

Chapter Three

"The Deceived Girl"

I couldn't remember if I'd had lunch, and I didn't want to raid Camden's pantry, so I got some of my orange peanut butter crackers and took them out to the front porch. October in Minnesota, where I grew up, consisted of two days of fall color if we were lucky, immediately followed by snow and ice. Even though it was late afternoon, the sky still beamed a rich clear blue and the trees sparkled gold and red. Fallen leaves swirled in the warm breeze. Squirrels chased each other around the tree trunks and up into the branches.

I sat down in one of the rocking chairs. Everything was peaceful and comfortable, but it wasn't what I wanted. I wanted my life to be the way it was before. I wanted to find the one thing I knew I couldn't find. Since my life would never be the same, and my dearest possession was gone, I'd better consider myself damn lucky to have found a place to stay and at least one friend I could still count on.

"Hello, David," a voice called from the hedge between Camden's house and the one next door. "Is Cam there?"

Lily Wilkes emerged from the foliage, her cotton-white hair poking out wildly from beneath a round straw hat decorated with plastic cherries. Lily must have the worst fashion sense in Parkland. Her choices today included a yellow parka over purple long johns, green socks, clunky sandals, and a clear crystal like the tooth of some prehistoric cat dangling from a leather string around her neck. She was carrying a wooden box.

"Sorry, Lily, you just missed him."

Lily hopped up the porch steps. "Shucks. I wanted him to feel these crystals." She cocked her head. Despite her weird clothes, Lily is very attractive in a spacey elf sort of way. "You look like you could use a crystal, David. Let me see what I've got for you."

She sat down in a rocking chair and opened the lid. Light caught on little spears of white, blue, pink, and purple.

I picked up one of the purple ones. "Those are nice. Where'd you get them?"

Lily hugged the box. "Oh, I couldn't tell you. These are special. I'm going to make some jewelry for the festival."

Parkland's annual Falling Leaves Festival is always held in October. It's a huge week-long street fair, crafts and food, musicians, tourists, the perfect excuse for anyone who thinks he's an artist to display wares along the sidewalks. People come from all over North Carolina, swelling Parkland's population to well over its usual two hundred thousand. One visit to the mass of humanity struggling to purchase metal wind chimes and ham biscuits had been enough for me. Maneuvering around town during Falling Leaves is an exercise in frustration. Trying to get a pizza delivered is hell. If you went anywhere near the center of town, your eardrums would be assailed with the worst bluegrass imaginable. Anyone with true musical talent would be light-years away.

Speaking of light-years, back to Lily.

"Did you get a booth?" Space was at a premium on Main Street.

She nodded, the cherries on her hat bouncing. "I am so lucky. Margery and Clark said I could have a corner of their table."

"Margery and Clark?"

"Two members of the ASG."

ASG stands for Abductees Support Group. Despite Camden's assurance that they've never been off the planet, Lily and her pals swear they've been abducted by aliens, not once, but many times. Lily has even told me her white hair is the result of alien experiments. That I can almost believe.

She rooted in the box. "Well, there was a very nice yellow one in here somewhere. Yellow's good for soothing your aura."

I tried to keep a straight face. "Does my aura need soothing?"

She gave me a long, serious look. "I sensed it the minute I saw you." She found the crystal she was looking for and handed it to me. It was clear with a faint yellow tint.

"Thanks."

"I put silver caps on all of them so you can hang it around your neck." She peered deeply into my eyes. "You want something, David. You won't be content until you have it."

"I think that could be said about everyone." Cute as she is, Lily was beginning to get on my nerves.

"This crystal will help you realize your dreams. Wear it in good health."

"Thank you very much."

She closed the box. "If I leave these with you, will you please tell Cam to check them?"

"Sure. What's he supposed to find?"

"Well, I don't want any with disruptive vibrations. Some could have been owned by bad people, you know. Some could have survived earthquakes. Some could have opposing minerals."

"That could hurt."

Lily always takes me seriously. "Especially if one's psyche is fragile. I won't need them back until the festival, so he can take his time." She set the box in another rocking chair and peered at me from under her absurd hat. "Are you going to find Cam's parents?"

The question took me by surprise. "It's not something we've discussed."

"Well, I think it would be a very good idea."

"Why? Has he said something to you about it?"

"I sense these things, as you know, and I feel Cam has a real identity crisis."

If there's anyone who knows what he wants out of life, it's Camden. He wants a home, a family, and, God knows why, he wants Ellin Belton. "I think you might be mistaken there, Lily."

She shook her fluffy head. Cherries flopped. "I've consulted the Tarot several times about this, and every time, I reach the same conclusion. Cam needs to know who he is. It's hampering his ability to grow as a person."

Camden has to be the calmest, most levelheaded person I know. "What makes you say that? He seems fine to me."

"He's denying his true self because he doesn't know who he is."

If there's anything I hate worse than UFO crap, it's amateur psychology. "Let's leave him the way he is, okay, Lily? If he wants me to find his parents, he'll say so."

She didn't look convinced. "Well, all right, but it's certainly something you should consider. After all, you can find them, can't you, David?"

I looked at her pixie face with its serious expression. I didn't need this today. "I'd give it my best shot."

"Would you? Would you, really? You're not too busy?"

I pulled a wry face. "Busy?"

She was immediately apologetic. "Guess things haven't been going too well, have they? I'm sorry."

"I'm sure things will pick up."

She got up and touched the yellow crystal in my hand. "This will help you."

"Can't hurt."

"Really. You have to believe, David, that's all it takes. I want you to consider finding Cam's folks."

"Well, what if I find them and they're horrible people? What if they come around and make a lot of trouble, ever think of that?"

"How could Cam's parents be horrible?"

"Their eyes could be on stalks."

She took two steps back and hugged her arms. "Don't say that!"

It's way too easy to tease her. "Just kidding. You know Camden thinks he's an alien."

She kept her distance. "Of course he does. Wouldn't you, if you didn't know where you came from, and you had all these amazing powers?"

"A lot of people are psychic. It's nothing that amazing."

"Not like Cam. I think his parents must be remarkable."

"I'll let you know when their saucer lands."

Lily shook her head, exasperated. A few cherries fell off her hat and tumbled over the edge of the porch. "Don't forget to use your crystal. Just believe, that's all it takes." She hopped back down the porch steps and disappeared through the hedge.

No, Sugar, it takes a little more than a piece of sparkly glass.

Cindy the cat came up the steps and hopped into the rocking chair. She sniffed the box of crystals and turned up her nose.

"I think you've got the right idea," I told her. "If it ain't edible, it's useless."

◇◇◇

I drove over to Food Row and bought a newspaper. When I came back into 302 Grace Street, again, despite my frustration at my current situation, I felt the same sense of peace when I walked in the house. Cindy was dozing on the back window seat in a pool of sunlight. The floorboards creaked slightly, but she didn't wake up. I could hear the ticking of the cow-shaped clock in the kitchen and the slight rustling of the oak leaves as they fell.

I stood in the parlor doorway, debating what to do. Finally, I went back to the porch and looked through the ads for apartments for rent. Most of the places were too expensive. Several were way out of town. I halfheartedly circled a few addresses and phone numbers, realizing the source of my indecisiveness was a certain attractive young woman who'd been in my thoughts since the moment I met her. Like one of my favorite jazz songs said, I'd found a new baby, but I had to find the best way to approach her. Better concentrate on other problems. As I closed the paper, something on the front page caught my attention.

"Smithsonian Director Found Dead in Office. Valuable Music Destroyed."

What?

I quickly read the whole story. A member of the Smithsonian staff had been killed last night and several folders filled with music were scattered in the hallway. Officials were trying to determine exactly what, if anything, had been stolen, but many of the fragile papers had been trampled. Washington police suspected the murder was a possible diversion while thieves broke into other sections of the museum, but this could not be confirmed.

Albert Bennett had been killed yesterday over a notebook full of old music. Melanie Gentry's great-grandmother might have been killed over old music. And now a third person murdered over old music.

What was going on? What were the murderers looking for?

I went into the office and went online for more details of the Smithsonian crime.

The murder victim was an assistant director in the antiquities department. He'd been working late and had forgotten to set the alarm on his hallway. Like Bennett, he'd been struck over the head and killed. The music folders had American folk music from the early 1800s up to the 1920s, and many pieces had been crushed and damaged beyond repair. No one was yet certain if anything was missing, but there was concern that some of the pieces may have been by Stephen Foster.

I'd studied Foster in elementary school, so I knew he was a writer of classic American folk songs such as "I Dream of Jeannie," "Camptown Races," and "Oh! Susanna." The paragraph in the newspaper referred to Foster as "The father of American music, the most popular composer of the nineteenth century."

The same time period as Laura Gentry's music. The same time period of this new PBS documentary Melanie mentioned. I didn't know a lot about folk music, but I did know anything by Stephen Foster was likely to be quite valuable. Is that what Bennett had in his notebook? But someone at the police department would've recognized a Foster tune, wouldn't they?

I called Jordan to make sure.

Jordan sounded even more irritated than usual. "Nothing that even vaguely resembles music here, Randall, and I believe we agreed you weren't involved with this."

A car pulled into the driveway. The sight of Kary set my pulse into double time. I quickly told Jordan good-by and closed my phone. She slid gracefully out of her friend's car, waved good-by, and came up the walk.

Maybe she'd like a drink. I ran around to the kitchen, grabbed the first soda I could reach, and I met her at the door. "I was just coming out to sit on the porch for a while. Care for a soda?"

"Thanks very much."

As she took the can, our fingers touched. I felt a tingle down to my socks and was intrigued to see a faint blush on her cheeks. "How was your day?"

"Pretty good. And yours?"

Improving at a fantastic rate. "Not bad. I've got a couple of cases going."

Now there was definitely interest in her eyes. "Anything you can talk about?"

"Sure. Have a seat."

We took seats in the rocking chairs on the porch. Kary put her book bag beside her chair. I noticed a little sparkly pinwheel, a roll of pink ribbon, and a bunch of artificial pink roses sticking out of the top of the bag.

"Are you working on a class project?"

She glanced down at her bag. "No, that's for something else."

The way she said it made me feel that matter was closed, and the sudden stillness in her face made me wonder if I'd said something wrong. But I thought I recognized this stillness. It was something I knew, but couldn't quite explain. Then her liveliness was back. Her smile was so radiant, I wasn't sure I could breathe. Her brown eyes gazed at me warmly. "Tell me about yourself. Cam says you're a detective and you might have your agency here."

I couldn't believe I said no. She looked so interested. What would it be like to have her as a partner? To sit in the island with her every night and discuss all those fantastic cases I was certain to solve? "No, I don't want to disturb the other boarders. I'm going to look for an office closer to downtown."

Dare I believe she seemed disappointed? "Oh, well, that's understandable. Did you always want to be a detective?"

"I thought I might own my own bar, like my dad, until I got tired of listening to everyone's troubles." Then I thought I'd be a father, and that didn't work out.

"You don't have a southern accent. I'm guessing you're not from here."

"Minnesota," I said. "I grew up in a tiny little southwestern town called Elbert Falls, population six hundred and eighty-four, location: nowhere. Actually, it was next to nowhere. The nearest town was Pond, Minnesota, population two hundred and thirty. Pond existed solely to make Elbert Falls feel like a grand metropolis."

"So you don't miss it."

"Not at all. It was cold. It was dull. It was eternally windy. I like that Parkland has four distinct seasons. Is Parkland your hometown?"

I wanted to ask her why she lived here. I wanted to know why she'd been sick, and if she was all right. I wanted to know a lot of things that had to wait.

"I grew up here." She immediately turned the conversation back to me. "How did you end up in Parkland?"

"I got a scholarship to the University of North Carolina, then decided to look into law enforcement and thought I'd be a private investigator. And you've always wanted to be a teacher?"

"Yes, my plan is to finish school in another year and find a job here in town."

"Camden said you were working your way through school on pageant money."

"Pageants have been a good way to make money for school, but that's all. You can only take so much parading around in your bathing suit."

An image that made me gulp for air.

"And speaking of school, this is really nice, but I have a paper to write." When she stood, her book bag fell over, spilling the contents. I hurried to help her pick things up and saw the Styrofoam circle down in the bag. I suddenly realized what the ribbon and roses and little pinwheel were for. Hadn't I seen dozens of those at Lindsey's grave? Kary was making a wreath. A wreath for a child. Now I knew why I'd recognized the stillness in her. I had it in me.

It was grief.

Our eyes met, and for a moment I thought, like Camden, she could see all the way into my soul. Then she smiled and said something that sounded like, "See you at dinner," but I was hardly listening. I was back in the cemetery, staring at the wreaths, the bizarrely cheerful stuffed animals and toys, the pinwheels rattling softly in the breeze, the little mound of dirt.

Lindsey, my precious little girl.

I was never going to forgive myself.

Chapter Four

"The Restless Dead"

The first thing I heard the next morning was Camden singing in the shower. This was a new song, some minor thing about a dead lover, faded flowers, broken promises. It fit my mood perfectly.

My love was true, my love was fair,
My love had lovely golden hair,
But now down in the earth she sleeps,
While flowers bend their heads and weep.

What a cheery little number. It took every effort to roll out of bed and into my own shower. Maybe Kary would change her mind. Maybe Donnie would be hit by a meteor.

Maybe I'd just give up.

You have a case, I reminded myself. An honest to God paying client. Get to work.

When I came down to the kitchen, Rufus Jackson was sitting at the counter, wolfing down some fluorescent cereal and milk, his thick shoulders straining against his faded tee shirt. Think professional wrestler having a bad hair day and you've got a good picture of Rufus. He's about six six, two hundred and eighty pounds, all muscle, including some places that weren't meant to be muscle. Before I moved south, I thought everyone in North Carolina was like Rufus and his pal, Buddy, overweight

ignorant rednecks who ran around dirt roads in old pickup
trucks, tossing Mountain Dew cans overboard and shooting
holes in mailboxes. Rufus actually likes to do this, but Buddy's
a serious stamp collector and a damn good woodcarver. And, to
be perfectly honest, there are rednecks in Minnesota, too. It's a
worldwide phenomenon.

His shrewd little eyes watched me as I stumbled around,
cursing as the hard butter crumbled the toast in my hand.

"What's your problem, Randall? You look like death eating
a cracker."

I no longer try to fathom these Southernisms, although this
was a new one and screamed for interpretation.

"Nothing."

Rufus munched another mouthful. "Wouldn't have anything
to do with Kary, would it?"

Living in this house must make everyone psychic. "What's
it to you?" I hacked at the butter. Did someone leave it in the
freezer overnight?

He shrugged. "I didn't think she'd go for Donnie Taylor,
either. He must have one hell of a personality."

"You think she'll marry him?"

His snort sent stray cereal bits across the counter. "You ever
know a woman to pass up a wedding?"

Since I'd been married twice myself, I had to agree. I gave up
on the butter and ate my toast straight, parking myself on a stool.
"What about her teaching degree? She ought to finish that first."

"You sound like her old man." He laughed.

"It's only six years. Get over it."

He laughed again and slurped up the milk in his cereal bowl.
He poured another bowlful, still chuckling. He was enjoying
his joke so much, I didn't want to argue. I changed the subject.
"Rufus, do you know why her parents don't want to have anything to do with her?"

"Guess you don't watch much Bible TV."

"I don't watch any Bible TV."

"Then you hadn't heard of the Ingrams." He crunched a mouthful of cereal. "One of them screechin', better give us money or you're goin' to hell preachers, him and his wife both. Got a program on one of the local access channels. Life Eternal or Eternal Life. Something like that."

I'd actually come across a program like this while channel surfing. Sometimes you can't avoid them. "Kary's parents are televangelists?"

"Yep."

"Did they kick their daughter out? What did she do, play cards on Sunday?"

"I don't know. Not something she talks about."

Maybe Kary, like Camden, was reluctant to play a part on TV. Maybe I'd find a tactful way to ask her. Maybe it was none of my business. "What about Albert Bennett? You know anything about the Bennett family?"

His brow furrowed, and he was off into the realms of arcane family knowledge that southerners relish. "Let's see now, Bennett. I knew a Stephanie and Ralph from over Torren way. No, wait, I'm thinking of Bertie and Ralph, not Stephanie. They've been dead for a coon's age. Bertie's wooden leg come off when she was trying to catch that pig, and she broke her neck, and Ralph, he wrapped his truck around a tree down by the highway. And then there was some Bonnetts over past Celosia. There was Sophie and Cletus and Bonnie." He gave a snort of laughter. "Heh. Bonnie Bonnett. Always did like saying that."

I cut in quickly before I was subjected to the entire Bonnett family history. "That's great, Rufus, thanks. I don't think that's who I'm looking for."

He wiped his mouth with the back of his hand. "What you doing here, anyway? Thrown out again?"

"Yes, not that it's any of your business."

Another snort.

"Speaking of TV," I said, "what's the deal with Ellin Belton?"

"Now that is one fierce little gal." He shook more cereal into his bowl. "They met at that Psychic Service, only now Cam's quit, and she don't believe him. She's over here all the time pestering him to do stuff he don't want to do. I don't know how he attracts all these women, anyway, the little squirt." He raised his head from the trough as Camden came in. "What the hell was that mournful song you were singing? Gave me the shakes."

Camden was tying his one and only tie. "What mournful song?"

"The one you were bellowing in the shower. Dead girls ain't no fun, something like that."

"I don't know. It just came to me. That bad, huh?"

"Naw, the melody was okay, but it sure was sorrowful."

Camden reached in the kitchen cabinet for a box of brown sugar Pop-Tarts. He was dressed for work, which explained the shirt and tie, but he was still barefooted. "Can you give me a lift to Tamara's, Randall?"

"Sure."

"Working today, Rufe?"

"If it don't rain. Looks kinda gloomy out. Buddy might come by later. I'm helping him get ready for the festival. He's got a boatload of ducks and fish he's carved."

"Tell him he can store some things here if he wants," Camden said. "Did he get a place on Main Street?"

Rufus nodded and slurped up bowl number three.

"Oh, that reminds me," I said to Camden. "Lily left you a box of crystals to feel."

He didn't even blink. "Okay." He put two Pop-Tarts in the toaster.

"Are you supposed to get some deep important messages?"

"She just likes me to check and make sure none of them belonged to mass murderers. Bad vibes, you know."

"Do you ever get anything from those rocks?"

"Not really." Cindy came in and wound about his legs. He picked her up and rubbed her behind the ears until his breakfast popped up. Then he set her down and put the Pop-Tarts on a plate.

"Ellin still bugging you about being on the show?"

He went to the fridge for a Coke. "She never lets up."

"Have you ever considered dropping her? Find somebody a little more agreeable? Lily, for instance, or Tamara, or perhaps any one of the ten thousand available women in this town. You're going to end up back in the Psychic Service, and you know what fun that was."

"No, I won't."

Rufus and I exchanged a look. "Stubborn as hell," Rufus said. "It's a perfect match."

Camden brought his Pop-Tarts and Coke to the counter, took another stool, and opened the box of crystals. When he touched the light yellow crystal, he frowned slightly.

"Uh-oh." I'd put the yellow crystal back in the box. "That one's mine."

"It's okay. Just a slight tremor."

"Let me guess. The previous owner died of a broken heart."

He put it back in the box. "It's nothing, really. I caught a glimpse of a young woman."

"Hope she was good-looking."

He took out another crystal. "She had to make a hard decision. Nothing life threatening, but it meant giving up her jewelry, including the crystal. It was a good luck charm, that's all." His eyes briefly glazed over as he felt the sharp edges of the next crystal. I wondered how it must be to see the past float up like faded photographs or old movies.

"As good luck charms go, it hasn't done much for me, either."

"Didn't you get your new client?"

"Yep, but her case is going to be tricky. I can't time travel as well as you. This happened years ago."

Rufus raised his head once more. "Speaking of time travel, Cam, that movie's on this afternoon. *The Time Machine*. Saw it in the *TV Guide*."

"If I'm not back, Rufe, would you record it?"

He shoved himself up from the counter. "I'll go set the DVR right now before I forget."

I showed Camden the article in the paper about the murder at the Smithsonian. "Some very strange things regarding music have been happening."

He scanned the article. "That's an odd coincidence."

"This PBS documentary that's coming to town, the show your sweetie wants you to be in. Same type of music. Why don't you ask her about it?"

"Why don't you ask her? I'm staying as far away as possible."

"Okay, I will, and I'm thinking Ms. Gentry's case may have a connection to the murder of Albert Bennett."

"Are you on the Bennett case?"

"Not yet."

When he put the paper back on the counter, it flopped open to the Apartments For Rent section. He glanced at this. "You can stay here as long as you like, Randall."

"At the Chateau des Rejects? No, thanks."

"French. That's impressive. A little harsh, but impressive."

"Okay, I wouldn't ever call Kary a reject, but you have to admit Fred looks like something out of a trashcan."

"Fred's had a hard life. His daughter didn't want to look after him, and he didn't have any money for a retirement home."

"I guess he's lucky he landed here."

Camden gave me a look. "You're lucky you landed here."

"It's just temporary until I find my own place."

I could tell he didn't believe me. "Okay."

"Use your vast psychic skills and find me an apartment, preferably in a building full of attractive single women."

Camden finished feeling the crystals, ate his Pop-Tarts, and announced he was ready to go when my phone rang.

"Hold that thought." I answered the phone. A woman's voice said, "David Randall? I'm Pamela Vincent. A friend of mine says you're very good at finding lost articles. Could you help me out?"

Two clients in two days. Not bad. "I'd be glad to, Ms. Vincent. What have you lost?"

I could hear the smile in her voice. "My heart."

"That's too bad."

"No, really, it's a gold heart-shaped locket my husband gave me. I'm very fond of it. I've looked everywhere, and I'm afraid it's been stolen. Would you have a chance to come see what you could do? I live in Greenleaf Forest just outside town."

"I could stop by this afternoon."

"Thanks very much."

Pamela Vincent gave me her address and I hung up. "The Randall Detective Agency has taken a definite upswing. Dead songwriters and lost lockets. Can't beat that."

I left a message on Byron Ashford's machine, asking him to call me, and then I called Harmon Lassiter again. He was home. In a rusty voice that reminded me of my granddad gargling, he said he'd be glad to talk with me tomorrow around noon.

As I drove Camden to Tamara's, he started another tear-jerking song, something about a maiden and a hangman.

"Good God," I said. "Can't you sing something more upbeat?"

"Upbeat?"

"'My dying wish another look from your eyes, oh, hangman, don't hang me now'? Where are you getting this stuff?"

"I don't know."

"Well, shut up."

Camden's always singing. Usually it's something he's practicing for church or for a wedding, but these dismal dirges were new. We got as far as Surry Street when he tuned up again.

Oh, bring my flowers to the grave, to the grave,
Mother, don't weep for me now,
And bury me deep in my bridal gown,
For my lover has betrayed me.

"Damn it," I said. "If you can't sing something cheerful, I'm putting you out on the curb and you can thumb your way to the shopping center."

"What is it with you?" he said. "It's just a couple of folk songs."

"Then sing 'If I Had a Hammer' or something. Anything but this dreck about dead brides."

"Oh." His tone meant I See All and Understand. "This is about Kary."

It was on the tip of my tongue to ask him if I had a future with Kary, but I was afraid to know. If he told me she would live happily ever after with this Donnie Taylor and grow old and fat with kids hanging all over her, I wouldn't be able to stand the news. But maybe it wasn't Donnie. Maybe there was hope for me. "Care to give me a preview of coming attractions?"

Camden was looking out the window and humming another damn minor song.

"Camden," I said to get his attention. He swung his power gaze back to me.

"I see two hearts singing," he said in that cryptic way that drives me and everyone who knows him crazy.

"Great. That helps a lot."

I dropped him off at Tamara's Boutique, an exclusive little clothing store in the shopping center. Tamara's an exclusive little gal herself, with a slow sensuous voice and brilliant green eyes. How Camden could pass her up for Ellin Belton is one of the mysteries of the universe.

Chapter Five

"The Angel's Kiss"

I drove on to the university to see if I could locate Tate Thomas. The music department was in one of the older brick buildings on campus. The faded gold hallways were decorated with dark photographs of past bands, orchestras and choruses, all members staring solemnly at the camera, probably wondering how they'd ever make a living. I could hear some soprano warbling scales and the muted thud of a drum. I passed practice rooms and larger rooms with risers, most of them empty. In one, I saw a few languid students going over a music score.

The secretary in Thomas' office said he'd be back in about twenty minutes if I'd care to wait. I sat down on a dark green plastic sofa and eyed the stack of music magazines. I didn't see anything that looked even vaguely like traditional jazz, so I reviewed my life instead. This took ten of the twenty minutes. The other ten I spent admiring a young violinist who sauntered through the office in search of a string. She was serious about getting the right string and ignored me. This single-mindedness reminded me of Kary, and I had a return attack of gloom. Who was I kidding? I'd been so dazzled by Kary's looks, I'd seriously misjudged her. She was beautiful, yes, but she was also a bright, intelligent young woman, as hell-bent as Ellin Belton to have a career, and with my track record, I'd be a fool to even think of marrying again.

The secretary's voice pulled me out of the depths. She had stopped typing and was talking on the phone to someone who was obviously upset. "I wish you'd calm down. I'm sure your job is safe. Yes, there will be cuts, but I don't see how this affects you. It's mainly the older staff members who are being let go." She paused. "Well, the arts always get cut first. Why don't you transfer to the P.E. department? There's no way they're going to get rid of the football team."

A trim man with gray hair and a Vandyke beard came into the office. Early fifties, I guessed. Looks just like a music professor. And he was.

"Mister Randall? I'm Tate Thomas. How may I help you?"

I stood and shook hands. "I just need a few minutes of your time, Mister Thomas. Melanie Gentry said you might know something about a songwriter named John Burrows Ashford. Any information you've got would be very helpful."

"Of course," he said. "Come into my office."

Thomas' small office had a window that looked out onto the tree-lined quad of the university. A bust of Beethoven and a bust of some other scowly guy sat on the bookshelves filled with volumes on music, conducting, and composing. Thomas sat down behind a small desk overflowing with papers and motioned me to a chair.

He made an attempt to straighten the papers. "Just finishing some arrangements for the chamber orchestra—if we're lucky enough to have a chamber orchestra next semester."

"Yes, I happened to overhear your secretary talking about budget cuts."

He sighed and shook his head. "Business as usual around here, I'm afraid. But we'll manage. Now what exactly do you need to know about Ashford? He was a fairly minor figure in folk music, but his works have been of surprisingly lasting influence."

"So it's your expert opinion that he wrote his own songs?"

"It's everyone's expert opinion. It's a fact."

"Melanie Gentry claims her relative, Laura Gentry, wrote the songs. Does she have a case?"

Thomas sat back in his chair and steepled his fingers. "Well, it's true that Laura Gentry and John Ashford had a close and somewhat volatile relationship. No doubt Laura contributed musical themes and ideas, but the bulk of the work is Ashford's."

"What can you tell me about their relationship?"

He took another long pause. "This is what I've learned from my studies, you understand, and what I've tried to explain to Melanie. I can't say how much of it is gospel. But there are great and tragic stories about nearly every composer. Musicians are very dramatic people. Very hard to live with at times. At least, that's what my wife tells me. Ashford and Laura lived together for a while, back when this was scandalous behavior. Ashford was a driven man, very egotistical, very much aware of society and how he could flaunt its rules. He came from a distinguished family and felt this gave him the right to act as he wished. Everyone else was ordinary, beneath his contempt, that sort of thing. When his music became popular, his head swelled even further."

"So his music was popular, despite this fling with Laura?"

"Oh, the relationship enhanced his popularity. He was the bad boy of folk music."

"And by folk music, you don't mean 'Blowing in the Wind'?"

Thomas shook his head. "No, not that kind of folk music. We're talking about the pure mountain strains that were brought to this country by the English and Scottish and Irish settlers, the real minor, atonal, twelve-note-scale themes. Ashford's sounded remarkably authentic, and people loved them. You must remember that turn of the century audiences enjoyed what were called 'Pathetic Ballads,' the real sob story stuff. Daddy's in Heaven, Mother's an Angel, My Child Shall Suffer No More."

"But you're saying Laura didn't write any of them."

"She may have collaborated on a few."

It was beginning to look as though I didn't have a case, either. Thomas got up and went to one of the bookshelves, hunted a moment, and took down a slim volume, which he handed to me.

"This may be useful to you. It's a biography of Ashford. Not definitive, by any means, but a good solid study of the man's life and work. It's the only one I know of."

"Thanks."

"I believe there may be some copies of his letters to Laura Gentry in the back."

I turned to the back of the book and glanced at a few of the letters. In earlier letters, Ashford had responded to Laura as a lover, but then he grew more and more distant until he was giving her the 1920s version of a brush-off. I felt he could've been a little kinder, but apparently, the woman was smothering him.

"I have given you my heart and soul!" the last letter said. "You must allow me my freedom! I have let you share in my innermost thoughts and desires, my music, my passion. You cannot cling to me so! What more do you want?"

Whew. I have given you my heart and soul. Too bad, buddy. She wanted blood.

"In your opinion, do you think Ashford murdered Laura over the songs?" I asked Thomas.

Thomas sat down and stroked his pointed beard. "Well, if you read the book, you'll see there was some controversy over Laura's death. She drowned. Some accounts say she and Ashford quarreled and he pushed her in. The death was ruled accidental, however, and Ashford killed himself soon afterwards. The mystery was never solved to anyone's satisfaction."

And it won't be solved today. Seems I'm several dozen years too late. "I'm also curious about Albert Bennett," I said. "You may have read about him in the paper. He was apparently killed over a music notebook, which was left behind on the lawn."

"Yes, I did see something about that," Thomas said. "I was actually acquainted with Albert Bennett. He taught here for about five years before he retired. I didn't know him very well, but still, a terrible tragedy."

"Did he have any enemies? Quarrel with anyone? Argue about music?"

"No, he was a very private man."

"Did the police ask you to decipher the marks in his notebook?"

He shook his head. "No one contacted me about that. I wouldn't have known what his notation meant, anyway."

"I'd like to know if there's anything about Bennett's music that connects to Ashford or Laura Gentry." It was a long shot, but it seemed an odd coincidence that a man had been murdered over a book of music just as Melanie Gentry approached me to solve a similar mystery.

"Well, Albert Bennett was not a composer, but his father was. Sort of." Again he reached for his bookcase and chose another large book. He thumbed through the pages. "Bennett, Bennett, ah, here we are. Horatio Isleton Bennett. Yes, he thought he'd revolutionize music by using his own symbols instead of the standard notes. It only made his works more incomprehensible." Thomas found the page he wanted and read aloud. "'Horatio Isleton Bennett, 1853–1940. Creator of the "Bennett System," an unsuccessful attempt to change the notation system. Bennett's compositions include "Swan Lake Revisited" and the experimental "Three Flats Lower." An example of his Bennett System follows.' And there are some of his symbols. My guess is that's what was in the notebook." Thomas turned the page so I could see the string of triangles and curls, the same little squiggles I'd seen in the newspaper account.

"Yes, that looks just like it."

"You've seen the notebook?"

"What was left of it. I arrived with the police the night of the murder."

Thomas closed the book. "Horatio Bennett is even more obscure than Ashford. I seriously doubt they ever met. But I can check some other sources for you."

I thanked Thomas for his help and promised to return the book. I checked my watch. Quarter to twelve. Plenty of time to drive to Pamela Vincent's. I might even make it back home to see some of *The Time Machine*.

A time machine would be very helpful right now. I never trusted history books or accounts said to be accurate. I have a theory that everything we call history is wrong. The only people who know the truth are the ones who lived through it, and they're long gone, just like John Burrows Ashford and Laura Gentry. Who knows? They could've been deliriously happy together and wrote fake love letters as a joke. So far, Laura's sounded like bad soap opera episodes.

◇◇◇

Unlike most locations in Parkland, Greenleaf Forest actually lived up to its name. The developers had left nearly all the trees, building large homes on private lots deep in the woods. Pamela Vincent's house was a beautiful redwood home with a wrap-around porch. Pamela Vincent was a stunning redhead. Okay, I've seen quite a few redheads in my time, but I can honestly state that Pamela Vincent is in the top five. Besides the glowing hair cut to swing just at her shoulders, she had a flawless complexion and dark brown eyes. She had on tight blue jeans, a white shirt, and diamond earrings.

She shook my hand. "Thanks so much for coming. Let's sit on the porch. This weather's wonderful, isn't it? I find it almost impossible to stay inside on days like today. Would you care for some tea?"

"Yes, thanks."

While Pamela Vincent went inside to get the tea, I admired the quiet woods around the house. Birds of all kinds jostled for position at the feeder near the edge of the lawn. A sparrow fiercely defended his patch of seeds against a bewildered-looking crow. Blue and white wildflowers swayed in the breeze. I found it hard to believe such a glorious woman as Pamela Vincent could hide away here and not be pursued. Maybe the husband was a huge hulking beast.

She returned with the tea and some sandwiches.

"I looked at the clock and realized it was lunchtime. Hope you like chicken salad."

"That's great, thanks."

We took seats in the rocking chairs. She pushed back her hair. "Now, about my locket. I remember wearing it to a party last Saturday night. I remember wearing it when we went to a friend's house on Sunday. Somewhere between Sunday afternoon and Monday morning, I lost it. I've turned this house on its head. Nick has searched every inch of the lawn. It's not some tiny flat thing, either. It's two inches wide and fat, very shiny gold on a thick gold chain."

"You've checked all your pockets."

"Yes, and in the car. We've retraced our steps. We'd feel silly calling the police for this, but still, it means a lot to me."

The sandwich was delicious. I took another bite and swallowed. "This friend you visited Sunday. Did he look for it, too?"

"I'm certain I had the locket on when we left his house."

"And you came straight home?"

"Yes."

"Do you remember taking it off?"

Here Pamela Vincent blushed a magnificent rosy blush that matched her sunset hair. "Well, actually, Nick and I took everything off. He always says the locket hits him in the nose when we, um, you know, so I took it off. I put it on the dressing table, and that's the last I saw of it."

"Was this in the bedroom?" She nodded. "Could I have a look?"

We finished our lunch. Then Pamela Vincent led the way through a large rustic living room and up wide wooden stairs to a bedroom decorated in shades of yellow. The dressing table where she'd last seen the locket was next to a window displaying an array of glass perfume bottles with colorful stoppers.

She pointed to the corner of the table. "I put it right here. I'm sure I did."

The cool October breeze gave the blue mini-blinds a slight rattle. "Has anyone been admiring that locket lately? Someone who might have decided to steal it?"

"A lot of people have admired it. I don't want to accuse anyone of stealing, I really don't. I just can't imagine anyone taking it."

"Has word gotten around town that it's missing? Have you offered a reward?"

"No."

I took another look around the bedroom, trying not to imagine Pamela in the bed. I looked out the window. The porch roof was conveniently flat, so someone could climb up the porch railing to the second floor. The thief knew exactly where to look, and if Pamela and her husband were busy—

"I take it you two didn't see or hear anything?"

She blushed again. "We were quite involved."

I was going to have to meet the lucky Mister Vincent. "Does your husband have any idea what might have happened to the locket?"

She sighed. "Well, here's where it gets complicated. Nick is a little scatterbrained sometimes. He's always forgetting or misplacing things."

"So he may know where it is and just forgot?"

"He's blaming himself, and I hate that. Something else must have happened to the locket."

"You're fairly isolated out here, Mrs. Vincent. A thief could've come in your window and picked up the first shiny thing he saw. Do you always wear those diamond earrings?"

She touched one. "Yes, they were a wedding present from Nick."

"Someone might have figured you'd have more expensive jewelry in your house. I'll ask around and check back with you in a day or two."

◇◇◇

Camden had given me Ellin Belton's phone number. She said she was very busy, but if I stopped by the Psychic Service, she might be able to answer a few questions. I didn't know why she couldn't answer my questions over the phone, but when I arrived at the address she gave me, I began to understand.

The Psychic Service used to send out its cosmic rays from an old shoe shop in a strip mall, but life in the cosmos must have picked up because now the service was located in one of the newer office buildings downtown, a tall rectangle of granite and glass. The receptionist's office was stylish, powder blue and pale pink with light wood trim. Very soothing. Decorations included a big fancy silk flower arrangement, muted lighting, New Age drivel permeating the airwaves, and a trim young woman in white sitting behind the pale pink desk. She had short white hair and big crystal earrings that dangled to her shoulders.

"Welcome to the Psychic Service," she said. "How may I help you?"

You oughta know, I wanted to say. "I'd like to speak with Ellin Belton. I'm David Randall."

"Yes, sir. One moment, please." She pressed a button on her phone. "Ms. Belton? There's a Mister David Randall here. Yes, I'll tell him. She'll be right with you, Sir."

"You have a fellow named Camden who works here? How's he with cats?"

She gave me a look as if I had suggested hiring Steven Speilberg to videotape a birthday party. "Mister Camden works only on the most difficult cases."

"So I couldn't see him?"

"I'm afraid not." She was as frosty as her hair. "He's taking a short leave of absence. However, I'll be glad to forward your request. He likes to help as many people as possible, and he's excellent."

Ellin came out, wearing a rose-colored suit that made her blonde hair an even richer gold. Her little earrings were crescent moons. "Good afternoon, Mr. Randall. Let me give you the tour."

She led me up and down the pastel halls, showing me private consultation rooms, the banks of phones occupied by crystal-wearing operators with mellow voices and earnest expressions, the horoscope division, full of more earnest people checking charts and maps of the constellations, and the other offices where, no doubt, people were being channeled and fleeced.

"I wanted you to see everything before you dismissed it," she said. "I know Cam's been telling you all sorts of stories."

"Actually, no. I have no idea why he'd want to retire and give up all this splendor."

Boy, if I ever want my hair curled, I'll remember the heat in Miz Belton's eyes.

"This is just the main office. We have a studio downtown where we'll be broadcasting our television shows." We paused in front of a large bulletin board. On the board were brightly colored posters announcing: "Ready to Believe," "Past Forward," and "News for the New Age." "These are some of the projects I'll be producing."

"Congratulations. Sounds like fun. What about this PBS documentary on music? What do you know about that?"

She perked up. "I see it as a huge opportunity for the Service. We have people who channel all sorts of musicians, spirit writing, phantom music. I want Robertson and his team to include us in his program, and Cam would be the perfect spokesperson."

I thought about the strange folk songs Camden had been singing lately and decided this was the last thing to mention. "What makes you say that?"

"Well, besides his looks and his singing voice, he's very receptive to spirits. I'm sure he could call up anyone they need."

This was so ridiculous I wasn't sure what to say. However, I'd figured out why she wanted to speak to me in person. "You think I can convince him to do this?"

"I don't see why not. The two of you seem to be good friends. I would appreciate it if you talked with him."

Like Camden, I didn't promise anything. "I'll see. When is Robertson coming to town?"

"In the next few days. I understand he's in talks with Morgan Freeman to do the narration."

"Sounds like a big deal."

Her eyes gleamed. "A really big deal." She straightened the poster for "Ready To Believe," even though it looked straight to me. "Actually, I'm one of three people being considered for the Psychic Network producer's job."

Oh, ho. "So this could be your big break?"

She made an unsuccessful attempt to sound casual. "Possibly."

"Do you know if there's going to be anything about Stephen Foster in the documentary?"

"I don't know. Is there a paranormal angle?"

"There might be a connection to the documentary. Did you hear about the break-in at the Smithsonian? A man was murdered, and some music was destroyed, maybe even stolen. It was all old American folk music, probably the same kind that's going to be featured in the documentary, including, I would imagine, songs by Foster."

I could almost see a little machine in Ellin's mind cranking out dollar bills. "Anything by Foster would be extremely valuable. That's something to consider. But I've researched Spiritualism. There was a popular song in 1853 called 'Spirit Rappings.' Can you imagine how wonderful it would be if Cam sang this in the documentary? It fits right in with the time period."

"If Camden sang this as himself, or someone else?"

"Well, it would certainly add an exciting dimension if there was an actual spirit involved."

"But this documentary, it's about the history of American music, right? Not the history of American ghosts."

"Whatever it is," she said, "I want in."

By any means necessary? Ellin Belton looked like a gal who just might do that.

◇◇◇

On my way back toward Grace Street, I pulled in at an apartment complex that had a "For Rent" sign out front. Despite a slightly shabby appearance, the buildings, parking lot, and grounds were clean. The swimming pool was closed for the season, but several children were in the small playground area, swinging and sliding.

The manager showed me the unit, a four room apartment, very basic, also clean, but just about as sterile and soulless a place as you could imagine: beige walls, brown carpet, tan linoleum in the kitchen. Even the light was wrong, a melancholy sort of light that said, well, this is all I can manage. I thought of the riot of color that was the Grace Street island living room and the way the sunlight poured in from the back bay window. I thought of the green bedroom with the view of the oak trees and the room that could be my office.

I thanked the manager and went out. I was just about to the Fury when I saw one mother help her little girl off the swings. She bounced the child on her hip and swung her around, laughing. I couldn't look away. They were so young, so spontaneous. I had taken Lindsey to the park to swing many times.

The mother hugged her daughter and started to carry her back home. That's when the little girl saw me. She smiled at me over her mother's shoulder, and then, to my amazement, she blew me a kiss.

My heart stopped for a moment and then began to pound furiously. I could see Lindsey dashing off to school, pausing to throw me a kiss with that same exuberant gesture, those same sparkling eyes.

A message. A message from Lindsey.

No, damn it! A coincidence! There were thousands of little girls in this city, and they all knew how to blow kisses. If I started reading deep significant meanings into ordinary occurrences, I'd go crazy. Get a grip!

But I stood there, unable to move, until the little girl and her mother had gone into their apartment. Why me? I didn't look like the kind of person who deserved a kiss. I looked exactly like what I was, a down-at-the-heels loser who was trying to get by. What made her smile at me in the first place? I hadn't encouraged her in the slightest. It was almost as if she had recognized me.

A sign. A message.

No!

No.

Chapter Six

"The Sorrow-Filled Dream"

By now, it was past five. I was tired and freaked out and wanted to head on home for dinner.

Head on home? What was I thinking? I didn't deserve a home like 302 Grace. I sure as hell didn't deserve anyone like Kary. I wasn't even sure I deserved dinner.

But when I pulled up to the house and sat for a moment looking at it, the place couldn't have appeared any more warm and inviting. Lights gleamed from the porch and the big front windows. Inside, nothing was beige.

One more night, I told myself.

As I made my way through the house, I could hear voices. Rufus and Buddy were in the backyard, making a hell of a mess. Buddy's a Rufus clone, only a little lighter and a little less hairy. He had on overalls and a baseball cap that said, "Old Fishermen Never Die, They Just Smell That Way." The two of them were surrounded by piles of wood shavings, pieces of wood, paint cans, tools, boxes, and cartons of Mountain Dew. I stepped out the kitchen door and gave them a wave.

Buddy squinted up at me. "What are you doing here, Randall? Thrown out again?"

"You should go on *Jeopardy*. You've got all the answers."

Both Rufus and Buddy can take a joke, which is good, considering how big they are. They snorted and snickered. Buddy said, "Well, I wanted to go, but Rufus here done beat me to it. Won ten thousand dollars, didn't you, Rufe?"

Rufus dug in the pocket of his overalls for a can of chewing tobacco. "Had all my categories. Dogs, Hunting, Famous Strippers, Fishing Lures, and Words That Begin With F."

"What's going on here?" I asked.

"Getting ready for the festival," Buddy said. "Say, Randall, I want you to find me a dulcimer player."

"A what?" I inspected the rows of wooden ducks lined up for a final coat of varnish. "A dulcimer player?"

"Yup. A possum bit Velmer's hand, and it's all swole up, so he's not able to play this year, and I need somebody to fill in."

I'd forgotten that Buddy and his fellow bluegrass musicians set up on a corner downtown and assaulted everyone's eardrums during the festival. Bluegrass music's fine in small doses, but Buddy and Rufus have been known to sing. The term "nasal" doesn't even come close to the barnyard sound these two can produce.

"I'll see what I can do," I said, "but I don't know many musicians. Did you ask Kary?"

Rufus used his screwdriver to pry open a can of paint. "Thought we would when she gets home. I told Bud the group was fine with just him and the others, but he don't believe me."

Buddy chipped carefully at a duck's beak. "Needs more than just banjo, bass, and guitar. The dulcimer's what brings in the tourists."

As far as I can tell, a dulcimer's a piece of piano you bang on with little hammers. The twangy sound's not quite piano, not quite harp. "Did you ask at the Crow Bar?"

"Yeah, we put some notices up. Kinda pushing it, though, to be ready by next week."

"I can play a kazoo if that'll help."

Buddy turned his head and sent a spray of tobacco juice across the yard. "Got a hot case goin'?"

"I wish. All I've got is a lost locket and a dead songwriter."
Insignificant cases, perhaps, but I needed them.

"Somebody must not've liked his songs."

I got a cola out of the fridge, checked to make sure the
recorder was working, and took a few minutes to watch Gene
Barry save America instead of London. Those creepy ships with
their headlamp eyeballs still give me the chills.

"Run out and sneeze on them, Gene," I said. When the world
had been saved, I picked the *TV Guide* off the coffee table and
looked through the listings until I found the channel for Bible
TV. The *Ingram Bible Hour* was on several times a day and had
fifteen minutes to go in this hour. The Reverend Gary Neil
Ingram, a large blond man with a red face, alternated between
pleading and threatening people to come to the Lord. Sitting
behind him was a large blonde woman in a lavender suit, her
hair poofed up in an array of curls. She gazed at the man ador-
ingly. Behind her was a row of men and women who nodded
and clapped their hands at everything the reverend said. I could
only watch a little of the program. I've always had difficulty with
a god who keeps score.

When the world had been saved again, not only by Gene Barry
but by the Reverend Gary Neil, I turned off the TV and started
dinner. I put some sweet potatoes in the microwave and hunted
in the cabinets for a can of green peas. I turned the potatoes for
their second nuking when the phone rang. It was Tamara.

"Hello," she said. "Who's speaking, please?"

"This is David Randall, a friend of Camden's."

"Oh, yes, David. We've met. I was just wondering. Cam's
been odd today, not quite himself. And if he doesn't stop with
the morbid songs, I'll have to fire him."

"I'll check with him when he gets home."

"Ellin picked him up about thirty minutes ago."

"We may never see him again."

Her voice was concerned. "It may not be anything, but several times today, he just started singing these sad songs. I'm not

sure what the customers thought. When I asked him about it, he looked at me like, so what? It was very unlike him."

Every so often, Camden does something like this, just goes off into space, or acts bizarre. "I'll see what I can do, Tamara."

She thanked me and hung up.

Kary came in around five thirty with some fried chicken. She set the red-and-white striped bucket on the counter. "Here's the main course. The sweet potatoes smell good."

"We'll be ready in about five minutes."

"Thanks. I'm going to practice a little."

In a few minutes, a lively melody I didn't recognize filled the house. What was I going to do about Kary? Trying not to think about her only increased the tension. I busied myself wrapping the potatoes in foil to keep them hot. This was crazy. I could not get involved with another woman. Not now. I'd wish her the best. Nobody would believe me, but I wanted her to have whatever she wanted in life, and if that meant Donnie Taylor, then okay.

I put the plate of potatoes on the table and then nuked the green peas. I filled the glasses with ice and set one at each place. The music spun itself out in ripples of notes.

Kary finished playing and returned to the table. "There should be some napkins on the counter next to the grocery frog."

"The grocery frog?" I looked around for a real one.

She pointed to a large green ceramic frog hiding behind her books on the counter. It had a scooped out back like a big dish. Various coins and bills lay inside. "That's the grocery frog. We all pitch in."

"I see." I reached over to the basket on the counter and took out two napkins, realizing it would just be Kary and me for supper. Rufus and Buddy had gone to the Crow Bar, their hangout, and Ellin had yet to return Camden. I didn't know where old Fred was and I didn't care. "That was a nice piece you were playing. What was it?"

She put a sweet potato and some peas on her plate and then took a drumstick from the bucket. "Oh, nothing really, just a little something I made up."

"You write music?"

She brought her plate to the table, sat down, and took great interest in arranging her napkin on her lap. "I just sort of play around. I'm not very good at it."

"I thought it was great." I filled my plate and sat down across from her.

"Well, thank you." Kary carefully peeled the foil from her potato. "I have to admit I'm intrigued by you, David." Before I could spring happy cartwheels around the table, she added, "I guess I've always been fascinated by people who want to solve crimes."

Okay, so she was intrigued by my job and not me, personally. It was a start.

She reached for the butter. "You're actually doing something to make things better in the world, not just singing about it."

"Singing?"

Kary looked flustered. "Did I say singing? I meant thinking. Thinking about it. You want to make things right."

"Well, I hope I can."

"You've been married before, haven't you?"

Whoa, where did that come from? Was this going to be a deal breaker in our fledgling relationship? Although peas and sweet potatoes are soft foods, I had a hard time swallowing. "Yes." I left it at that. No need to trouble her with the details.

"I'm sorry it didn't work out."

"My fault entirely."

"Any advice?"

Don't do it, I wanted to say. You are my dream girl, my soul mate. Give me time to prove I can be the one you want.

Are you insane? The other part of me said. What makes you think you'll manage any better with Kary? But something inside insisted she was the one. I was just as delusional about Kary as Camden was about Ellin.

"Well, it's tricky. You have to be certain you and your partner want the same things. Got somebody in mind?"

"I've been seeing someone for about six months."

A whirlwind courtship. Terrific. "And he's the one?"

Her gaze was disconcertingly steady. "I don't know. There are still several things we need to work through."

This was encouraging.

Then she said something very discouraging. "I know he's planning to give me a ring. He wants to make it an official engagement."

"Right now it's unofficial?"

"Yes."

"So suppose tomorrow the two of you go out to eat and you find a ring under the hamburger bun?"

"Like I said, there are still some things to work out."

"What about your folks? What do they think of him?"

I thought for a moment I'd gone too far. She averted her gaze and gave all her attention to her plate. "They aren't involved."

"I'm sorry."

"And if they were, they definitely wouldn't approve. Donnie's a scientist."

"Your folks don't approve of science?"

"My folks don't believe in evolution. In fact, I'm a bit surprised they believe the earth is round." Again she fixed me with her steady dark brown gaze. "I, however, believe in evolving, which is what I'm trying to do."

I wanted to say, "I will be happy to help you evolve," but decided this might be a bit forward. "Trying to create a new life for yourself. I can relate."

"Is that why you're here at Grace Street?"

"It's part of the reason."

"Right now, I'm figuring out where Donnie fits in. Or if he fits in. Or if there's something else. I don't suppose you need any help with your cases?"

She asked the question so casually, so offhand, I almost didn't process it. This time I could hardly swallow from amazement. Was it possible I was the something else she was looking for? I managed to get the sweet potato down. "I—well, sure."

She pushed her plate aside and leaned her elbows on the table. "I think I could help. I want to do something practical, something that actually gets results. I don't mean chasing bad guys down dark alleys, but maybe something in the area of research? I know my way around the Internet."

I was still so stunned by her offer it took me a few minutes to reply. "That would be great, thanks."

"I don't want to intrude, or get in your way, I just—I'm not sure how to explain this."

"No need to explain. I'm sure something will come up, and I'll be glad to have your assistance."

When she smiled, I was surprised the light didn't bounce off the walls. "Thanks. More chicken for you?"

"I'm all done." Boy, was I ever.

"I'll take care of the dishes."

I helped her carry the dishes to the sink and then went into the parlor office and shut the door.

Damn.

Now this doesn't mean what you think it does, my practical side warned. Lots of people are charmed by the idea of investigating. Don't start thinking of Kary as your partner in crime.

I needed to convince her I was the one before Donnie declared himself. If she saw Donnie as a way to a better future, I wasn't sure I had much more to offer, but if she saw Donnie as a way to spite her parents, I was an even better example of Evolution in Action.

I had to find something to take my mind off this, so I picked up the book Tate Thomas had given me. I was thirty pages into Ashford's biography, all of it pretty dull, when Melanie Gentry called for a progress report.

"I met with Thomas. From what he tells me, the music community sides with Ashford."

"Yes, that's the standard answer. You see what I'm up against." I could imagine her looking down from her throne at her unruly subjects. "What about Lassiter?"

"Meeting with him tomorrow. You don't have any proof your great-grandmother wrote these songs, any scraps of paper with notes, or rough drafts, or anything?"

"No, but Lassiter might know someone who does. And I'm almost certain Byron Ashford has proof, proof he's kept locked up away from my family. He'd do anything to discredit our claim, Mister Randall. I'm counting on you to get to the truth."

"Well, what if the truth is something you don't want to hear?"

"I have every faith in you, Mister Randall."

That was nice to hear, even if I wasn't sure I could help her. "I'll let you know something tomorrow. And it's David, please."

"Thank you, David."

I read some more of the biography. Ashford didn't have to worry about rags to riches. He was born rich and never had to struggle for anything. Songwriting was more of a hobby for him, and when he found he could make it pay and become a popular stud, he set to it. Although the book was written in a neutral tone, I got the distinct impression that Ashford was a real jerk, selfish, egotistical, and certainly not the kind of guy who was big on sharing. After a while, I'd read enough and decided to take a break.

I could hear the TV, but when I stepped out into the foyer, I could also hear what sounded like sobbing. I cautiously peered around the corner. Kary had her face down in her hands, her shoulders shaking with sobs. On the TV screen, I caught a glimpse of the large blond preacher and his wife. The sound was low, but I could hear his strident voice over the organ music. I didn't want to intrude, but when I stepped back, I stepped on a creaking floorboard. Kary looked up. She grabbed the remote and turned off the TV.

"I thought you were upstairs." Most people don't look their best when they've been crying, but even with her face streaked with tears she was appealing.

"Sorry I startled you. Are you okay?"

She took a quick shuddering breath and got her emotions under control, debating what to tell me. "I was watching a very sad program, that's all. You know, those starving children in Africa. It gets to me." She got up, wiping her eyes. "I'd better say good night."

"Good night."

She passed me without another word and went up the stairs. I turned the TV back on. The *Ingram Bible Hour*, with the preacher and his wife singing about love and forgiveness.

Well, apparently that didn't include their daughter. I wondered if this had anything to do with the pink roses and little pinwheel I'd seen in Kary's bag and the aching sadness in her eyes. Was it possible she'd lost a child? Maybe a younger sister or brother. Did her parents blame her? Or maybe she was making a wreath for a friend. There was so much I didn't know, and I already felt guilty for having invaded her privacy.

I was lounging in the island, eating some popcorn and trying to divert my thoughts with *Invaders From Mars* when Camden came home. He had a wild-eyed look.

"There's some chicken left if you want it," I said as he staggered to the sofa.

"No, thanks." He flopped down and loosened his tie. "Ellie and I had Chinese."

"And some strong words, I take it."

He pushed his hair out of his eyes and blew an exasperated sigh. "This show of hers. It's going to kill us both. I don't want to get started on this TV thing. If I help one person, I'll have to help a thousand."

I passed the popcorn. "She doesn't strike me as the kind of woman who'll ever let you alone, you know that. You might as well give up."

"You're a lot of help."

"You're such a wuss. Tell her no and mean it. Or marry her and make her stay home looking after the kids."

This was so ridiculous, we both laughed, although the idea of Ellin Belton as a mother gave me the chills.

"So what is the deal with this show?"

He checked the clock. "It's on now. You can see for yourself."

"It's on now? I thought all those psychic shows came on around two a.m., right after the Creature Feature."

"Midnight is the witching hour." He found the remote and clicked on channel forty-seven. There it was, the Psychic Service Network, Your Channel to the Stars.

You've seen these things. A paid audience whoops and cheers and applauds at all the right places. Phony psychics make phony predictions and paid actors dramatize the events. Everyone listens intently to stories of love found and valuable objects restored. It was all here, presided over by a good-looking blonde in flowing celestial blue and an equally good-looking brunette in flowing pink.

"I didn't see those two around the service," I said.

"Bonnie Burton and Teresa Perello. They used to work in horoscopes."

"They can chart my day anytime."

There was a question and answer section, and then a slick guy in gray told the weekly astrological forecast.

I threw some popcorn at the screen. "There's our old pal Haverson the Hog. I thought Ellin didn't want him on."

"That was the centerpiece of our argument tonight."

Haverson was plainly enjoying himself as God of the Universe. After him, there were some testimonials from the audience.

"Pretty cheesy, huh?" I said.

No response from Camden. First I thought he'd fallen asleep; then I saw he was sitting very still, his eyes wide open, unblinking.

Uh-oh.

He doesn't often do this. It usually means trouble.

"Camden?" I reached over and carefully shook his arm. "Camden, come back."

It must not have been a deep trance, or maybe I caught him before he got in over his head. I only had to call his name a few times before he stopped doing his stuffed animal impersonation and blinked at me.

"What did you see?"

He looked at me as if he'd never seen me before.

"Camden?"

"That's not my name," he said.

"Okay, then, who are you?"

He winced. "No. Wait. That's not right."

I wasn't in the mood for mysterious messages from beyond, or weird unexplainable events that would cost me. "Your name is Camden, and Earth is your home planet. We're watching TV, remember? Come back right now."

"Wait." I couldn't tell if he meant me or someone in his vision. "I'm not—I don't want you to—no!"

He suddenly flung himself off the sofa and landed on the floor. I jerked in surprise, sending popcorn flying.

"Damn! How about a little warning?"

I helped him onto the sofa, and he slumped back, dazed.

"What the hell was that about?"

His eyes were still rolling. He shook his head as if to clear it and gave me a confused gaze. "What happened?"

"You zoned out, spoke in tongues, and fish-flopped on the floor. What were you seeing?"

He rubbed his elbow. "Nothing. I was watching the show. Next thing I know, I'm on the floor."

"You didn't see anything? No disasters? Floods? Famines? Snowstorms?"

He shook his head. "One minute: horoscopes. The next minute: carpet."

I sat back down in my chair. These trances of his never make sense to begin with. "Maybe you were a performing seal in your past life."

He seemed okay, so we watched the rest of the show. Then I checked the recording of *The Time Machine*. "You want to watch this?"

"Didn't you watch it this afternoon?"

"Just the last part. I can watch it again. I'm not sleepy." This time I got the Deep Look. I held up a warning finger. "Don't say anything. Do not say one word. After your acrobatics this evening, I'm not sure I can trust your predictions. And you really shouldn't stare like that. I can hear the villagers rustling their pitchforks." I swear I could almost hear him walking around in my mind, opening drawers and cabinets to find what he wanted, but he didn't say anything. After a while, he fell asleep on the sofa, and I dozed off in the blue armchair.

When the dream came, I caught a glimpse of white dress, ribbons, a small hand flipping long brown curls over one lacy shoulder. I pushed the dream away. No. I'm tired and confused and I can't handle this even when I'm feeling my best. Go away.

I managed to struggle awake. The house was silent. Faint light came from the kitchen where the light over the stove had been left on. A warm breeze lifted the curtains at the front windows and made the porch swing sway. It creaked softly.

There was someone in the swing.

At first, I thought it was Camden, for the figure was small and dressed in white, but he was still asleep on the sofa. When I realized who it was, my whole body began to tremble.

No. No. I'm awake now, I know I am.

She didn't say anything. She sat in the swing, her little feet dangling in their black patent leather shoes. Lindsey. My God. Lindsey.

Part of me wanted to scream and run away, far from what I didn't want to see: her accusing eyes and sad downcast little face. Part of me wanted to run and grab her and never let go. But she didn't look at me.

I couldn't be dreaming. There was the rest of the popcorn, my shoes, my keys and wallet tossed on the table with the rest of the household junk. I could smell leftover chicken and Kary's perfume and the fragrance of the old wooden house. I wasn't dreaming. But I had to be.

Cindy wandered in from the kitchen and stiffened, whiskers alert. The cat's green eyes glowed as she looked out the window toward the swing, and she growled a curious sound, as if asking a question.

"Do you see her, too?" I whispered.

This had to be the height of desperation, talking to a cat about a ghost in the middle of the night. Cindy trotted to the window and hopped up on the sill. When she turned her enigmatic gaze back to me, I could see the empty swing behind her, creaking softly in the night breeze.

Chapter Seven
"The Good Old Man"

Somehow I found myself in the green bedroom the next morning. I swung my feet over and sat on the edge of the bed, trying to find some sort of meaning in the images I'd seen. Damn, if Camden's house was haunted, all the more reason for me to get out.

The dream stayed with me no matter how hard I tried to push it away. At breakfast, I was so distracted I didn't realize Kary had spoken to me until she tapped me lightly on the shoulder.

"David, did you want some scrambled eggs?"

"Oh, yeah, sure." I rubbed my eyes. "Sorry. Thinking about my case."

"That's okay. One egg or two?"

"Two, please." The sight of her finally registered on my tired brain. She had on a white terry cloth bathrobe that was a little big for her, so it kept slipping off her shoulder, revealing more of her creamy skin. Any other time, I would've appreciated this, but the white robe reminded me of Lindsey's white dress and I couldn't concentrate on admiring Kary as much as I wanted to.

She avoided eye contact. Was she embarrassed I'd caught her at an emotional moment?

"Look," I said. "Last night, I didn't mean to startle you. I heard somebody crying, and I was just concerned."

"Thanks, but I'm all right."

She didn't look all right. She was still a vision, but a lot of her sparkle was gone. She gave the eggs her full attention until a wizened elderly little man wearing faded striped pajamas wandered in. Sprigs of hair grew from his ears and around his bony skull. It was Fred, Camden's oldest and moldiest tenant. He looked like a stalk of celery that had been left out overnight.

"Good morning, Fred," Kary said. "Do you want some scrambled eggs?"

He gave a snort that Kary interpreted as a yes and cut his beady eyes my way.

"Who are you?"

"David Randall."

Another snort. "Guess Cam lets anyone in."

Camden came into the kitchen, yawning and pushing his hair out of his eyes.

Fred turned on him. "This a friend of yours? How long is he staying?"

"As long as he wants." Camden gave me a look but didn't say anything about last night. I would've bet money he'd had the same dream.

Fred glared at Camden accusingly. "Did you eat the last Pop-Tart?"

"No, there's a whole box."

Fred gave a sniff. "Hurry up with them eggs, Kary. I got to get to the park."

Camden went to the stove and gave Kary a hug. For a moment, she put her head on his shoulder.

"You're sure about this?" he said, and she nodded. "You don't want to call them? Your mom might want to hear from you."

"The only thing they'd want to hear is that I'm coming back, and that's not going to happen." She gave the eggs a quick stir. "Almost done, Fred."

Rufus was the next one in, taking his place at the dining room table. He refused an offer of eggs, choosing his cereal instead. There was casual conversation about his construction job, the weather, and how many jack o'lanterns Kary wanted Buddy to carve for the front porch. I ate my eggs and tried not to think about the dream.

For some reason my ex-wife Barbara came to mind. Damn it, I didn't want to think about her. Barbara would be crying, but not for me. I wondered if she ever stopped crying, if she ever found any measure of happiness again, any consolation at all.

And I was a big help, wasn't I? Just a big help all around.

◇◇◇

On the hour drive to Oakville, I listened to the CD of Ashford's songs Melanie Gentry had given me. Selections included "The Restless Dead," "The Sorrow-Filled Dream," "The Deceived Girl," and "The Hangman's Daughter." Carefree stuff. Camden must have been listening into her brain waves, because the songs sounded exactly like the dirges he'd been singing lately. There was one about a baby left in the woods; one about a phantom haunting her lover; one about angels leaving heaven to comfort a grieving father. Love lost, love betrayed, love gone wrong— Ashford had a one-track mind.

After a while, they all ran together into one big sobbing mess. I took out the CD, surprised it wasn't soggy, and replaced it with the New Black Eagles Jazz Band. It's impossible to be maudlin with "Fidgety Feet" pounding through the car. Now this was real music, real man-eating jazz, clarinet and trumpet and trombone trading harmonies and racing toward the conclusion like runaway trains. I wondered if Kary liked this kind of music.

Kary. My thoughts always came back to Kary. I turned up the volume and tried to concentrate on the case.

Oakville, like Parkland, is a large busy city, but because it's closer to the mountains, some of the streets angle up steep inclines and others look like they'd plunge over the end of the world. Large trees shade old houses and traffic crams the roads. October's prime time for "leaf lookers," as the locals call the tourists who swarm the hillsides, searching for the peak colors. Roadside booths all along the highway proclaimed the best cider, apples, and pumpkins, usually on misspelled signs. This used to bug me until Camden pointed out that visitors to our fair state expect a certain amount of rural cuteness.

There was nothing cute about Harmon Lassiter. He matched the raspy voice I'd heard on the phone, a rail-thin man with bony fingers and a fringe of gray hair clinging to his knobby skull. He looked like one of those walking stick insects carefully side-stepping its way around a bush. He met me on the porch of his ancient Victorian home on Evenway Avenue, and although the weather was chilly, we sat outside, as though this was as far as he wanted me to get. He had on a ratty gray sweater with broken buttons, faded corduroy slacks, and dingy slippers the color of oatmeal. In an odd way, it was like looking at Tate Thomas through a warped glass. He had the professor's academic air of condescension and dry lecture-speak. Tate Thomas on a really bad day. Tate Thomas when the grant money ran out.

His long fingers toyed with the broken buttons on his sweater. "My mother knew Laura Gentry and John Ashford. They were friends for a while. She even went to some of their parties, but they were uncontrollable people, she said. Way too emotional. Enough emotion for a hundred people. Everything was a production, everything. A mere trip to the bakery was fraught with significance."

"And what's your opinion about authorship of the songs?"

"I'm almost certain Laura wrote 'Little Jenny Jones' and 'Field Mouse Dance.' I can remember hearing her play them. 'Course, I was just a little tad, but I liked that 'Field Mouse Dance.' She played them here, in this house. Used my mother's piano."

"Then why hasn't she received the credit?"

He grimaced as if he had to share his branch with an impertinent aphid. "You'll have to ask Byron Ashford. Lord Byron, I call him. Tone deaf upstart! Had the gall to call me up and ask for a copy of my notebook, as if there was anything in there he didn't already know."

"Your notebook?"

"Where I wrote down my songs. My first efforts were pale copies of Laura's work, just like a beginning author often copies his idol's style."

"It would help my investigation if I could have a look at your notebook."

He looked at me a long moment, like an insect that has come to a crack in the walk and isn't sure how to cross over. "You're working for Laura's great-granddaughter, that's what you said?"

"Yes, she hired me."

"I've already told her I don't have anything of any use to her."

"I'd still like to see it."

He sighed and pushed himself out of his rocking chair. I heard old bones pop and creak. "I'll be a moment."

I sat in the chill afternoon air and watched traffic successfully maneuver up and down the steep road in front of his house. Must have been twenty degrees cooler in Oakville. Most trees were in their last flame of color, and more than one flock of birds flew past, heading south.

Lassiter returned carrying a large dog-eared notebook. He handed it to me and sat down. "You a musician?"

"Not really."

"Then it won't make much sense to you."

I opened the notebook. First I thought a party of ancient ants had raided their last picnic: tiny black dots and scribbles filled pages of lines. I turned the page. More dead ants.

Lassiter gave a rusty chuckle. "If you can't read music, it must look like a mess of nothing to you. It's just a few tunes, not very original. Had to make my own staffs. Couldn't afford the fancy paper."

I looked through page after page of Lassiter's cramped notation. "Why would Byron Ashford be interested in your first compositions?"

Lassiter's tone was scornful. "Guess he was afraid Laura Gentry might've squirreled away a secret song or two that belonged to his great-grandfather. Laura never wrote in my book. Hell, I didn't show it to my own mother. Too embarrassing."

"But you said you copied Laura's songs at first to get the hang of writing music, right?"

"There are a few of them in there, but nothing Byron Ashford hasn't heard."

"Would you show me those?"

He took the notebook and thumbed through the limp pages. "Here's 'Field Mouse Dance.'" He handed the book back to me.

"Field Mouse Dance" looked exactly like the other clumps of ants. "And this is a copy of Laura's original song? Would you mind if I made a copy of this? I'll need it to compare with Ashford's version."

He shook his head. "This notebook doesn't leave my house."

"All right," I said. "I'll bring Ashford's version with me tomorrow. You've still got your piano here?"

"Course, but don't count on me to play anything." He flexed his bony fingers. "Haven't been able to play much in a long time."

A brilliant plan formed in my mind. "Don't worry about that, Mister Lassiter. I know somebody who can play the piano."

◇◇◇

I picked up a burger and fries and drove to Greenleaf Forest feeling pretty pleased with myself. Kary wanted to help on a case, and I'd found the perfect thing for her to do. We'd take a leisurely drive up to the mountains. She could play the ants for me and tell me how to decipher their strange tracks. And then—well, something was bound to happen.

As for Pamela's locket, I'd recalled how one of my mom's rings had slipped down a heating vent. Wouldn't hurt to check the bedroom vents of the Vincent house.

I drove into the driveway of the country home, parked, and got out. A man was using a garden hose to wash some window screens propped against the porch. He was of average height and slim, with light brown hair. He was wearing dirty sneakers, torn jeans, and a plain green shirt with the sleeves rolled up. Was this Mister Love Machine?

"Nick Vincent?"

He looked up. He had that same abstracted air Camden gets sometimes, that oh-the-dream's-over-I-can-wake-up-now look. His green eyes brightened his calm face.

"You must be David Randall. Nice to meet you."

We shook hands. I wasn't sure how such an ordinary-looking guy had managed to snag a babe like Pamela. Must be the eyes. Women are always going on about Camden's eyes. It's a girl thing. Either that, or Nick Vincent knew a special sex trick.

He turned off the hose. "Any leads on Pamela's locket?"

"I'm afraid not."

"I offered to buy her another. That didn't go over well."

"Not when it's a favorite trinket." I'd been through this several times with both wives. "Getting your spring cleaning done early?"

He grimaced at the screens. "We've had them off during this nice weather, but Pamela wants them back on now. She said if the screen had been on the bedroom window, the thief might not have gotten in."

"I wanted to check something in your bedroom."

"Go on up. I want to finish these."

I went up to the yellow bedroom and looked for heating vents. There was one right under the window, but the grate was way too small for anything the size of a locket to fall through. I looked out the window, feeling the cool breeze. No screen certainly made it easier for the thief—if that's what had happened to the locket.

I came back outside. Nick Vincent was shooing the black birds from the feeder.

"Scram! Leave some for the cardinals." He turned to me. "Any luck?"

"No, sorry."

His shoulders slumped. "I can't believe I lost it."

"What makes you think you lost it?"

"Because I lose everything. And if I'm not careful, I'm going to lose Pam. One day, she's going to get fed up with me and pack her bags—if I haven't lost them, too."

"I doubt it's that serious."

He shook his head. "I don't know. Want a beer?"

"Sure."

We sat on the porch, drank our beers, and Nick told me everything he'd misplaced since they'd moved to Greenleaf Forest. I could understand the flashlight, extension cord, paint roller, and coffee cups, but when he got to the lawn mower and spare tire, I knew I was dealing with someone who was one doughnut shy of a dozen, as Rufus would say.

"It's ridiculous, I know," Nick said, "but I've always been this way. I get distracted and forget where I put things."

"Well, you don't have any security around your place. It's possible somebody checked out the house and decided to have a look inside. Nothing else was taken, right?"

"Not that we know of."

"Where's Pamela today?"

"Grocery shopping. That's usually my department, but we swapped chores today. She doesn't mind going to the store, but it takes forever because people like to stop and talk."

"She has a lot of friends?"

"Hundreds."

"Has Pamela ever received any weird letters or phone calls?"

"I'm pretty sure she'd tell me if she did."

"Usually beautiful women have at least one admirer who's a little cracked."

"That would be me. I still don't understand what she sees in me."

"Trust me—you'll never figure that out."

"Well, there's the age difference, too."

They both appeared to be in their late twenties. "Age difference?"

"Ten years."

"You're kidding."

"Pamela's older. You'd never believe it, would you? She could've had any man in the world, and she wanted me."

"I'm sure you went down kicking and screaming."

"From the first time I saw her, I was lost."

"I know how that is." I took another drink. "Anybody have a grudge against you? You haven't lost anything vitally important, have you?"

"Nobody's got a grudge." His gaze went to the shadowy wood that surrounded the house. "I'd call that locket vitally important, though."

A white Camry drove up and parked. Pamela got out and pulled a bag off the front seat. Nick and I went to help with the groceries.

"Well, I'm glad I bought more beer," she said. "What are you two talking about?"

Nick kissed her cheek. "You'll be happy to know we're talking about you."

She put her other arm around him and gave him a kiss. There was no way to tell which was older. They were a perfect match. Would Kary and I look as right together? Would I ever have the chance to find out?

I carried a bag of groceries into the kitchen and set it on the table. Thinking of Kary made me want to be home when she got in from school.

Pamela put some packets of seeds on the counter. "Nick, you were going to pull that ivy out of the flower bed for me."

"I'll do that right now."

I helped Pamela fold the paper bags. "Nick happened to mention the age difference. I never would've guessed."

"Not quite ten years. He'll be twenty-nine this year, and I'll be thirty-eight." She said this with all the confidence of a woman who knows she'll always look terrific. "It was love at first sight. I saw Nick at an office party. I'd been invited by a friend. Nick was standing with another man, his boss, I think." She chuckled. "The boss thought I was coming across the room to him. I can see him now. He sort of pushed Nick to one side, puffed out his chest, and stepped forward—poor guy! I went right past him to Nick, who looked at me with those beautiful eyes—oh, I can't tell you how I felt. My search was over."

My search was over. I couldn't have put it any better.

"If you don't mind me asking, has the age difference been a problem?"

"Not at all. Oh, occasionally he'll mention something I've never heard of, or I'll say, you remember when such and such happened, and he'll say no, and then I'll remember he was only six at the time. But we're soul mates. I think I could've been a wizened old Asian woman and Nick a seven foot Masai warrior, and we still would've found each other." She gave me a keen gaze. "But your question wasn't an idle one, was it? Who is she? Does she feel the same way about you?"

"I don't really know how she feels about me. And she's engaged to someone else."

"I'm sorry."

I shrugged. I didn't want to talk about this. "I'm going to check out some pawn shops for your locket."

"That sounds exciting. May I come along?"

"If you like. Foster's, Limited, on Tenth Street is usually a good bet. Let me have a look first, and I'll call you if I see anything that looks like your locket."

She thanked me. I waved good-by to Nick tugging at the ivy and got in my car. On the ride back to Grace Street, I wondered why I'd let the age difference between Kary and myself stand in my way. Things were working out great for the Vincents.

Chapter Eight
"The Lass From the Low Countree"

When I got to the house, I thought I'd get some peanut butter crackers and plan exactly how to approach Kary. When I came in sight of the island, I saw Camden lying on the sofa, and this huge woman leaning over him. She was the biggest woman I had ever seen, easily six five, well over three hundred pounds. I didn't even want to think about what she was doing.

"Hey! Back off!"

She moved like a glacier, two tiny eyes gleaming in a broad fleshy face surrounded by lank brown hair that fringed over her forehead. Her expression was grim. She wore a massive pair of green shorts and a shapeless brown tent top she must have ripped off a circus. She had something in her hand that looked like a towel.

Good lord, I thought. Some mammoth maniac has broken in and she's strangling him with a dishrag. How am I going to get him away?

"Back away, I said! Leave him alone."

"You Randall?" Her gruff voice sounded as if she'd smoked since conception.

"Yes, and who the hell are you?"

She shifted her attention back to Camden. "It's okay. It's Randall."

I managed to get around her to the sofa. I saw now she was pressing a dishcloth to his shoulder. Camden's eyes were open. "It's okay, Randall. A little accident, that's all."

"He just walked right out into the traffic like a blind man," the woman said.

Camden looked up at me, his eyes full of concern. "I don't remember. I woke up on the sidewalk."

The woman straightened. It was like watching the continents shift. "Yeah, I may have yanked a little hard, but I had to act fast. Pulled his arm out of joint, didn't I, Shorty?"

"Walked into traffic?" I couldn't believe it. "Where?" Grace Street had hardly any traffic.

"Out on Food Row. I'd walked over to get some burgers for dinner. I have no idea what happened."

Food Row! It was a miracle he wasn't a smear on the highway.

The woman glanced at me. "This happen often?"

I felt she deserved an explanation. "Usually, when he has trances, he doesn't go anywhere. He just zones out. Sleepwalking is something new."

She screwed up her face in disbelief. "Trances?"

"He's clairvoyant."

She gave a snort. "So how come he didn't see himself almost becoming roadkill?"

"I never see my own future," Camden said.

"What were you seeing when you took your Stroll of Death?" I asked him.

"Nothing. Just like last night. Nothing."

"Oh, brother." Where the hell was all this leading?

The woman heaved herself toward the kitchen. "I'll get some more ice."

"Do you mind if I ask who the hell you are?" I said.

She fixed me with her little eyes. "My name's Angie Dawson. I happened to be heading toward the 31 Flavors when I saw Junior here drifting into the westbound lane. Said to myself, it seems a shame to let such a cute little guy become a hood ornament, so I reached out and grabbed him, brought him home.

He said you'd be home soon, but I thought I'd hang around to make sure. You got a problem with any of that?"

"No," I said. "Thank you."

I watched as she maneuvered herself around the corner to the kitchen. Then I faced Camden. "Tell me what's going on."

"I told you already. After Tamara dropped me off, I worked on the gutters for a while and then decided to get some cheese-burgers for dinner. I remember walking over to Food Row. I remember thinking Wendy's might be better than the Quik-Fry, and the next thing I know, I'm lying on the sidewalk with my arm nearly out of its socket, and Angie is saying, 'are you okay?'"

"Were you able to walk home?"

"With her help. I was really disoriented, but she knew where Grace Street was." His eyes were larger than ever with worry. "Randall, I've never blacked out like that. When I have those really deep visions, I'm always seeing something, even if it's something I don't understand."

"I wonder why you couldn't have been rescued by something human."

He started to give me a withering reply, but was interrupted by Angie's slow return to the sofa. She had a sort of shuffling walk, arms swinging forward as if to propel the rest of her. I couldn't imagine how she'd been able to react fast enough to save him.

"Okay, kid, here's some more ice. If your pal's going to stay, I'll get on home."

I took the ice and wrapped it in the dishtowel. Camden thanked her and was going to say something else when Rufus came in the front door and saw Angie, and Angie saw him. They stopped and stared at each other. I swear I heard an audible "boinnng" as their eyes met. Rufus looked as if one of his con-struction buddies had whacked him with a two-by-four. Angie's eyes glowed with the delight of a tyrannosaurus rex spying a limping stegosaurus.

Like me, Camden had difficulty controlling his expression. "Angie, this is Rufus Jackson. Rufus, Angie Dawson. She saved my life this afternoon."

Rufus came out of his stupor. He grinned. "She can save my life, too, if she likes."

"In your dreams," Angie replied, but she grinned, too.

They shook hands. Camden and I winced at the crackle of bones, but this hearty exchange of strength sealed Rufus' fate. His smile now took up his entire face.

"What's all this about saving Cam's life? You okay, Cam?"

"Fine," he said. "I just wasn't paying attention."

Angie decided to be equally modest. "Wasn't no big thing. He'll be more careful next time."

"Well, I was just on my way to the Crow Bar for a drink," Rufus said. "I'd be mighty pleased to buy you a drink to show you my appreciation. Cam here's a good friend of mine. You can tell me all the details."

"I believe I'd like that," she said.

The two of them lumbered out to Rufus' car, a blue Bigfoot truck with the obligatory giant wheels, gun rack, deer lights, and mud flaps printed with silver silhouettes of naked women. He'd rejected my offer of a pair of fuzzy dice, saying that would be tacky. They managed to squeeze in, looking pleased with themselves and ridiculously shy. If the giant tires sank a bit, it wasn't noticeable.

I came back to report this to Camden. He sat up and slowly rotated his shoulder, wincing. "As Rufus says, a perfect match. She must have been fated to come here."

"Don't start with that," I said. "You don't know what's going on any more than I do."

"Just don't tell Kary about this. She'll fuss."

"As long as you agree to see a doctor. I don't like this blacking out business."

"What kind of doctor? You think a doctor would know what's going on? A witch doctor, maybe."

"I'm sure there's one in town."

"It's this damn talent." He rubbed his forehead. "I suppose as I get older, it'll manifest itself in all sorts of screwy ways. That's something to look forward to."

"You're really cheering me up."

"On top of everything, I didn't get the cheeseburgers."

"Well, if you'll stay put, I'll go get some."

"I'll stay right here."

Because it was past five, it took me about thirty minutes to drive to Food Row, get the cheeseburgers and drive back. Camden was still sitting on the sofa, but he looked so odd, I said, "Camden? You okay?"

He gave me an unfriendly stare, stood, and drew himself up. "My name," he said in a cold voice, "is John Burrows Ashford."

Holy shit.

Okay, I'd play along for now. "David Henry Randall," I said with equal stuffiness.

He looked around. "And where is this?"

"302 Grace Street, Parkland, North Carolina, USA. Earth," I added, just in case.

He stared at me. "Parkland? Parkland! How did I get so far from the mountains?"

I caught his uninjured shoulder and turned him to face me. "All right, whatever's going on, just stop it right now. Camden, stop it."

I saw a flicker in his eyes like that weird membrane snakes have. Flick. The other personality was gone. Camden looked at me.

"What?" he said, as if I'd asked him a question.

"What the hell was all that about?"

"All what?"

"A minute ago you were John Ashford. I thought mediums usually channeled Indian chiefs named Mombasa."

He looked puzzled. "I had another blackout."

"You said you were John Burrows Ashford, the man my client says cheated and killed her great-grandmother." I went into my office and brought out one of the booklets Melanie had given me, *The Collected Folk Songs of John Burrows Ashford*. On the front cover was a picture of mountains in silhouette, trees, and a crescent moon. Inside, there was a picture of the great Mister

Ashford himself, a tall, dark-haired man with a permanent sneer. He was dressed in a black suit and vest, his chest puffed out like a rooster's, his prominent nose up. He reminded me of that pompous Colonel Winchester on *M.A.S.H.*

"What does it mean? What does he want?"

"Well, I don't know," Camden said, exasperated. "What did he say?"

"He wanted to know where he was and why he was so far from the mountains."

"And you said—?"

"What I always say when you get like that, 'cut it out.' I think my actual words were, 'stop it right now.'"

Camden took a long look at the picture and shook his head. "This is something new."

"Don't do it again."

"I don't remember doing it the first time." Then his eyes went wide. "Do you suppose during these blackouts, Ashford has been trying to come back through me? I don't like this idea at all."

"Me, neither." Although it had occurred to me this would be a simple way to solve my case. The next time Ashford popped in, I'd give him the third degree. No, this was ridiculous! Ashford was dead. Camden was having one of his breakdowns, that's all.

"But why Ashford?" he asked.

"You must be picking up some vibes from me."

He was unconvinced. "I suppose."

"Don't worry about it. The burgers are getting cold. Let's eat."

Kary came in and had a burger and so did old Fred. So did Buddy, who showed up with another box full of wooden animals. Conversation was normal, although I kept giving Camden glances to make sure he was still Camden. I was so concerned, I almost forgot to ask Kary for help.

Almost. "Kary, what's your schedule like tomorrow?"

She thought a moment. "Learning styles seminar in the morning and a talk with my advisor in the afternoon."

"Can you skip the talk? There's something you can do for my case."

"Great!"

Ignoring the evil eye Buddy sent my way and Camden's amused grin, I explained. "I need you to play some music for me. The owner lives in Oakville. He's an elderly man who doesn't want me to take or copy the songs. He can't play them for me, but I know you can."

She took another French fry. "I really need to meet with my advisor tomorrow. How about Friday?"

"That'll work."

Buddy made a snorting noise.

I put my burger down. "What's with you?"

"Nothing," he said. "Kary, honey, did you remember to ask about a dulcimer player?"

"Yes, I did. I think one of the music majors at school might be able to play. Let me get her number." She left the table to get the information for Buddy.

Buddy grinned at me. "Help on a case, my ass."

"Will you mind your own business? I don't remember inviting you to dinner, anyway."

He took another handful of fries. "Just 'cause your two-bit detective agency is here, don't think you own the place. Tell him, Cam."

When Camden didn't answer, we both gave him a quick look. His eyes were starting to glaze over. I reached out and shook his arm. "Hey. Don't do that at the table."

He blinked and came back. "Sorry, I drifted off for a minute."

"No drifting."

Buddy frowned in concern. "You feeling okay? Seeing something spooky?"

Camden decided this was the safer route. "Yeah. Some accident out on the highway. It's okay. Nobody got hurt."

Buddy nodded and chewed his fries. Everyone who knows Camden is used to this kind of thing. I raised my eyebrows as if to say, was it another blackout? Camden shook his head. I figured he was still shaken from his close encounter with Angie and the westbound traffic.

In a few minutes, Kary returned. "Buddy, I called my friend, and she can't play with your group. She's going to be out of town that weekend."

"Shoot a monkey," Buddy said. "Well, thanks for asking her. We'll have to try somewheres else. You're gonna come hear us, right?"

"Oh, I wouldn't miss it." She took her seat and picked up her cheeseburger. "Donnie has to work all day that Friday, but Saturday, we plan to come to the festival."

My cheeseburger tasted like dust. I set it down again. What a great basis for a successful marriage. Yes, we both love the Falling Leaves Festival.

Buddy chuckled. "Well, the two of you have a real nice time. You stop by and we'll play something special for you."

The food I'd already eaten struggled to the surface. "Excuse me. I just remembered there's a phone call I need to make."

I went back to the parlor office. I needed to contact Byron Ashford. He'd gotten my message and said he'd have time to talk to me tomorrow.

"I'll be glad to tell you my side of the story, Mr. Randall. Stop by any time after ten in the morning."

I thanked him and hung up.

I went online to check for an apartment, but after looking at about ten likely places, I sat back. Besides wanting to know more about Kary, I was a little concerned about Camden's mental state.

You need to stay here and look after both of them, I told myself, while my more rational side said, You're just looking for excuses. Putting off the inevitable.

After a while, I heard Buddy leave and then I heard Kary talking on her phone.

"But I thought we discussed this. You know how I feel."

Hmm, sounded like a problem.

"Donnie, for goodness sake. Don't be like that. No, we need to settle this. You know this about me. You know how I feel about children. I told you." She listened a while and then made an exasperated sound. "Well, maybe I don't want to wait. No, you don't understand! No, just forget it!"

Then there was a furious burst of music as she pounded on the piano. I didn't recognize this tune, either, but I imagined it was called "You Stupid Jerk." It was a good song. I enjoyed it. About the time she wound it up, a car horn beeped outside. She came to the front door and paused, startled, at my office door.

"Oh. Sorry about that, David. I keep forgetting you have your office there now."

"Anything I can help you with?"

"No, everything's fine. I just—have a few things to work out."

The next person to stop by my door was Camden, who said he was going to Lily's. "The Abduction Support Group meets this afternoon."

"See if Ashford has any advice for them."

"I'm sure Lily will let me know if he beams in."

"Did you hear Kary's 'Sonata in Rage'?"

He leaned against the door frame and put his hands in his jeans pockets. "I believe the whole neighborhood heard it."

"A quarrel with Donnie. Have you met this paragon?"

"'Paragon.' Ten points."

"Come on, that's worth twenty."

"Yes, I have met him."

"So is he the one for her?"

"No. But she thinks he is."

What? I sat up in my chair. "Good grief, tell her."

"Oh, I think we both know how well that would go over."

"Seriously. Is this prewedding jitters, or is she having second thoughts?"

"Let me put it this way. Kary has a definite plan for her life, and if someone doesn't fit in, she's going to leave them by the wayside."

And why wouldn't Donnie the Paragon fit in? That was a mystery I wanted to solve. Because if he wasn't part of her plan, maybe I could be.

Chapter Nine

"Where Have You Been,
My Own True Love?"

After Camden left for Lily's, I read Internet news about the Robertson PBS documentary. Some of country music's biggest stars were already attached to the project, and, as Ellin had said, Morgan Freeman was being considered as the narrator. Special preview showings were scheduled in L.A, Boston, New York, and D.C. before being broadcast on PBS nationwide. It was indeed a Big Deal. Robertson said, "We hope to include everyone, from the big cities to the humblest small towns, with songs representing all areas of our country. No contribution is too small or obscure. This is the peoples' music, our music."

I took a break on the porch. Camden and Lily came back through the hedge and up the front walk. Lily wore a ruffled blouse that hung down way past the waist of her patchwork skirt. The hat of the day looked like an old fisherman's hat, but instead of lures, it was decorated with pins. Probably souvenirs of all the planets she'd visited.

She tugged the hat. "But don't you see the significance of her dream, Cam? That white room, what could it be?"

Camden paused at the porch steps. "It's just a white room. Marsha's been thinking of repainting her den."

"But that tall guy, he'd really been abducted, hadn't he?"

"He really thought he had." By the tone of his voice he was letting her down easy. "He's read a lot of accounts, seen a lot of those TV dramatizations, and he was drinking a lot that night."

Lily wouldn't give up. "The aliens could've gotten him drunk, couldn't they?"

Most aliens I know carry a spare six-pack in the old saucer. Never know when you'll need a quick pick me up.

Another pause from Camden. "I don't think so, Lily."

"And what about Bummer?"

"All flashbacks. He took a few too many trips back in the sixties."

"Cam, weren't *any* of them abducted?"

"No." He looked sincerely sorry.

She sighed. "But we were so sure this time."

"Look at it this way," he said. "At least your support group is in place. When someone actually has a close encounter, you'll be ready."

"But they have all these stories. One of them has to be true." She glanced up at me. "Have you ever seen a UFO?"

"More times than I can count," I said.

"Really? Do you feel you've had an alien encounter?"

I'm having one right now. "Entirely possible."

I could have reeled her in if Camden hadn't said, "Randall never gives a straight answer. I don't think he believes in anything."

"Oh." She absorbed this radical concept. "That's too bad. So I don't guess you believe in ghosts, either, Mister Randall?"

A little figure in white, brown curls bouncing, a presence in the house. "No. No ghosts, no monsters, no Bigfeet, no Elvis sightings."

She grinned, her elfin face glowing in the sunlight. Damn, woman, get rid of that hat. "Well, I draw the line at Elvis sightings myself, but you have to believe we are not alone in the universe."

Honey, we are more alone than you could possibly imagine. "I think if there were intelligent life elsewhere in the galaxy, it would have contacted us by now."

"Oh, but it has!" she said. "We're just not able to interpret the signals."

"Yes, well, leave that to the expert here." I indicated Camden. "Your own neighborhood satellite dish."

She beamed at him. "We really appreciate his help. Most people think we're a little cracked. I can't blame them, I suppose."

"You know you can call on me anytime," Camden said.

Dark eyes sparkling, she put her hands on his shoulders. "Thanks, Cam. You're a sweetheart." She kissed his cheek and hopped back around the house.

I settled back in one of the rocking chairs. "Wow, she's a cutie. Space travel must agree with her."

"She certainly brightens up the neighborhood." He took his seat in the porch swing.

"Speaking of alien encounters, did Ashford return?"

"No, and if he had, I'm sure Lily would've told me."

"What's with this little support group of yours? They pay you for your time?"

"No. They don't ask me very often."

"Is there some reason you keep doing this?"

He watched the goldfinches hanging upside-down to tweeze thistle seeds out of their feeder. A few fat doves pecked at the grass beneath. "I saw a cartoon once. A man looking up at a flying saucer and little bug-eyed aliens looking down at him. The man says, 'Take me with you,' and the aliens say, 'No, you're too ugly.'"

"Actually, that's pretty amusing."

"Okay, I'll admit it's funny, but it's the ultimate rejection. Lily and these other people have been rejected by everybody, even aliens, or the aliens they think they've seen. They want to belong. I can understand that."

"So you go over and depress them further by telling them nobody's really been on a spaceship."

"They need to know the truth. They need a little reality."

"And you're just the man to give it to them."

He looked out across the lawn. "You bet. Somebody who sees things all day long, things nobody else can see."

"Why do they believe you?"

"I don't know. I guess they have to believe someone." He got up. "I'd better refill the bird feeder. Bring you anything?"

"No, thanks."

He put more seeds in the feeder and returned to the porch swing. Some shiny little blue bird joined the cafeteria line under the goldfinches. All the birds whirled away in alarm as Ellin's silver Lexus swung into the driveway. She slid out, beaming. For a moment or two, I could understand why Camden was so crazy about her.

She ignored me and went right to Camden. "Exciting news! I have a meeting with Robertson tonight. He's actually interested in a paranormal angle for his series. He likes the idea of tying it in with the Spiritualist movement. I want you to come meet him."

Camden, predictably, was not impressed. "No, thanks."

Ellin's voice went up an octave. "Why not?"

"I told you I don't want to be on TV."

"Good God, if I had your talent, I'd be touring the country!"

"Ellie." He remained baffled by her inability to understand. "Don't ever wish for something like this. It's not at all what you think. I'd trade places with you in a heartbeat except I wouldn't wish my kind of talent on anyone."

Oh, brother, I realized. Ellin isn't psychic at all.

Ellin turned away. Her hands gripped the top of the porch railing as she stared out into the yard, obviously trying to control her temper. "I thought by working closely with psychics, something would take, something would rub off or sink in, but I'm just a blank."

"Don't be so hard on yourself."

"You know everyone in my family is successful. Everyone! Mother is head buyer for women's clothing at Shay's Department store. My sisters head up their own companies." She faced him, her arms folded tightly across her chest. "I want a top position at the Service. I want to be the producer of the PSN. It's my one chance to prove myself. I'm not musical, I can't make clothes or cute little craft items, I'm not particularly athletic, and don't even ask me to dance."

He tried to stem the flow. "Ellie—"

"But I have excellent administrative skills, I'm well-organized, I can make tough decisions, and I work really well under pressure!"

And you're going to explode. She gave me a glare I read as, "You were supposed to help me convince Camden." I shrugged. These two were on their own.

"Ellie, you don't have to be psychic to get the job," Camden said.

"But you are, and you'd be perfect for this program. If you're not going to help me, then what am I supposed to tell Robertson?"

"I have other obligations."

"You're not doing a damn thing."

"It's Wednesday. I have choir practice."

She couldn't have looked more surprised if he'd bitten her on the leg. "You could skip one practice, couldn't you? I'm sure they have more than one tenor."

"I have two more solos."

Ellin plopped into a rocking chair. "I don't believe this. Cam, for heaven's sake, can't you let it go for once? The other choir members would understand."

"They're counting on me. And I want to sing."

She started that whine up again, but Camden stopped her with a look. "Ellie, I need to sing. It's important to me. The choir is important. Those people helped me out during some hard times."

"All right," she said. "All right!"

She propelled herself out of the rocking chair and down to her car. Camden sat on the swing for a while.

"And this woman is the one?" I couldn't help but ask.

He sighed. "Well, sometimes I wonder if I could be mistaken. I don't have visions about what's going to happen to me.

Sometimes I get a little glimmer of feeling from her, but it's never enough for me to be sure."

I was surprised there was even a glimmer. "Then she's not the one. Forget it. What about that cute little Lily from Jupiter? She's an alien, just like you."

"At the risk of sounding melodramatic, it's Ellie or no one."

"And you plan to marry this woman and be faithful to her forever?"

"If she says yes."

"You really are an alien."

Camden took another drink. "I need her, Randall. Besides being attracted to her, her lack of psychic ability can block the bad vibes."

"The blank she was talking about. So she's like your own personal force field."

"Don't tease her about it. It really bothers her." The birds had returned to the feeder, and he watched them for while, his expression withdrawn. "I'm using her, too. Why anyone would want this kind of thing is beyond me. I've spent my life either hiding the talent or constantly having to explain it."

"But it's useful, too. You've found things, found people. You can't say it's been a total loss."

He didn't answer for a moment. "Sometimes I'm afraid I'm going crazy."

"Well, you probably are. Your enormous brain just can't fit in your head anymore and it's leaking out."

"No. I mean, I think I might be—" he faltered, "—not human."

"So what do you think you are?"

His eyes were intent. "Doesn't it sort of make sense? I have all this strange psychic power. It had to come from somewhere. I don't know anything about either of my parents. Suppose one of them, I don't know—" he faltered again.

"Suppose one of them was a Martian? Okay. Sounds reasonable to me."

"No, listen. Suppose some of my visions are some kind of race memory?"

"You mean a message from Your People?" He looked so damn serious, I had to laugh. "Camden, for God's sake, you have O.D.'d on all those science fiction movies you watch. You're not an alien."

"Well, how the hell would you know?"

"Because I'm an alien, and we don't let weirdoes like you in the club. You need a ride to church tonight?"

Finally he managed to grin. "You read my mind."

◇◇◇

Victory Holiness was a little gray stone church in a rundown but neatly kept neighborhood. The houses along the street were small, but each one had a porch, a little yard, and some kind of fall flowers. The church sat on the corner next to a softball field and a small graveyard surrounded by a low border of stones. The sign out front said, "You Have Friends at Victory Holiness Church. Come Join Us." The early evening air was warm. A trace of cooler breeze hinted at a thunderstorm. The church's stained glass windows glowed softly. People entered the front door, calling to each other, shaking hands, laughing. Everything was warm and friendly, a perfect little Hallmark scene.

I knew then I couldn't go in. I could feel emotion rising in me and knew I wouldn't be able to take it. "I'll wait for you in the car," I told Camden.

The church had a small playground with some benches, so I sat down on one, and tried to pull myself back together. The breeze stirred the swings on the playground. I thought about the little girl who had blown me a kiss. I thought of my own little girl, who would never blow me a kiss again. I thought of the many times I'd taken Lindsey to school and waited until she was safely inside. I thought of the many times I'd picked her up, how she'd come skipping down the sidewalk, book bag swinging, long curls bouncing. She'd tell me how her loose tooth wiggled, how she lost her very best pencil, how Mrs. Andrews said her picture of Brown Bear was excellent, how yucky the potatoes tasted at lunch.

I shoved away years of memories. The choir sang a hymn, something about standing on promises. I'd promised to love, honor, and cherish—twice. I'd promised to look after Lindsey.

I changed position on the bench to look at the church, glowing more golden as the daylight faded. I tried to think of something else, my old church in Elbert Falls, bare wooden pews and cold white floors and windows of plain blue glass that made everyone look frozen; the uneven voices of our tiny choir, six members on a good Sunday, our faithful bellowing alto, a few weak and off-key sopranos, our thin reedy tenor, who would've killed to have had a voice like Camden's, clear and steady and not too high. I could hear it now, supported by the rich chords of the choir.

Cross the river to the promised land
With the angels I will stand
Close to my Lord, my Savior, there,
Fill my days with song and prayer.
When my days on earth are done,
I'll cross the river and fly to the Son.

There wasn't any promised land. Why were they bothering to sing about some fairy tale? They were just deluding themselves. This was it, right here, and if you screwed up, if you lost something valuable, something precious, it was gone, and there wasn't a damn thing you could do about it.

I have burdens, care and doubt,
Sorrows deep within, without,
Still I know the Lord will be
Close beside to comfort me.

The chorus swelled like a rush of cool air in the summer heat. The congregation sang along. It seemed the little church would burst with song.

Fly to warmth and fly to light,
Endless day for endless night,
When my days on earth are done,
I'll cross the river and fly to the Son.

Back in the car, I turned on my music, searching for something loud and raucous. The Black Eagles were stomping through their tenth anniversary concert when Camden got into the car. I turned the music down. He gave me one look and stayed silent. All the way back to the house, occasionally, I'd glance his way. He kept his gaze forward. But he knew. He knew everything.

◇◇◇

In my room later that night, the lamp made a pool of gold on the green spread. The rain-scented breeze lifted the curtains, and thunder rumbled faintly. Before morning, we'd have one of those rip roaring storms that bent trees and made houses shudder.

From upstairs, Camden sang yet another mournful song.

Where have you been, my own true love?
Where have you been today?
Alas, I am so far from home,
I fear I've lost my way.
If you would only take my hand
I'd lead you back to me,
For you're the fairest maiden
That ever I did see.

I thought about telling him to shut up, but I didn't. I let him sing it again.

Chapter Ten

"The Unquiet Grave"

Early the next morning, I was in the office on my cell phone with one of my better sources, Bilby Foster, asking about gold lockets, when I heard a voice in the hallway. Camden stood in front of the hall tree, an odd piece of furniture he said came with the house, a cross between a coat rack and a bench. It also has a mirror. Camden was staring into the mirror, holding up a lock of his untidy hair.

"What is this?" he said in that alien and superior tone. "Good Lord, doesn't this man own a comb? This is disgraceful! And he's so small!"

Oh, brother. Ashford again. "So what were you?" I asked him. "Mister Universe?"

He whirled to face me, his presence making Camden's youthful face look hard and old. "I was taller than *you*. Six six, a hundred and ninety pounds, well-groomed, in peak condition." He turned back to the mirror. "I can't imagine dealing in such a body as this! How old is this man? He looks like a street urchin."

"So go pick on somebody else."

"Oh, no. I've been trying for years to make contact with a sympathetic soul, a soul that understands music, that understands loss." He touched Camden's reflection and then his face. "I've heard him singing here in this house. My songs sound well in his voice. It will be difficult, but I'll look past the physical limitations."

"You can't take over like this."

His eyes gleamed in a way Camden's never did, a cold, calculating glitter. "I promise I will only use him for a short while, until my music is in the right hands."

I didn't like the sound of this. "I can do that for you. Tell me what needs to be done."

He shook his head. "I'll do it. Then I'll leave, I promise." He preened for a while in front of the mirror. "Even though he's woefully small, he's kept himself in shape."

This was creeping me out. "I want you to leave now."

"I shall come and go as I choose."

"No, you won't."

He laughed. "You're going to stop me? I don't think so."

I took a step forward, then realized any move I made would be toward Camden.

Ashford laughed again. "You hit me, who gets the black eye?"

An awkward situation, to say the least, but it could work to my advantage. "You're going to need help. To the rest of the world, you're Camden. If you want to get anywhere as Ashford, no one's going to take you seriously."

He eyed his reflection. "You may have a point."

"Tell me what needs to be done."

The look he gave me was full of loathing. He detested having to work with such an inferior slug. "Very well. But not now. Soon, I promise you."

Then Ashford was gone, and Camden was back. He swayed slightly, as if someone had jostled him on a crowded street, and blinked.

"We have a big problem," I said.

His gaze went to something behind me. "Randall, don't start with the remarks."

"What remarks?" I heard floorboards creak and for a moment thought Ashford was creeping up on us. I turned. It was Angie

Dawson in the flesh—and I do mean flesh—a large suitcase in one hand and a large CD player in the other.

"Where do you want me to put this stuff, Cam?"

He started for the stairs. "I'll show you."

The she-behemoth was moving in? Angie lumbered up the stairs behind Camden. When he returned, I had my arms folded and my eyebrows up. I probably looked as pissed as John Ashford.

Camden looked defensive. "I could use another tenant."

I glanced up, expecting the ceiling to sag. "You're joking, right?"

"It was Rufe's idea, and what could I say? I owe her, plus she's been kicked out of her other apartment."

"For what? Eating the other tenants? I don't think our place can stand the strain."

He was getting annoyed. It was a pale imitation of Ashford's exasperation. "She needs a place to stay, and I could use the extra money."

"Oh, she's going to pay rent? Excuse me."

"Rufus said he'd help her out."

"'Clash of the Titans.'"

"Just be nice, okay? No cracks about her size."

I glanced at the ceiling. "Oh, there'll be cracks, but I won't be making them. That wasn't the big problem I meant. I just spoke with Ashford, or don't you remember a blank moment?"

His eyes went wide. "Just now?"

"Before Angie came in."

"No. I remember you saying something about a big problem. I thought you were making a rude comment about my latest houseguest."

"Ashford's back and meaner than ever. Can't you tell when he's around?"

He gave no immediate reply. I could tell something had happened by the way he was staring at Ellin, who just arrived. This was not Camden's usual Glad to See My Girl stare. This was amazement and a predatory gleam.

"Do you mean to tell me *this* man has *this* woman? I am impressed!" He went to Ellin and folded her in his arms. "You are one of the most beautiful women I have ever seen."

"Camden," she said in surprise. "What on earth—?"

"Forget Camden!" Ashford said. "You need a real man, someone who can truly appreciate you, who can give you everything you desire."

She pushed against his shoulders. "Cam, this macho shit isn't funny."

He gave her a shake, his eyes hard. "I'm not Camden. He can't possibly be man enough for you."

Ellin surprised me with her impressive self-defense skills. She broke his hold and would've kneed him where it hurts if she hadn't been so perplexed.

Ashford gripped her arms again, and I said, "Ashford, back off." When he glared at me, I added, "Remember our conversation?"

Reluctantly, he let go. Ellin stepped back, rubbing her arms. "What the hell is going on? What's wrong with you?"

"Camden's not himself today," I said. "He's possessed by the spirit of John Burrows Ashford, songwriter and all-around prick."

As I expected, Ellin didn't have any trouble believing this. Still, she was a little taken aback.

"Oh, my lord, when did this happen?"

"He put in his first appearance yesterday."

She made a move as if to touch Camden's arm. "How long does he stay?"

Ashford drew himself up, or as far as he could in Camden. "As long as I like."

"No, you don't," I said. "Go on, take a hike."

"If by that cryptic phrase, you mean vacate this body, I suppose I shall, but if you continue to toy with me—"

"Yeah, I'm shaking. Get out."

As Ashford jumped ship, Camden sagged, and this time, Ellin's hands went to his shoulders to support him. He looked understandably surprised to be in her embrace.

"Hi," he said.

"Cam, Randall said you were possessed."

He glanced at me. "Again?"

"Big time. And he was even more of a snot this goaround, making passes at Ellin."

He reacted with alarm. "What?"

I thought the light in Ellin's eyes was relief. I should have known better. "Cam, this is fantastic. How often do you channel Ashford? What does he want?"

He pushed his hair out of his eyes. "I don't know. I don't remember his visits."

"But you probably could, couldn't you? This is wonderful! This is just what I need for my show. This is my way in!"

Even though I suspected she'd say something like this, I still didn't believe it. "You have got to be kidding."

She shot me an Ashford-quality glare. "Shut up, Randall."

"This is serious. Ashford wants to take over. The last thing we want to do is encourage him."

"Nonsense. Everyone knows spirits come back to resolve unfinished business. Once Ashford does this, he'll be gone."

"I don't think so. Unlike you, he wants Camden's body. We've got to get rid of him."

Camden cleared his throat to get our attention. "I'd really appreciate it if someone would tell me what's going on. I just got here, remember?"

Ellin's eyes danced with enthusiasm. "Cam, this is a major psychic event. We haven't had a true possession in months, and here I've actually talked to the man. If this happened on the show, our ratings would be supernatural, and you know this is going to be perfect for the PBS documentary."

Was there any way to derail her? "If this happened on your show, no one would believe it," I said. "They'd just think Camden was acting. How would you prove he was possessed?"

Another glare. "You stay out of this." She held onto Camden's arm. "Cam, how often does he drop in? Do you remember anything about how it feels?"

He pulled away. "Ellie, please don't get so excited. I don't remember a thing. Total blackout. Whatever business Ashford has, let's let him complete it and go back to the Great Beyond. I'm not interested in making a fool of myself on TV."

"Why don't we ask Ashford how he feels about it?"

"Ashford won't even know what TV is," I said. "He died in 1929. Talk about possession! Ashford could take lessons from you. Camden, you see what she's doing, don't you?"

"I'm not going on TV, and neither is Ashford."

"Cam, don't you see what an opportunity this is for me? Yes, it's awful he just comes in whenever he feels like it, but it's not going to be forever."

"How do you know that, Ellie? If I can't remember when he's here, what if I forget how to be me?"

If Camden hadn't looked peaked and wan, I think Ellin would've hauled him off to the TV studio right then. As it was, she backed down a little. "All right, would you at least let me know the next time he's here so I can have my camera crew or Robertson's film him? He could be an invaluable source of historical facts."

"He's only interested in himself," I said. "You'd get the facts according to Ashford."

Ellin rounded on me. "This has nothing to do with you."

"Yes, it does. I'm trying to find out why people keep getting killed over who wrote what song. It's the feudin' Gentrys and Ashfords."

"And you haven't asked Ashford anything while he's in Cam?"

"I've told him to get out."

"Oh, I don't believe that's all you've said. You can't accuse me of using Cam when you've parked yourself in his house with a front-row seat to everything that goes on here."

I didn't get a chance to defend myself. She turned back to Camden with his orders for the day. "Stay right here. I'll be right back with my crew. We'll film Ashford, let him say whatever he wants, and then maybe he'll leave, have you thought of that? Maybe all he wants to do is tell his story. Just stay here."

Out she went, punching a number into her cell phone.

I gave Camden another suggestion. "Run while you can."

He shook his head and went up the stairs to see if Angie had gotten settled. In a little while, Angie tromped down. "So what's the deal with Blondie? Man, that tongue could open tin cans."

"She's Camden's dream girl. Don't ask me why."

She jerked a massive thumb toward the stairs. "He'll be down later. I told him to take a nap."

"Yeah, he could use one," I said. "Things tend to get a little crazy around here."

She ambled toward the kitchen. "Who's this guy Ashford?"

"A dead composer who's decided to take over Camden's body."

She gave me her glacier stare. "Yeah, right."

I shrugged. "If you're going to live here, you'd better get used to this kind of stuff."

She continued her slow march to the food. "What about that brunette he works for?" She reached the counter and paused for breath.

"Tamara Eldridge."

"Nah. That'll never work."

So she was the expert now? "Why not?"

She grinned, her cheeks rising to cover her eyes. "Tam and Cam? I don't think so."

This surprised a laugh out of me before I could stop it. "I knew something wasn't right."

She edged around the counter to the fridge. "Used to work for a guy named Gayford Rayford. Painful. Downright painful. 'Gay Ray', everybody called him. Parents must have been crazy."

"My former boss is Gordon Morton."

"That's a mouthful." She gave me another cheeky grin. "How 'bout Chip Dipp? I swear that was the boy's name. And my momma knew a Bo Peep Thacker."

"That's nothing. I went to school with Thumbelina Andersen and Hiawatha Quisenberry."

Chuckles shook her rolls of fat. "Damn it, you're kidding now."

"Scout's honor."

"All right." She was suddenly serious. "Scout's honor. What's really going on around here?" She took a Coke from the fridge. "There's a beauty queen whose folks don't care where she is, an old man who looks like he's got mold growing on him, a little guy who sees things, and a struggling private detective who looks like some TV star, I forget his name, and this Ellin woman with the screechy voice."

"Welcome to 302 Grace Street." I checked my watch. "I've got to talk to someone about my latest case. Would you keep an eye on Camden? If Ashford shows up again, see if you can convince him to leave."

She eyed me. "Yeah, sure. Too bad I tossed my proton thrower and ghost trap away."

◇◇◇

From what Melanie had told me, I expected Byron Ashford to be a Class A jackass, but he was surprisingly civil and cooperative. In looks, he reminded me of an older, more polished Reg Haverson, tall, sandy-haired, tan and self-assured.

"There's nothing to hide." He led me into his spacious country home in Lesser Lake, one of Parkland's more exclusive suburbs. I'd parked the Fury beside a shiny black Corvette Sting Ray. "Melanie Gentry is simply a misguided young woman with too much time on her hands."

We went into a den decorated in neutrals, and Ashford indicated a tan leather sofa. "Could I get you a drink, Mister Randall?"

"No, thanks." The room was just as polished as its owner, oak-paneled walls, bookcases filled with leather-bound volumes and golfing trophies, a wide-screen TV, DVD, stereo CD player, all the latest toys. The beige curtains were drawn back to reveal tennis courts and an indoor swimming pool in the backyard. Lesser Lake gleamed a bright blue in the October sunshine. A speedboat bobbed at the dock.

"Do you write songs, too, Mister Ashford?"

"Not me." He gave a self-depreciating laugh. "Great Granddad had all the musical talent in the family. I can't tell one note from another." He sat down in a matching tan leather chair. "But I do know the value of my great-grandfather's work. The original copies are in the museum in Elenna. You can see for yourself who the author is."

"Do you know about the upcoming PBS documentary on early American music?"

"Yes, I do. In fact, I've been approached about being interviewed for the program."

"Ms. Gentry seems to think they will ignore the contributions of her great-grandmother entirely. Is this a valid concern?"

Byron Ashford sat completely at ease in his chair, his hand smoothing the soft leather. "What contributions? She's nothing but a footnote, if that. And if by some wild chance Laura Gentry had anything to do with those songs, who better to discover it than the experts?"

"You'd have no problem with that?"

"No problem at all. I told you, there's nothing to hide, no deep dark secret. My great-grandfather wrote those songs and that's all there is to it."

"What about Laura Gentry's death? There seems to be some question about how she died."

"You mean did John Ashford kill her? Mister Randall, I think Laura Gentry killed herself. She was emotionally unstable, living with a man in a time when this was beyond sinful, and when he could no longer handle her wild outbursts and demands and asked her to leave, she simply couldn't take it. All you have to do is read her letters."

From my own reading, I knew Laura's letters had become increasingly emotional, from the early simple letters filled with "I love you so much" to the more distraught "I cannot live without you."

"You've read her letters?"

"Yes, Melanie let me read them some time ago. She wanted John Ashford's letters, but I'd already promised them to the museum. She's certainly welcome to go there and read them. When you read his, you'll see how much he cared for Laura and how he tried to keep her from becoming so dependent. He knew the relationship was falling apart, and he was trying to soften the blow."

John Ashford was sounding more and more like a saint, and I knew from my brief encounters with him via Camden that couldn't be the whole picture. What would this smug man say if I told him I'd met his great-grandfather and thought he was a horse's ass?

"Suppose my investigation turns up information that proves Laura wrote these songs?"

His smile was more of a smirk. "That's highly unlikely."

"Coauthorship, then. They both get credit."

At last he displayed some of the famous Ashford snobbery. "Why should the Ashfords share credit with someone who doesn't really deserve it? But your questions are hypothetical. Go to the museum and see for yourself. Or ask any reputable musician or scholar. Melanie Gentry does not have a case. I hope she's paying you well for wasting your time. Was there anything else?"

"Yes. Do you know Albert Bennett? Would your great-grandfather have known anyone named Bennett?"

He thought it over. "I don't recall that name. Does this Albert Bennett have anything to do with the Ashford family?"

"Just checking." I'd had enough of this guy's attitude. If Melanie was the queen of her small country, then Byron was king of the neighboring province, glaring at her over the border and daring her to start a war. "I'll see myself out."

Chapter Eleven

"John of Hazelgreen"

When I entered his pawnshop, Bilby Foster looked exactly like a troll hunched over a king's treasure. He gestured to a glass cabinet. "Told you on the phone I had a few. Take your pick."

There were three lockets that fit Pamela Vincent's description of her missing necklace. "Can you put these aside until my client comes?"

"Got yourself another sweetie?"

"One can never have too many." I took out my cell phone. "Pamela, it's David Randall. Do you know Foster's Pawnshop in Parkland? He's got three lockets here you should have a look at."

"I'll be right there, thanks," she said.

I closed my phone. Bilby was inspecting a tray of rings, his thin mouth pursed as if each ring had come out of a box of Cracker Jacks. I walked up the aisle to the front of the store, passing the rows of guitars, banjos, mandolins, and other instruments hanging on the wall. Had people given up trying to learn to play them, or had their dreams for glory and success gone awry? This piano, too—did an aspiring musician have to pawn his treasured instrument for food or to pay the rent? Was he hoping and praying it would still be here when he had the money to claim it?

Would Kary take her piano with her when she left?

The thought of her leaving the house was like a blow to the chest. But if she married Donnie, she'd leave, and she'd take every trace of her: the piano, the colorful needlework, the silly-looking cow-shaped clock, the stained glass butterflies hanging in her bedroom window—it would be like a death in the family.

I sat down on the piano bench. My God, was that what was really bothering me? The thought of losing another—

I tried to keep Lindsey from my thoughts, but she came in anyway, smiling her perfect smile. She will always be perfect, eight years old, with her long brown curls and dark eyes, dressed in her best Sunday dress, all white lace, the dress we buried her in, the dress she was wearing as she sat in Camden's porch swing—

You don't deserve Kary. After all, you couldn't take care of one little girl. What makes you think you could take care of another?

It's not like that!

Pamela arrived before I managed to tie myself in mental knots. The sight of her changed Bilby's screwed troll face to open-mouthed admiration.

I escorted her to the back. "Three choices here. I hope one's yours."

Bilby was still staring. Pamela looked carefully at the lockets. "May I see this one?"

She had to repeat her question. I tapped on the glass top of the counter. "Bilby."

He snapped out of his stupor. "Oh, yes. Yes, indeed. One moment." He pulled out the tray and set it on top of the counter. Pamela picked up one of the lockets, and with a sigh, put it back in the tray.

"That's not it."

Bilby wilted as if he were personally responsible.

"Mine has the slightest tracing along the edge, and the chain isn't quite this thick."

He perked up. "I'll certainly be on the lookout for it. If you'd care to leave your number—"

"You can call me, Bilby," I said. "I'll see that Mrs. Vincent gets the message."

"Yeah, sure, okay."

Pamela viewed the surroundings. "You have a very nice shop, Mister Foster. Everything's so clean and well-organized. I'm afraid I had a completely different idea about a pawn shop."

"Please look around," he said. "Make yourself at home."

He watched as Pamela went up and down the aisles. "Randall, how do you do it?"

"She's a client. A married client."

"She's absolutely gorgeous. Reminds me of my mother."

"Your mother?" I'd always imagined Bilby as the offspring of a toad and a tree stump.

"Had that same beautiful red hair." He noticed my disbelieving stare and glowered. "Took after my dad."

Pamela came back with a smile that made the gold jewelry in the case seem dim. "This is quite a place, Mister Foster. I expected something dark and crowded."

"I'm very sorry I don't have your locket."

"And he's never sorry about anything," I said. "Thanks, Bilby. We're going to try Del's."

"He's got nothing but junk."

"We're going to try him anyway."

Pamela thanked him, and we went out. She sighed. "You know, I wish we could find the locket, but I'm really more concerned about how Nick is taking this. I keep telling him it's not his fault."

"Is his forgetfulness a problem for him at work? What does he do for a living?" I could just imagine Nick Vincent as a surgeon or a lawyer, one of those professions where you might need a good memory.

"Oh, he's the only child of a very rich businessman, so he's independently wealthy. He's always had plenty of money to buy whatever he liked, so if he lost something, or forgot where he put it, he'd just buy another."

"I believe he offered to buy you another locket."

"And I should've said yes right away, but I didn't. Now he's obsessing about finding this locket."

"We'll find it." Although I wasn't really sure how yet.

Pamela was still pondering Nick's background. "Maybe being an only child made him more scattered. Maybe his parents gave him too much attention."

I'm an only child, but I had a happy, normal childhood. I thought of Kary's parents. Since they turned out to be so heartless, was she afraid to trust anyone else? Was she afraid one mistake and she'd be thrown out again? Did Donnie seem safe and normal to her? What did that make me?

Something else I didn't want to think about.

"Let's head over to pawn shop number two," I said to Pamela. "And sorry, but it's just as clean and nice."

She pretended to be annoyed. "My goodness, for what I'm paying you, you should at least find one grimy hole in the wall."

◇◇◇

Although it was pleasant being in Pamela Vincent's company, we had no luck at any of the pawnshops we visited. She went back to Greenleaf Forest. I headed back to 302 Grace to see if Ellin had made good on her threat.

I expected to find TV vans, camera crews, and anxious paparazzi clustered at the windows. The front yard looked surprisingly normal. Camden was in the kitchen putting some food in Cindy's dish.

"Has the media circus already left town?" I asked. "I'd hate if I missed it."

"Ellie forgot she'd sent her camera crew to Greensboro to film the Wicca Convention. However, she's contacted Robertson's people, so I'm sure they'll all descend on us at some point."

"Ashford pop back in?"

"Not that I'm aware of, but then I never know when he's here."

"Well, Byron Ashford's convinced Laura Gentry had nothing to do with Ashford's work and is getting himself ready for a spot in the documentary. Maybe the two of you can share a segment."

I went back to the office and pulled out the folder full of Laura Gentry's letters to look through them again.

"My dearest John," one read. "You can't begin to imagine the emotions that swell within me as I pen these lines. Like the forgotten bride in the 'Resurrected Sweetheart,' like the heroine in 'John of Hazelgreen,' I can live only for the 'glance in your darkling eyes.' You must come see me. You must keep your promise."

"Trash. Sentimental trash," intoned the superior voice.

I looked up. Ashford was back on board, his presence making Camden's posture rigid and his eyes cold. He tossed his head back like some maestro about to conduct the philharmonic.

"I don't suppose you found anything of use."

"Your great-grandson's tone-deaf."

He decided whether or not to get angry before snorting. "Genius skips a generation or two. The important thing is that I have it."

I closed the folder. "What do you need Camden for, then? You're so brilliant, you find another way to come back."

He sauntered forward as if he owned the room. "I like the way my songs sound in his voice. The way he craves music, just as I do. It's too bad he doesn't know who he is."

"What are you talking about?"

Another snort, another head toss. "This pitiful young man has no idea about his family. I am John Burrows Ashford! My mother was Clara Barrows, a first lady of Virginia society. My father was John Davis Ashford, a wealthy and influential land-owner and politician. I can trace my ancestry back hundreds of years to the Stuarts of England and Scotland. What does Camden know? His mother gave him away. He never knew who his father was. He has no real family. Why, even his name isn't really his."

"Then why bother with him?"

His eyes glowed. "Because music is in his blood, in his very being, like me! I can give his life meaning. He can be everything I am and more. I can make him famous."

"He doesn't want to be famous. He just wants to be left alone."

"I never heard such nonsense. Why spend his life in this rundown old house when he could live in a mansion? He could travel, have concert tours around the world!"

"Look, he's been that route, and he doesn't like it. His clairvoyance brought him more than enough fame, usually the wrong kind. He wants a normal life."

The crafty look came across Camden's face. "Does he? You're not seeing it from my point of view, Mister Randall. I have the inside story, so to speak."

"Nice try," I said, "but Camden doesn't remember anything."

"Really?" His grin was sly. "Perhaps he says he doesn't remember, but I think he does."

"It doesn't matter. As soon as your business is finished, you're out of there."

Another calculating look. "And if I refuse?"

"I'll make you leave."

His laugh was harsh. "I don't think so."

I wanted to smash that superior look off his face. I hauled back my fist but my arm was grabbed and almost wrenched out of the socket by Rufus, who glared from his immense height like some wrathful hillbilly god.

"What the hell you think you're doing?"

How to explain, in twenty-five words or less, that I wasn't trying to hit Camden, but his evil alter ego? To make matters worse, Ashford, the bastard, fled like smoke up a chimney, leaving Camden to stare at us with wide confused eyes, which infuriated Rufus even more.

Rufus shook me. "Pick on someone your own size, you jerk."

My teeth rattled. "Same to you! Let go, you big moron. I'll explain."

Rufus let go and turned to Camden. "This clown was about to deck you. What's the deal?"

"Uh-oh," Camden said to me. "Was he back?"

"Beyond obnoxious. I almost lost it, sorry."

Rufus looked back and forth between us. "Who was back?"

"You'd better tell him," I said to Camden. "He's not going to believe me."

Camden sat down while Rufus hovered, still expecting me to attack. "It's like this, Rufe. I'm being possessed by the spirit of John Burrows Ashford, and apparently, he's a real son of a bitch."

Rufus may look like the poster child for intermarriage, but he always catches on to this kind of nonsense. "Well, who's this John Burrows Ashford and what makes him so special? Does he just step in whenever he feels like it?"

Camden rubbed his forehead. "Unfortunately, yes, and I can't tell when he's here."

"I can," I said. "He's one big mean son of a bitch."

Rufus got right to the point. "What are we gonna do about it?"

"I don't know. Ashford first said he'd leave after I solved my current case, but now he's making noises like he wants to stay."

Camden looked alarmed. "Stay? You mean, take over permanently?"

"Hell, he can't do that," Rufus said. "What case you talking about, Randall?"

"I'm trying to find out who wrote the songs in *Patchwork Melodies*, and who killed Albert Bennett and Laura Gentry. I'd like to blame Ashford, but I don't have proof."

"Well, find some. We aren't gonna have some dead guy parking himself in Cam whenever he wants."

Camden was still concerned. "Did he say that exactly, Randall, that he was going to stay?"

"That's not going to happen. I'll find some way to get rid of him."

My cell phone rang.

Rufus gave the phone a glare. "That better not be Ashford."

Fortunately, it was Pamela Vincent.

"Hello, David. Hope I'm not interrupting anything."

Just a little out-of-body session. "Not at all. What's up?"

"I'm calling to say thank you for trying, but we've decided the locket's gone. Nick's going to buy me another. It won't be the same, but I'll be more careful with this one."

First Ashford and now strike two. "I'll be glad to keep looking."

"That's all right. I'll send you the rest of your fee. Thanks again."

She hung up.

"You got another ghost calling you?" Rufus asked.

"No, that was Pamela Vincent. I'm trying to find her locket. She called to say don't bother, but I'm not ready to give up yet." Plus, I'd never asked Nick about his technique. "And I'm not going to give up on getting rid of Ashford, either."

A horn honked. We went out to the porch. Buddy had arrived to work on his woodcarvings. Three large pumpkins gleamed from the back of his pickup.

Buddy waved. "Thought I'd get a start on Halloween. How many you want, Cam?"

"As many as you like."

"We'll line the porch steps. Scare the little goblins."

He and Rufus set up shop in the backyard. I didn't feel like gutting pumpkins, so I called around to a few more pawnshops, asking about the heart-shaped locket. Ashford didn't make a return appearance. After a while, Buddy and Rufus were joined by two more men, and they began to practice their music. It was hard to concentrate with an intensely nasal version of "Fox on the Run" reverberating from the backyard. I decided I needed a peanut butter cracker or two.

I found Camden sitting at the dining room table, a plate of Pop-Tarts and a glass of tea untouched. He gazed out across the backyard. The leaves shone brilliant yellow and red; the oak leaves, glossy brown. Little breezes chased the leaves on the ground and sent others spiraling from the branches. Faint smells of toast and coffee lingered in the kitchen where the cow-shaped clock ticked quietly.

I kept my tone neutral. "Thinking about those gutters, huh?"

"Among other things."

I sat down. The backyard concert paused while Buddy reattached a string to his banjo. The silence stretched. Cindy padded in and hopped up in the window to watch the leaves.

"Mrs. Rosalie Camden," Camden said. "I'm thinking about her, too."

"Your foster mother?"

"The last one." His gaze, like Cindy's, was still on the leaves. "In Virginia. She was very kind, but her husband was never comfortable around me."

More silence. There wasn't anything to say. I knew he'd been passed around from one family to another until he was old enough to strike out on his own. Despite his good looks and calm disposition, his talent had been too spooky for normal folks.

I could tell that Camden's gaze was way beyond the leaves now. "So Camden isn't my real name. It's hers."

He never mentioned his past or made any reference to how it must have been. I knew he'd been born in Virginia and had grown up in several foster homes. I knew he'd dropped out of school and traveled around the country before settling in North Carolina. He'd never seemed depressed about it. This was the work of John Burrows Ashford, undermining his confidence, softening him up for the final takeover: your life is so pitiful, so worthless, let me live it for you. I knew Ashford wasn't going to give up so easily.

Outside, the band tuned up and started something slow and melancholy. The guitar player strummed his guitar and sang about traveling a lonesome road.

Camden listened for a while. "John Camden. Not very imaginative, is it? Practically every boy at Green Valley was named John. Sort of like a scene from *Buckaroo Bonzai.*"

"At least she didn't name you Rosalie."

This brought a grin, a slight one. "Or Hubert. That was his name."

I was probably one of two people who knew his first name. Too bad it was the same as Ashford's. This had to be working in the songwriter's favor.

"Does it matter?" I tried to sound casual. "Lots of screwed-up people came from wonderful upstanding parents. Having a certain name doesn't guarantee success."

"No, it's just that I've never been able to find out my real name, if I ever had one. And the only thing I know about my mother is what Mrs. Camden told me. She said she was a young woman who couldn't keep me. It's as if my parents never existed."

"Maybe they're using their super-secret powers to block you from finding out your true identity."

He grimaced. "A kryptonite shield, perhaps?"

"Ashford's the reason you're feeling like this. He thinks he can win you over with his lofty family tree. Don't let him get to you."

"I can't remember anything he says. I wake up, you tell me he was here, I go on as usual."

"There has to be some way for you to make contact with him. He's working on you from the inside. How are you going to fight him if you can't remember anything?"

"I don't know, Randall. I've never had this happen before. What am I supposed to use for ammunition?"

"He wants the mystery solved. He wants the world to know he is the author of those songs."

"I thought he was."

"Well, obviously something's wrong, or he would've stayed dead."

Camden picked up his sneakers. "I have to get to work."

It was unsettling to think that spacey little Lily was right all along. Maybe she did have a direct line to the stars.

"Camden, there's a way out of this problem. I'm the hotshot detective here. Why don't you let me find your parents?"

"No, thanks. If they didn't want me before, why should they have anything to do with me now? I'm not interested."

With eyes like his, he's a terrible liar. "If you know more about them, you could keep Ashford from taking over. Don't you have a birth certificate somewhere?"

"I don't know where it is."

"It's bound to have your mom's name on it if nothing else. You don't remember?"

"When I left home, I didn't take a lot of things with me."

"Would Rosalie Camden have a copy?"

"She died a long time ago."

"So who got her stuff?"

He shook his head. "Forget it. I appreciate the offer, but no, thanks. We'll have to think of some other way to get rid of him."

"Okay." I'd already put my mind in gear. He didn't know it, but he'd given me enough information to start my search. He could thank me later.

Chapter Twelve
"The Wild Daisy"

Tamara picked Camden up before I turned on my computer. Until now, I'd kept out of Camden's personal affairs, figuring if he wanted me to find his folks, he would've said so long ago. This was the first time he'd ever mentioned any names or places. I started with "Green Valley" and "Virginia." Several items came up, including the Green Valley Home for Boys in Bell City. I clicked on the web address and found an address and phone number. It was doubtful anyone at the home would give me Camden's information. In certain circumstances, adoption records were sealed in Virginia. But if I could find someone who knew Rosalie or Hubert Camden, I might be able to learn his mother's name. Bell City was about three hours from Parkland. If I left now, I could make it there and back today.

I found Kary at the piano, looking through her sheet music. She set the stack of music aside and opened the piano bench. "You haven't seen my copy of Chopin's Ballades, have you? I think I'll play the G minor for the Miss Falling Leaves Pageant."

"So you're definitely going to enter?"

"First prize is five thousand dollars."

"I'd walk around in my bathing suit for that."

She closed the bench. "Where could that book be?"

"I'll help you look."

"Maybe it's in the bookcase. It has a yellow cover."

There were several patchwork cushions in the island, the kind that are large enough to sit on. I could tell Cindy had used a few of the tassels as cat toys. I pulled two over so we could sit down to look through the music. Outside, the Nasal Boys continued with "Foggy Mountain Breakdown."

Kary set another stack of books to one side. "Now where is that stupid book?"

I pushed the old encyclopedias over, disturbing a tiny spider. "Why don't you play one of your own pieces?"

"They aren't nearly good enough."

"I think people would like them. What about that one you were playing the other day? It was very nice."

"David."

I waited for her to continue, afraid I'd pushed too hard.

She sat back on the cushion. "I love music, and I've always written little tunes and songs. I thought at one time I'd be a composer. I had a scholarship to the Kirby Music School in Charlotte, but I had some health problems and couldn't go. I had to give it up."

I started to say "I'm sorry," but she put up her hand.

"It's okay. You didn't know. That's why I'm telling you. I write some music every now and then, but just for fun. Cam's already been after me to have them published, so don't you start, too."

"That's a very good teacher voice you've got going there."

"Thanks. I like to keep in practice."

"Are you studying to be a music teacher?"

She tugged at a folder that had gotten stuck under a large dictionary. "I thought about it, but there are so few positions in the arts. I'd like to teach second grade." The folder came loose, but it didn't have what she was looking for. "I've done some practice teaching in second grade. Second graders can usually tie their own shoes, and they haven't become jaded. They're still open and excited about life. You can teach them anything."

Lindsey had loved second grade. She'd loved school. Hell, she'd loved everything. There were so many things she'd never experience.

I was glad Kary was focused on her search because my expression must have been grim before I got it under control. I pushed another row of books over and caught a glimpse of something yellow with "Chopin" in black letters. The music book had fallen behind the bookcase, which fortunately didn't have a back.

I tugged it out. "Is this it?"

"Yes! Thank you!"

When I handed her the book, our fingers touched. Kary held my gaze longer than I expected. Then she blushed a little and got up. "Thanks."

To cover my confusion, I used my best TV promo voice. "I'm a detective. I find things. That's my job."

I made her laugh. She went to the piano and began to play. I put the rest of the books back on the shelf and headed out to Virginia. I was a detective and it was time for me to do my job and find something very important.

◇◇◇

There were quite a few Camdens listed in the Bell City phone book. I started with Allen Camden, asking about Rosalie or Hubert, and worked my way through down one column until I reached a Daisy Camden, who sounded pleasant if slightly concerned.

"Rosalie Camden was my mother. What's this all about?"

"My name's David Randall, Miss Camden. I'm trying to find out some information about Rosalie's adopted son, John. Did you know him?"

"Oh, you mean Johnny? The one with epilepsy?"

Well, this was news. I wasn't sure what to say. "Yes."

"Poor little thing. He left home when he was just sixteen. I don't know how in the world he could get along having those fits of his."

Ah, the mysterious fits. "Staring into space? Seeing things? Maybe not remembering where he was?"

"Yes, exactly. Why are you calling? Has something happened to him? I can't be much help to you, and Mother and Father are dead."

"Miss Camden, if you don't mind, could we meet somewhere? Camden—that is, Johnny—needs to know about his birth mother, and I was hoping you or another relative might have a copy of his birth certificate."

"That would be in Mother's things."

"Would it be possible for me to see it?"

A long pause. If she hung up now, my best chance would be gone.

"Well," she said, "I don't suppose there's any harm in it. I'm on Cross Street, near Circle Drug, number three-fifty-five. Come on over."

◇◇◇

Daisy Camden met me on the porch of her small blue house. If she took after her mother, then Rosalie Camden must have been a large shapeless woman with soft wrinkled features and wispy hair trying to escape an untidy bun.

"Thanks for seeing me, Miss Camden."

"Well, it's nice to see you, Mister Randall. Come have a seat."

We sat down in white plastic chairs. Daisy smoothed the skirt of her billowy flowered dress. "You know, I often wondered about Johnny and hoped he was all right. You say you're a friend of his? How's he doing?"

"He's doing fine," I said. "He works in a clothing store in Parkland."

"My, my. Got those fits under control, I hope."

"Yes. He never mentioned a sister, though."

"Oh, he probably don't remember me. I was a good fifteen years older and out of the house by the time Mother took him in. Mother said nobody wanted him on account of his problem. Just remember he was a cute little thing, always humming or singing."

"He still does a lot of singing."

"Is he married? Got kids?"

"He has a girlfriend."

"That's good. Now what was it you wanted to know?"

"His birth mother's name."

"Well, I got no idea where that birth certificate is, but we can look for it."

The bare front porch sporting only two plastic chairs gave no clue to the amazing disorder within the little blue house. I stood in the doorway, appalled. I'm not the kind of guy who keeps his clothes sorted by color, but neither am I the kind of guy who leaves empty pizza boxes and beer cans on the floor. I sure as hell don't leave everything I own on the floor. Daisy led the way through the piles of clothes, papers, and empty food containers, following a narrow trail through the debris. I expected an entreating skeletal hand to rise from the depths. Save me! Or a tribe of feral cats oozing around the stacks of newspapers and plastic bags.

"It'll be back here somewhere. That's where I put all of Mother's things."

Mother's things were crammed into another room from floor to ceiling: furniture, boxes, books, more clothes, and lots of things I didn't recognize. Camden had said Rosalie died a long time ago. I didn't want to think about what had been growing in this room since then.

Daisy began to root around in the mess. "Should be a box in here with papers."

I was afraid she'd cause an avalanche. "A file box, maybe?"

"Shoe box, most likely."

Great. Wishing I had some plastic gloves, I started digging. I caused several crashes trying to retrieve what looked like shoe boxes from the elephants' burial ground.

"Sorry, Miss Camden."

"That's all right. Just push it over to the side. And call me Daisy. I feel like we're kinfolk."

What side? There was no side. I managed to rearrange enough junk to get to another stack. Daisy must have rented a forklift to clean out Rosalie's house. "Did your mother have a family Bible? Sometimes important papers are kept in Bibles. Or a photo album, maybe."

"Mother didn't take any pictures. As for a Bible, I don't remember seeing one."

"Do you remember seeing anything from the Green Valley Home for Boys?"

"Can't say that I did."

"Did your mother have a desk?"

"Oh, yeah. It's under here somewhere."

After thirty minutes, we'd cleared a path to the desk, a medium-sized rolltop. It took another thirty minutes to move enough stuff so that we could roll the top back. Papers were crammed into every possible space, letters, envelopes, receipts, recipes, scraps with names and addresses, prescriptions, old birthday cards, and coupons. I was just about ready to give up when Daisy tugged the bottom drawer free and said, "Is this what you're looking for?"

She pulled out a faded green folder with "Green Valley Homes for Boys" written across the front and handed it to me. I opened the folder and caught the thin piece of paper before it floated out. *Certificate of Live Birth.* "This is it."

"Well, how 'bout that?"

We stood knee-deep in the trash and read the certificate. John Camden had been born in Bell City Memorial Hospital on February 22 at eight p.m. He'd weighed all of six pounds. Under "Father of Child" was written "Unknown." Under "Mother of Child" was written "Denise Baker." Her age was listed as sixteen.

Denise Baker. "Thank you, Daisy."

"Why don't you take that along? Seems to me Johnny should have it."

"He'll appreciate that."

"And bring him to see me."

◇◇◇

On the way home, out of curiosity, I drove past the Green Valley Home for Boys. I had a mental image of a grim stone prison, but the series of brick buildings looked more like a small college campus, complete with shade trees, a soccer field, and a basketball court. It didn't look like a bad place to live, but then, I'd never been an orphan. I had what I came for, though. I had a name. With any luck, the Internet and my best search engines would be able to locate the Denise Baker who was sixteen thirty years ago and lived in Bell City.

As soon as I got to 302 Grace, I fixed some peanut butter crackers and a Coke and set to work. On PublicRecords.com I typed in "Denise Baker" and "Bell City, Virginia." This brought up a list of Denise Bakers, all too old or too young to fit the requirements. Next I tried "Denise Baker" and "Richmond, Virginia," thinking maybe Denise had left the Bell City area. Checking this list, I found several good possibilities, so I wrote down the addresses. Five had phone numbers. Definitely worth a try.

The hard part would be convincing her that her son was possessed by an angry, bitter composer and finding her might just save his life.

Chapter Thirteen

"True As Silver"

I wasn't too thrilled to find Fred in the kitchen the next morning, dunking his toast in his coffee and scowling. I'd hoped he was already in the park, arguing with other old geezers about the space program. Fred must have harbored some secret desire to be an astronaut, and if any of his cronies dared to suggest the moon landing had been faked, he'd start trying to chew their legs off. Every day, Camden gave him money for a newspaper and a cola. Every day, Fred came home purple in the face over something he'd read. When I asked Camden why the hell he let Fred buy a paper if it upset the old man so much, he said getting riled was the only thing in life Fred truly enjoyed.

"Morning, Fred."

The scowl made Fred look like one of those bizarre dried apple dolls people sell at the festival. "You still here?"

"I'm just as surprised as you, Fred."

"Cam know about this?"

"Yes. I have his permission."

Another scowl. "You pay rent?"

"Do you?"

He pulled his coffee cup closer, as if afraid I might snatch it, toast crumbs and all. "Ain't none of your business."

While I was scrambling some eggs for my breakfast, Kary came in, tying the sash of her white robe, her golden hair loose around her shoulders, an absolute vision of just-out-of-bed perfection.

"Good morning, David. Good morning, Fred."

Fred made a "Huh" sound that could've meant anything.

"Good morning," I said. "You can still go to Oakville this afternoon, right?"

"Yes, I'm looking forward to it."

As she went past to the fridge, I caught Fred's eye. He was looking at me as if he'd caught my hand up her robe.

"You better watch your step, Mister."

"Fred, my intentions are completely honorable."

Another "Huh!" I knew what this one meant. He shook a piece of toast at me. The limp corner that had been in the coffee fell off on the counter. "She'll be leaving soon. She won't have to fool with you drooling over her anymore."

I wasn't in the mood to be lectured by Space Geezer this morning. I scooped my scrambled eggs onto a plate and turned as if recalling something. "Isn't the shuttle going up in about ten minutes?"

He gave a start. "Where?"

"I think you can see it from the park."

"Damn." He crammed the rest of the toast in his mouth, washed it down with the coffee, and trotted around to the stairs. "Cam! Cam, I need my money!"

Kary reached into the grocery frog on the counter and pulled out a handful of quarters. "Fred, Cam's in the shower. Here, take this."

He hurried back to the kitchen, grabbed the change, and ran out the front door. In a few minutes, he was back to snatch his coat off the hall tree. The door slammed.

Kary brought her cereal and milk to the counter. "What was that all about?"

"You know how Fred is." I put my toast on the plate and brought it to the counter. Kary sat down across from me, and

I had about five minutes to enjoy this peaceful domestic scene before Rufus wandered in to get his cereal.

"Festival opens today," he said. I got a dark look. "Still no dulcimer player."

"I haven't forgotten."

He gave me a scowl old Fred would've envied and indicated Kary with a slight nod. "Nah, you've had other things on your mind."

At the risk of angering this mammoth, I said, "And how's your new girlfriend enjoying life here at 302 Grace?"

Surprisingly, he backed off. "We're getting along just fine."

Camden came in, dressed for work, his hair in all directions. "Morning, everyone."

"You own a comb?" Rufus asked.

He pushed back his bangs. "I'll make the attempt when it's a little drier."

"I take it you need a ride to Tamara's," I said.

"Yes, please."

"How about you, Kary? Need a ride anywhere?"

"If you could drop me off at the college, that would be great."

"Just call me the family chauffeur."

Camden took his box of Pop-Tarts out of the cabinet. "Larry over at Parkland Motors still has that Festiva you were interested in, Kary."

"The one that's Day-Glo green? It's cute and definitely memorable. I wouldn't even need headlights."

"Kind of bright, is it?" I asked.

"It looks like a nuclear pea," Camden said. "I told her she should get it. Actually, I told Larry he should pay her to take it off his hands. It's got about thirty thousand miles on it, new tires, already inspected. You're going to be driving what, maybe three miles a day? The Festiva would be perfect for you to drive back and forth to school."

"I'll think about it."

Rufus shook the last of his cereal into a large bowl. "Squished a Festiva against my forehead once, just like a beer can."

Kary laughed. "I hope not."

"Just kidding."

I figured the Festiva issue was as dead as a flattened beer can, finished my breakfast, and announced the Randall limo service would be leaving whenever the passengers were ready. Kary went upstairs to get dressed. Camden managed to wrangle his hair into some sort of order and filled his glass with Coke.

Rufus took a big gulp of coffee. "That Ashford bothering you today?"

"As far as I know, he hasn't dropped in."

"Doing anything about that, Randall?"

Actually, yes, I wanted to say. I may have found Camden's mother. Whether or not she can be of any help is the question. "I'm on the case."

"Seems like you're on everybody's case today."

I had a few minutes, so I went into the office and called the first Denise Baker on my list, Denise B. O'Brien. She was pleasant but firm.

"You have the wrong number, sir. I never had any children, and quite frankly, never wanted any."

Strike one.

The second Denise Baker was Denise Baker Hofsteder. The house sitter informed me that the Hofsteders were in Africa and wouldn't be back for a month.

"Denise and I have been friends since grade school," the woman said. "I would've known something like that. And her family was very wealthy. If that had happened to her, they would've provided for the baby."

Strike two.

The third Denise Baker, Denise Baker Sommers, said she wished she could help me, but she wasn't the one I was looking for and she was the only Denise Baker she knew. The fourth Denise wasn't home, so I left a message on her machine, and the phone number for the fifth Denise was no longer in service. By now I'd run out of strikes. There was one more Denise, Denise Baker Rice, and her phone number wasn't listed. Still, I had her address.

It wasn't long before Kary came back down the stairs in jeans and a rust-colored sweater decorated with gold leaves. She even had on little gold leaf earrings. Camden obligingly took the back seat so she could ride up front with me.

"I really like your car," she said as I got behind the wheel. "What kind is it?"

"A Plymouth Fury. It was my dad's."

She smoothed the burgundy vinyl seat. "Well, it's not a Day-Glo Festiva, but it's nice. Isn't it a little conspicuous, though, when you're on a stakeout?"

"It strikes fear in the hearts of evil-doers everywhere."

"Well, I hope this music you want me to play helps you catch an evil-doer."

"As clues go, it's a long shot, but it's worth a try."

She turned to Camden. "Are you coming, too?"

"It sounds like fun, but I have to work all day today."

"Such a shame," I said.

When I pulled up in front of the community college, Kary gave my arm a squeeze before she got out. "I'm excited about this. See you later." She waved and went inside.

Camden slid into the passenger seat. He gave me a sidelong glance.

"My intentions are completely honorable," I said. "And if you decide to come along, I'll toss you off the first scenic outlook."

On the way to the shopping center, he didn't say much, but he didn't break into mournful song, either, so I figured he was all right. I wondered if I should mention Daisy and my trip to Bell City, but something told me to hold all the family information in reserve until I knew for certain I'd found Camden's mother. Camden seemed himself today. Maybe Ashford had given up and gone back to the Other Side.

Like most of the shops, Tamara's Boutique was decorated for Halloween, black plastic torsos in the window draped in orange and gold, little bats hanging from the ceiling, and pocketbooks shaped like half moons dangling from the mannequins' wrists.

I pulled into an empty parking space. "Put Tamara on Ashford Alert. If he comes back, she can give me a call."

"Okay."

"Tell her the window looks great. Very festive. Ask her what she's going to be for Halloween."

"She's made herself a very fancy witch costume."

"And what are you going to be?"

He got out of the car and leaned back in the window for a moment. "I hope I'll be me."

I drove down to Mayes Street where the stores were decorated for Halloween, too. The big half-price clothing store had an array of masks and children's costumes in the windows. I remembered every single one of Lindsey's costumes. There were pictures somewhere. Barbara had them. Barbara had all her things. Her first Halloween, we'd dressed her in a little pumpkin suit. Then she'd been an angel, a teddy bear, a fairy, a gypsy for the next two years, and then a princess.

And now she was back to angel.

God, I didn't want to think about that. If I'd had any idea the pink princess dress with the real lace and gold spangles and jeweled crown she so adored she even wore it to bed was going to be her last Halloween costume—well, what could I have done differently? Her last Halloween, her last Christmas, her last Valentine's Day—would I have cherished those special days more?

Nothing special about the holidays anymore.

Disgusted with myself for getting into such a mood, I turned back up River Street West and headed downtown, determined to do something constructive and find Pamela Vincent's locket. People would be setting up for the festival this morning. Somebody who dealt in jewelry might have a lead for me, and some of my sources might have news about Albert Bennett's murder.

A few streets had already been closed off, so I had to park several blocks away and walk through the confusion of festival setup. Parkland's Main Street is a wide boulevard lined with maple trees, brilliant red leaves carpeting the sidewalks. Large stores such as Montgomery Ward and Sears had gone out of business or moved to outlying malls, and instead of letting the buildings fall into ruin, clever developers had chopped up the space into little specialty shops, restaurants, and luxury condos.

There was a strong smell of coffee and bacon from the corner café. The street echoed with the whack of hammers, the whine of electric drills, and the clang of dropped metal posts as people scrambled to get their booths assembled. Trucks, U-Hauls, and vans backed up and unloaded the stacks of tee shirts, boxes of candles, and piles of baskets. Further down the street, I found Buddy and a friend putting together the shelves that would hold all his carvings.

He gestured me over. "Randall, come hold this side."

I held one end while he slid the other piece into a groove.

He straightened and dusted his hands. "That's got it, thanks. We'll put the ducks here, Velmer."

Velmer was another large man in overalls, his long untidy brown hair sticking out from under a cap that said "Squirrels Unlimited." His scraggly beard hung off his chin like Spanish moss. One hand was bandaged, apparently from the possum bite. He squinted at me. "This the Randall you was talking about, going to find us a dulcimer player?"

"That's what he says."

"No luck yet, fellas, sorry."

"All the good ones is taken," Velmer said. "Told you we shoulda started looking sooner, Bud."

"Well, hell, that ain't my department. Hand me the ducks and quit being such a butt."

Velmer moved back to Buddy's truck to grapple with a cardboard box. Buddy reached under a table and pulled out another box. "Don't let Velmer rile you, Randall. He's a few pickles short of a jar, if you know what I mean. I know you're doing all you can."

"I've got several things going at the same time," I said, "but I haven't forgotten the Nasal Warblers."

"You mean the Frog Hollow Boys."

"Is that what you're calling yourselves now?"

"Velmer wanted us to be Goose Creek Fever, but another group's got a name kinda similar."

Velmer returned with the box of ducks. "Well, Frog Hollow Boys ain't too much of an improvement."

I didn't want to spend the day discussing the merits of Frog Hollow Boys over Goose Creek Fever. These guys were going to sound pretty rough no matter what they called themselves. "Anybody setting out jewelry yet?"

Buddy gestured with a duck. "On up the street. Fella's got about a ton of belt buckles. Thinking of getting one with a salmon on it, what do you think?"

He pronounced it "sall-mon," so it took me a minute to realize he meant the fish. "Sounds good."

"And that feather woman's here, the one with all the tattoos. She's got some nice bracelets."

"Thanks." I walked up a few blocks. Feather Woman wasn't hard to find. She was about six feet tall, her unnaturally black hair pulled back in a long ponytail with what looked like two eagle feathers. She was wearing jeans and a short-sleeved tee shirt. Every inch of her muscular arms and what I could see of her neck and shoulders was covered with small multicolored tattoos, most of them intertwining flowers and vines. Her booth was already assembled. She was putting out cases lined in black and filling the cases with silver bracelets, necklaces, rings, and earrings.

"Morning," she said. She had strong features and dark eyes. She continued to work.

"Beautiful stuff," I said.

"Not selling yet. Come back this evening."

"I'm looking for something in particular, a gold heart-shaped locket."

"I only deal in silver, and I don't do hearts."

"Safer that way."

She gave me a thin smile. "True."

"Anybody in the festival deal in gold?"

"Several people. You might try up at the corner, Tommy Fairbanks and Annie Blum. Or you might buy something more your style." She picked up a ring shaped like a skull. "Here's a nice little conversation piece."

"No, thanks."

"Not into death? How about a lightning bolt?"

"I thought you weren't open yet."

She shrugged. "Somebody looking for a heart, I make an exception."

"This heart was stolen."

"Aren't they all?"

I walked past more booths. A tangle of wind chimes made uneven melodies in the brisk breeze. Slick wooden chairs and tables were stacked up under one tent, as well as wooden key holders, napkin holders, and candleholders. I passed a large woman unloading framed photographs of lighthouses and two stout men in overalls pushing a cart filled with apples.

"David! Over here!"

Lily waved from a tent made of spangled purple netting. I wandered over to admire the celestial glory of the ASG's Festival Tent. Bright plastic stars hung from the corners. Three tables were covered with crystals resting on purple velvet. Lily was covered in some sort of ghastly red-and-white polka dot shawl, her white hair under something that might have been a sombrero decorated with one of the plastic stars.

"Look what a great place we have this year!"

I wasn't sure what was so great about being wedged between a booth full of oddly colored pots and a booth selling peanuts, but I made all the right replies.

Lily continued to color-coordinate her crystals. "You see, everybody loves peanuts, so we'll always have a crowd. Last year we were beside these really expensive paintings and Emma Lou's Country Jumpers that cost forty dollars apiece. We didn't do well at all, but this year, we'll be able to do really well, I think."

"I think so, too, Lily."

She beamed at me. "Do you still have your lucky crystal?"

"I carry it with me everywhere."

"Are you buying someone a present?"

"Looking for a stolen necklace. I haven't had much luck."

"You'll find it. You're very good at finding things."

I almost told her I might have found Camden's mother. "Thanks." I left her pondering whether or not to put a big clear crystal beside a blue one and went on up the street.

Tommy Fairbanks and Annie Blum were in the middle of an angry quarrel. Fairbanks was a big, soft-looking man dressed in jeans, cowboy boots, and a flannel shirt. His loose, fleshy face contrasted with Annie Blum's sharp bony little features, but his pale blue eyes and her dark gray eyes were filled with the same furious glare.

"I told you to bring the chains," he said. "What were you thinking? Now I'm going to have to go all the way back to Lewisville to get them."

"You didn't say bring the chains." Annie Blum had on tight jeans, a blue shirt, and a leather vest. Under normal circumstances, she might have been pretty, but anger had screwed her face until she looked ready for a broomstick ride. "Am I supposed to read your mind? We didn't need the chains in Asheville. We didn't need the chains in Meritsonville. What makes you think we need so many damn chains here?"

Tommy Fairbanks gave the side of his head a slap. "Hello! I can't believe you're so stupid. This is Parkland! Two hundred thousand people and the biggest street festival in North Carolina. We need all the chains we can get."

From what I could see of their booth, they had dozens of gold and silver bracelets, gemstone rings, and quite a few chains. Not enough, apparently.

Annie Blum blew out an exasperated breath. "I'll go back to Lewisville and get them."

"Oh, no, you won't. I know how you drive. The festival will be over before you get back. You stay here and run the booth. I'll go get them."

"And leave me to do all the work?"

"If I leave now, I'll be back by seven tonight."

This quarrel showed no signs of slowing. A small crowd had gathered to watch this bit of street theater. I thought I'd circle around and check with the happy couple later.

A fellow named J.W. dealt only in semiprecious stones. Fergus McNeely, despite his Scottish-sounding name, was an Asian man, and his specialty was jade. His business cards said, "Fergus Hiroshi McNeely," which I found very melodic.

By the time I returned to Fairbanks and Blum, Tommy had gone to retrieve the all-important chains, and Annie was sitting in a lawn chair behind a bank of glittering bracelets, glaring and smoking like a dragon guarding her treasure.

I wanted to say, Got any chains?

She took the cigarette out of her mouth. "We're not open."

"I'm looking for something in particular," I said. "A gold heart-shaped locket."

"We don't have anything like that." Her fierce expression dared me to ask another question, but I'm so used to Ellin's glares, this one seemed almost anemic.

"Do you know anyone who does?"

She took a long drag on the cigarette and blew a stream of smoke. "If you'd like to wait a couple of days, you could ask my partner."

Lily and her sparkly purple tent looked amazingly normal after all that. She was still alone, still fiddling with the crystals as if trying to find the perfect alignment.

"Did you have any luck?" she asked.

"Tommy and Annie seem a bit fractious."

"Oh, they don't like each other," she said.

"But they're partners?"

"I know. Isn't it odd? They always come to the festival."

"You'd think they'd find other people to work with."

"Well, Annie does the designs, and Tommy puts the pieces together. Their jewelry is really in demand. They make a lot of money."

"It always comes down to money."

"I guess that's why they put up with each other."

I looked around. "Did your pals get abducted? I thought they were bringing drinks."

She pointed to a can of Diet Coke. "They did. Now they've gone to find lunch. Do you want to stay and eat with us?"

"No, thanks." I'd had enough festival for now. "See you later."

◇◇◇

I found my own lunch at Janice Chan's, one of the few restaurants still downtown. Janice and her partner Steve make the best hot dogs I'd ever eaten, fat and juicy in soft steamed buns. As usual, the little place was busy, but I didn't mind waiting. Janice caught my eye and nodded. She'd have my order ready by the time I got through the crowd. Janice, a slim dark woman of Chinese ancestry, and Steve, red-haired and taciturn, made as odd a team as Tommy Fairbanks and Annie Blum. Steve was always in the back, cooking and cleaning, rarely emerging from the clouds of steam. Janice ran the front, pausing occasionally to push strands of her silky black hair behind one ear.

Most of the customers were picking up their dogs to go, so I found a seat on one of the red leather stools at the counter. After a while, there was a lull in the action, and Janice brought over two hot dogs all the way, fries, and a Coke.

"David."

"Hello, Jan. Seems a little more crowded today."

"It's the festival. Always brings in more people."

"You mean not everyone wants pork rinds and apple sauce?"

"You'd be surprised." She wiped up a spill of cola.

"Janice, I'm looking for a gold heart-shaped locket that's missing from a home in Greenleaf Forest. Have you heard anything about that?"

Thanks to a steady stream of talkative customers, Janice hears everything that happens in Parkland. "No. Things have been pretty quiet lately. Everyone's been discussing the festival. Do you need to know about a certain warehouse shipment, or perhaps the latest leak at the city council?"

"No, thanks. What about Albert Bennett, fellow who was murdered late Sunday night, maybe early Monday morning?"

"Over by where you used to live?"

"Yeah. The only thing taken was a notebook the police found on the lawn. It has some strange music notes in it."

"A notebook with music in it?"

"That's all."

"Oh," she said. "Then you might be interested in this."

Janice gets all kinds of newspapers for her customers to read. She handed me a copy of the *Washington Post.* "Page two."

I folded the page back, and Janice pointed to an article. I read, "Officials now believe the man who attacked and killed an assistant director at the Smithsonian was looking for a sketchbook containing the works of American song writer, Stephen Foster. An expert in the field of early American songs and folk music said the original sketchbook is in the Stephen Foster Memorial Museum at the University of Pittsburgh and the murderer may have mistakenly thought it was in the Smithsonian."

Good grief. Another notebook! I read on.

"Foster, author of some of America's best-loved songs, including 'Oh! Suzanna,' 'Camptown Races,' and 'Beautiful Dreamer,' kept a sketchbook to draft ideas for song lyrics and melodies. A digital copy is readily available online, courtesy of the University of Pittsburgh and the Center for American Music. Police are continuing their investigation."

And I'd better continue mine.

Chapter Fourteen

"My Hopes Have Departed Forever"

I had a few minutes before meeting Kary, so I went back to the college. I noticed a black Corvette just like Byron Ashford's in the visitors' parking lot. I wanted to talk to Tate Thomas, but he wasn't there. His secretary looked as if she'd been crying.

"Are you all right?" I asked.

She sniffed and blew her nose into a tissue. "Sorry. One of my friends was let go this morning."

I wondered if this was the same friend she'd told not to worry. "That's too bad."

"She's not the only one. Professor Thomas is worried he might be next."

"Doesn't he have some kind of seniority or tenure?"

"He's sixty-eight and the college is really coming down on the professors who haven't published anything lately."

Thomas hadn't looked that old to me. "Is this a real possibility?"

She nodded and blew her nose again. "I'd hate for that to happen. I'd be out of a job, too. But I think things are going to change for the better. Professor Thomas has a meeting with Kendal Robertson this afternoon, you know, the man who's filming a documentary about early American music? Professor Thomas is certain to be interviewed for the film. If he's chosen for this documentary, it would be a huge boost to his career, and then I doubt the college would let him go."

"Is Thomas that well-known?"

"No, but he will be. He's been very excited lately about the possibility of finding something very important. He couldn't tell me the details, of course. It's not unlikely for another professor to steal his ideas. It can get kinda cutthroat in the academic world."

The possibility of finding something very important. Could Ashford's music be more valuable than Thomas let on?

She gave her nose one last pat. "Can I give him a message?"

"No, thanks. Just one other thing. Has a man named Byron Ashford been by to see Thomas?"

"Yes, he came in just before you."

"Has he been here before?"

"Yes, I think Professor Thomas is helping him locate some of his great-grandfather's music."

"Thanks," I said. "I'll try to catch Thomas later."

As I was going out the door of the music building, Melanie Gentry was coming in. "Oh, hello," she said. "Have you been to see Thomas?"

"His secretary told me he's meeting with Kendal Robertson."

She jumped right on this. "Really? When?"

"Now, I believe."

"Has he found something? Have you found something?"

"Not yet. I'm going to Harmon Lassiter's this afternoon."

Her fierce look faded. "Oh. Well, that's good."

"Tell me something," I said. "Is Ashford's work worth more than anyone suspected?"

"I don't think Ashford's work is worth spit," she said. "Laura's, however, is priceless."

"Did you know Thomas is also talking with Byron Ashford?"

"Yes, but I have every faith you'll find what I'm looking for first. If Lassiter has any sort of notebook, I want to see it. Under no circumstances should Byron Ashford get his hands on it."

"Thomas' secretary said Thomas has been excited about the possibility of finding something important. Was she talking about this notebook?"

"Good heavens, no. Tate Thomas would not be that interested in Laura's work or Ashford's. She must have been talking about something else. He's doing research on Beethoven. Maybe he's on the trail of a lost symphony."

I wasn't sure I believed her. I knew enough about Beethoven to know he wasn't an American composer. If Thomas was trying to get a part in Robertson's documentary, he wouldn't meet with him to discuss anything Beethoven might have lost. "Well, I hope I can have good news for you by later today."

"Excellent," she said.

◇◇◇

And excellent was the word I used to describe the sight of Kary waiting for me in front of the community college. It was a perfect October afternoon, the sun at just the right angle in the bright blue sky, and the cool air filled with the smell of burning leaves, but as I leaned over to open the door, I noticed she looked distracted.

"Those pesky teachers pile on the homework?"

She tossed her book bag on the backseat and slid in. That's when I saw the tiny sparkle of light on her left hand. My heart went down for the count. The only thing that saved me was her preoccupied expression. She didn't look like a woman who'd just been given an engagement ring. It's been my experience that delighted gasps and ear-splitting squeals are involved as well as an uncontrollable impulse to inform the entire world.

I cleared my throat. "Are congratulations in order?"

She glanced at the little diamond. "Yes, thank you."

Maybe she was stunned. "Was it in your hamburger?"

This finally brought a smile. "You almost called it. The ring was around a carrot in my salad. We have a joke about his aversion to vegetables."

I couldn't believe she was going to go through with this. "So when's the happy day?"

"Oh, that's a ways off. We've got so many things to get straight first. I want to get my degree and a teaching job, preferably here in Parkland. He wants to finish his degree. He's already been offered some great jobs. The only problem is most of them are out of state."

Do you really love him? I wanted to ask. Is he worth all this frustration? "Would you want to move?"

"I don't know. I always thought that if I stayed here, maybe someday I could—" She swallowed hard. "Do you still have your parents?"

"My dad died five years ago. My mom lives in Florida."

"Did you get along with them?"

"I was really lucky. They were the best. My mom still is."

"You could talk to them? Explain things?"

"Yes."

She didn't say anything for several moments, her gaze on the houses and fast food restaurants that lined the street leading away from the college. I wasn't sure what to say. What had she done that required forgiveness? Or was the only sin her parents' one-sided view of the world? I had the worst suspicion she was marrying Donnie not only to goad them into contacting her, but also because he could offer her stability and security. I was neither stable nor secure at this point, but I damned well planned to be. And I wasn't giving up. She wasn't married yet.

She looked back at me, her expression puzzled, as if she couldn't quite decide what to say, either.

"You've got a lot to think about," I said.

She waved her hand as if erasing the subject. "Tell me some more about the case."

As we drove toward the interstate, I told her as much as I knew about John Ashford and Laura Gentry and their ill-fated love affair. I was glad I had to keep my eyes on the road. If I'd had to look into her face, I'm not sure I could've driven very far, my emotions were so scrambled.

"That's sad," she said when I'd finished the Ashford/Gentry saga. "So obsessive."

Since I was teetering on the edge of obsession myself, I decided not to comment.

"Kary, you're a musician. What do you know about Stephen Foster?"

"I know there are a lot of myths about him that aren't true."

"Such as?"

"Well, he wasn't a Southerner. He was born in Pennsylvania and made only one trip to the south, to New Orleans. You know the song, 'Camptown Races'? Camptown is in Pennsylvania."

"I always thought that was way down south somewhere. What about 'My Old Kentucky Home'? You're saying he never lived in Kentucky with the old folks at home?"

"I think he was seeing that as everyone's home."

Like 302 Grace, I thought. The ideal.

"And Foster wasn't an untrained musician who just sort of floated around gathering melodies," Kary said. "He was a professional songwriter."

"Any mysteries about him? Any missing songs or legends of lost operas?"

She thought for a moment. "There was a stage work that was performed but never published, but that was early in his career. I don't know if that would count."

But it might, I thought. Somebody's after something. Albert Bennett's screwy little notes, John Ashford's folk songs, Laura Gentry's—forget it. A lost work of Stephen Foster's would be worth a fortune.

Kary's attention was on the flame-colored leaves rushing past. "He died young. He was only thirty-seven with just thirty-eight cents in his pocket. And a piece of paper that said, 'Dear friends and gentle hearts.' Dear friends and gentle hearts. I've always thought that was so sad."

I did not want her to be sad, not even the slightest bit melancholy. "Here's where your research skills come in handy. Anything else you can find out about Foster would be very helpful."

"Okay."

I was ready to change the subject. "So how are you and Angie getting along?"

"Great. She and Rufus make a perfect couple, don't they? Rufus told me she was as cute as a speckled pup, and she says Rufus is as fine as frog hair."

"They were made for each other."

We finally reached Oakville and Lassiter's house. As I'd hoped, Lassiter was charmed by Kary and invited us into the dark cave of his home. The man owned every issue of *National Geographic* ever printed. We carefully maneuvered past the tall neat yellow stacks to a musty parlor. An old dark piano crouched in one corner. It looked pretty decrepit to me, but Kary gave a little cry of delight and hurried forward.

"How beautiful!" She opened the piano and smoothed her hand over the yellow keys. She played a few chords. "What a nice tone! How old is it?"

Lassiter beamed. "Over a hundred years. Was my mother's."

Kary sat down on the piano stool and began to play a Chopin waltz. Lassiter's face softened even further. "Haven't heard it sound like that in years."

Kary rippled through the waltz and stopped. "What did you need me to play, David?"

Lassiter dug his notebook out of an ancient bureau. He found the right place and handed the book to Kary. She didn't even blink at the sight of the music.

"'Field Mouse Dance.' That sounds cute."

She set the notebook up on the piano and began to play. I turned on my recorder. "Field Mouse Dance" was a perky little tune with a lot of high notes to indicate mouse noise. Kary liked it well enough to play it again. Lassiter stood as if transfixed. Well, why not? An angel had come down from heaven and was playing his song.

After "Field Mouse Dance," Kary played "Little Jenny Jones" and three Lassiter had written. His were okay, but lacked a certain spark and harmony. I recorded all of them. Lassiter sat in a dark cracked leather armchair, his thin fingers playing the notes along in his lap.

Kary finished and turned to face him. "These are very nice. I've tried to write music. I really envy you."

"Wish I could play like you," he said. "That's a true talent you've got there, Miss Ingram. Hope you plan to do something with it."

"I'm going to teach school."

"That's good, that's good. Don't stop playing, though."

"Oh, I won't." She looked through the notebook. "This is pretty here, this 'True As Silver,' and I really like this title, 'Two Hearts Singing.'"

I see two hearts singing. That's what Camden had said several days ago, when all this started.

Lassiter made a face. "I have to admit I stole that title from one of Laura Gentry's songs. It was just too good to pass up."

"That's okay," Kary said. "There can be more than one song with the same title."

"Her song's right much better. It's on the next page. I copied it down, too."

"Play both versions, please, Kary," I said.

She played Lassiter's first, a straightforward little tune, nothing remarkable. Then she played Laura Gentry's. It was evocative, plaintive, charged with emotion, the kind of tune that gets in your head and doesn't go away.

She finished and sat back. "Wow."

"You see," Lassiter said. "No way I'd be as good as that. She wrote that when she first fell in love with Ashford, but it's so sad, you have to wonder if maybe she knew things weren't going to work out, one of those mind things, like a hunch."

A premonition. I know all about those.

Kary played it again. As the sad sweet tune filled the dark little parlor, I couldn't help but think of Lindsey and the happier days of the past, of love lost and love betrayed.

Damn. Now they had me doing it.

Kary played the last soft chords. The music trailed away like a sigh. The three of us sat for a while until I shook myself from the memories. "Thanks very much, Mister Lassiter. I think I've got all I need." We shook hands and he started to replace the notebook back into the bureau drawer. Then he turned and looked at Kary.

"You'd take good care of my book, wouldn't you, Miss?"

Kary looked puzzled. "Of course I would."

Lassiter gazed at the faded cover for a long moment and then handed the notebook to her. "I'll let you take it for over the weekend, so you can record everything, as long as you make me a copy. It's been so long since I've heard these tunes, and you play them so beautifully."

Kary's cheeks turned a becoming pink. "Why, thank you, Mister Lassiter. This will certainly help David's case."

He grinned. "Ain't doing it for him, Girl. This is between you and me. Now don't rush off. I may have a soft drink or two in the Kelvinator."

I thought we'd better leave before he changed his mind. "We ought to get back. It's a long way, and Kary might have some studying to do."

He elbowed me in the ribs and winked. "You're a lucky dog, Randall."

"Yeah, that's what they tell me."

Kary closed the piano and shook Lassiter's hand. He held on for a moment. "Did my heart good to hear my old piano played like that. You tell Randall here to bring you back any time, you understand?"

"I'd like that very much," she said with her million-dollar smile. I hoped Lassiter's old heart could take the strain.

He kept her hand in his. "Ain't nobody left in my family but me, nobody who likes these old songs. But somebody needs to remember them."

"You're right, Mister Lassiter. I think it's important to keep all kinds of music alive."

"Well, you do that, Miss. I certainly appreciate it."

We got in the car and started for home. "Thanks," I said. "You've saved me a lot of time."

She had Lassiter's notebook in her lap, and she smoothed the cover. "I loved playing that piano. The songs were so engaging, especially that one about the hearts."

The sunset was a mass of purple and pink clouds, the trees, dark silhouettes against the brilliant sky. I drove just under the speed limit, wanting to prolong my time with her as much as possible. I finally had to come right to the point.

"Speaking of hearts, Kary, I realize this is none of my business, but why did you accept the ring? You don't seem very excited about it."

"I am. It's just such a big step. I feel overwhelmed."

"There's no rush, you know."

She kept her gaze forward. "Well, I didn't want a nose ring or a tattoo, so I chose the first atheist I could find."

It took me a moment to realize she was making a joke. "You don't have to take the first atheist you find, do you? Give the rest of us a chance." She didn't say anything. I gripped the steering wheel. I risked a glance at her. "Kary, I know we haven't known each other very long, but I feel we have a connection." I was startled by how normal my voice sounded. "I think we're both looking for the same thing."

She was so quiet, I thought I'd upset her. I took another glance in her direction. She looked straight ahead, her perfect face in the twilight revealing nothing.

"Maybe. But I think we're in very different places in our search."

But my search is over, I wanted to say.

Chapter Fifteen

"The Drowned Lover"

We got back to the house around six. Kary went up to her room, and I slumped into the office. We hadn't said very much the rest of the way home. I'd stopped short of begging her to call off the engagement and marry me. I couldn't believe I had that much restraint.

I was going to call Melanie, but there was a call on from Nick Vincent, a distraught Nick Vincent.

"David, my watch is missing. I can't find it anywhere. I don't know what's going on. I can't believe this!"

"What happened?"

"I can't find my watch. I know I had it yesterday when we were on the porch. I've looked everywhere." His voice was on the rise. "I can't possibly be this careless. It was a birthday gift from Pamela. She will kill me."

"Okay, take it easy."

"Thank goodness Pam's at her friend's house. I haven't told her. She's going to flip out."

"Nick, take a deep breath and relax. I'll stop by first thing in the morning."

"First the locket and now this. She's going to leave me."

"I doubt that. We'll find your stuff, don't worry."

I heard him take some unsteady breaths. "Okay."

"You going to be all right? Do you want me to come to your house now?"

"No, no. Tomorrow morning will be fine. Pamela won't be here. She has an art class or something." He gave a slight laugh. "I know I'm forgetful, but honest to God, I can't be this stupid."

"I'm sure there's a reasonable explanation."

"Thanks, David."

He sounded a lot calmer, so I hung up. Reasonable explanation? I didn't have an explanation of any kind about either of my cases. What did I have? Lost jewelry, a pile of teary love letters, a recording of sappy tunes, a possessed friend, and a broken heart. I could write my own song.

Speaking of possessed friend, I thought I'd better check on Camden. He wasn't in the island watching TV or in the kitchen. I went up the stairs to his third-floor bedroom. He wasn't there, either.

I came down to the second floor and knocked on Kary's door. "Have you seen Camden?"

"No," came her reply.

I tried Angie's door, but heard only thunderous snoring. I hurried back out to my car. I knew what had happened. Ellin had taken advantage of this situation, as usual, and carted him off. If I didn't hurry, Ashford was going to be broadcasting his woes all over town, and people were going to think Camden had lost his mind.

WPKD's across town. I cut down Tenley and made an illegal left turn onto Marsh. Took me twenty minutes. The station's a small brick building surrounded by impressive electrical towers and satellite dishes. Ellin's car was parked in the lot. I went in and told the receptionist I was a guest on Psychic Service Network, I was very late, would she please show me the correct studio.

She hardly looked up from her romance novel. "Fourth door to your left."

I thanked her and went down the short hallway to door number four. The dark studio had a high ceiling full of jungle wires and a floor crawling with snaky cables. Brilliant white light illuminated the Psychic Network set: tasteful chairs and a table with a huge bouquet of pink, blue, and white flowers, those soothing psychic colors. A stagehand was fastening a microphone on the low collar of one of the hostesses, either Teresa or Bonnie. Audience members searched for their seats. I saw Reg Haverson in all his glory, preening in front of a small mirror. Ellin stood by one camera, discussing something with another stagehand, and there was Camden. I should have said there was Ashford, because I could tell by his stiff posture and the way he scornfully surveyed his surroundings, the songwriter was definitely in the house. He had on Camden's best dark gray suit and burgundy tie. When he saw me, he smirked as if to say, "Fooled you."

Ashford may have been inside, but Camden was still five seven, one hundred and thirty-five pounds. I took his arm and pulled him along with me. "Party's over."

He tried to get away. "Unhand me! This is none of your business!"

I hung on. "Oh, yes, it is. For one thing, you're trespassing. For another, this is my case, not Ellin's, and I'm going to solve it my own way."

Ellin spotted me and rushed forward like a freight train out of control. "Randall! Leave him alone!" She didn't say, "He's mine!" but I knew she wanted to. She grabbed Camden's other arm. "How dare you come in here and disrupt the program? We're on in five minutes."

She was not going to win this tug of war. "You're on in five minutes. Camden's coming with me."

She held on. "He isn't Camden right now. He's Ashford, and he wants to be on the show."

"Are you crazy? Do you want everyone to see Camden like this? Will you think of him for once?"

Her face turned red. "Randall, he wants me to be happy, doesn't he? He wants to help."

Our argument attracted the attention of the audience. Reg Haverson strolled over, brushing imaginary lint off his perfect suit. "What seems to be the trouble? Do we have competition for our program tonight?"

"There's no trouble," Ellin said. "Randall was just leaving."

I kept a firm grip on Camden's arm. "Not without Camden."

She dug in her heels. "How many times do I have to tell you he isn't Camden right now? This is John Burrows Ashford, and he's our guest for the show."

Ashford decided to put in his two cents' worth. "I have promised Ellin I would speak on her television program."

"Well, you're not," I said. "I told you I'd help you, but you have to cooperate, and making a fool out of Camden on TV isn't part of the bargain."

He puffed up. "Make a fool out of him? What utter nonsense! I shall make him famous."

Reg checked his watch. "You know, this is really interesting, but we're on the air in three minutes. If you can't come to some agreement, we'll have to find another topic."

"No," Ellin said. "It's settled. Ashford wants to do this, Randall. You have no right to stop him."

"And you have no right to drag Camden into this without his knowledge or consent." Time to play dirty. "Reg, you could fill in, couldn't you?"

From the way he grinned, I knew he'd been waiting for just such an opportunity. "As a matter of fact, I have something on hand in case of emergencies."

Ellin's voice shook with anger. "We are not going to do a program on reincarnation."

"Let me get my notes."

Now she had to let go. "Reg!" She turned the full fury of her anger to me. "Damn it, this is my show! I call the shots!"

I pulled Camden away. "Tonight it's Reg Haverson and his past lives. If you don't want him to take over the entire hour, you'd better see what else you can dig up. Camden and I are out of here."

Ashford protested and Ellin threatened death and lawsuits, but I hauled Camden out of the studio, down the hallway, and past the bored receptionist. He was still Ashford in the car and still Ashford all the way home, griping about being manhandled.

"Doesn't my opinion count?"

"Not much," I said. "Besides, what good would it do to tell your story on TV? Only music scholars know who you are. Nobody's interested in a sixty-year-old murder case except Laura's great-granddaughter, me, and you."

He crossed his arms and sulked. "The way Ellin explained it, my words would have gone out all over the city. Someone might have useful information. You have denied me access to my public!"

"And you've denied Camden access to his life. Will you go away? Let me handle this. Or at least help me and keep away from Ellin."

This brought his predatory grin. "She is a fantastic woman, so fiery, so independent! Laura was like that."

"Yeah, and look where it got her."

He scowled. "I did not kill her, Randall. She was headstrong. She shouldn't have gone out in that storm. She wouldn't listen to anyone."

I hadn't heard about a storm. "Tell me what happened." Okay, so I was taking advantage of the situation, too, but not in front of thousands of people.

"We quarreled, as usual. We could never agree. I told her we were not good for each other. She was too demanding. I wanted to see other women. Instead of accepting my offer of a ride home, she said she would walk. There was a terrible storm that night. She slipped on the riverbank, fell in, and drowned. Of course, I blamed myself. I became despondent and could not write. And then I didn't want to live."

Tate Thomas had told me what had happened.

"You killed yourself?"

"Yes."

I pulled into the driveway and turned off the motor. We sat for a long while in the darkness. The porch light cast such eerie shadows on Camden's face, I could almost see Ashford's features.

"My last memory of Laura is seeing her in her coffin, so very white, her dark hair spread out on the pillow. She held two white roses in her hands. At the graveyard, two ravens came and sat on her tombstone." His voice faltered. "I had just written a song about a raven plucking a ribbon from a dead lover's hair. Such an eerie coincidence. I felt it was an omen, a sign I should follow her."

I didn't want to feel sorry for Ashford, but I did. "Why are you here? What do you really want?"

For the first time, he was uncertain. "I'm not really sure."

"To prove the songs are yours."

"But of course they are. There's no question about that."

"Where's the proof? What's it going to take to get rid of you?"

"Perhaps it is destined that I come back in this man. Perhaps it is his destiny, too. My music needs to return to this world."

"I doubt it's Camden's destiny to have you poking around in there."

"But my music. Surely my music must live on."

"I hate to tell you, pal, but your music is antique. Hell, people hardly listen to classical music any more, much less some folk ballads. The only composer people know and the kids might study in school is Steven Foster."

"Foster! My work is just as good as his! I took what he had created and built upon it, improved it!"

"I don't think so."

"Oh, so you're a music expert now?"

"Ashford, you're what we call an also-ran. Nobody knows your stuff. You may have a small band of fans in academic circles, but your music's been out of style for decades."

"That's not true."

I turned the motor on and switched on the radio. "Okay, listen up." I moved across the dial, letting him hear pieces of what passed for music these days. There was some indecipherable noise off Rock Ninety-Two, some R & B yearning and moaning, a little bit of orchestra stuff on public radio, and a lot of talk.

"That's it," I said. "That's what people listen to. They're more concerned with airing their views than singing a song. I'm sorry, but that's the way it is."

For once, he had no angry comeback, his expression, lost. On the radio, a loud woman's voice demanded free abortions for everyone and an equally strident man's voice told her she was a moron and a murderer.

"Turn it off," Ashford said.

I turned off the engine. Silence filled the car.

"I wonder if any of this matters," he said. Then he was gone. Camden looked at me, bemused, like a kid that's fallen asleep in the car and has no idea where he is.

I held my thumb and forefinger a few inches apart. "You came this close to being a TV star."

His eyes clouded over a moment, and then he said, "Don't let anyone have the notebook."

Chapter Sixteen

"For My Love Has a Roving Eye"

I was already debating what to do about the notebook, and with Camden's warning—or possibly Ashford's—I decided not to call Melanie right away. Saturday morning, I tried the fourth Denise Baker's number again. She still wasn't home. I left another message and then I drove out to Greenleaf Forest. Nick Vincent met me at the door.

"Okay," I said. "Let's find this thing. What does it look like?"

"It's platinum with a chain band. I'm going to check the living room. Why don't you look in my study? I've already checked, but you may see what I've overlooked."

His study was on the second floor, across the hall from the bedroom. It was not the mess I expected. It looked like every other study: a desk with a computer, swivel chair, bookshelves, and file cabinets. The walls were covered with photos. Not surprisingly, all the photos were of Pamela. Pamela as a child, all eyes and red curls. Pamela as a teenager, hair down past the waist of her low-cut jeans. Pamela with a group of people who were obviously her family, huge red-haired brothers and model-tall red-haired sisters, all mugging for the camera.

But no watch.

Nick came in. "Find anything?"

"No, sorry."

"Does Pamela have a study?"

"I've looked in there, too, but come see for yourself."

Pamela's study was also neat, neat and plain. Cream-colored file cabinets flanked an oak desk. On the wall were two large paintings of flowers, a framed photo of Nick looking very poetic, and a large white calendar with appointments written in black marker.

"Hers doesn't look quite as lived in."

"That's because she's rarely in it," Nick said. "She prefers to be on the porch."

"Have you checked outside?"

"Yes, all around the house."

"Let's look again."

Pamela came home while we were rooting through the trashcans. "Oh, hello, David. I thought you weren't going to look for the locket anymore."

Nick froze. She must have been an expert at reading his expressions, because she put her hands on her hips.

"Okay, what have you lost now?"

"It's nothing, Honey, really."

"Nick."

He gave me an imploring look, but I didn't think Pamela would appreciate any more lies. "Tell her, Nick. She might know where it is."

Pamela continued to glare. "Where what is?"

"My watch."

"The one I gave you for your birthday?" He nodded. "The platinum one?" He took several steps back before she exploded. "Nicholas Harold Vincent, I don't believe this! Your brand new watch? The very expensive brand new watch?"

"Please don't be upset. David is helping me look."

"You're impossible." She held up both her hands as if distancing herself from both of us. "I don't want to hear another word about it."

"Pam, Honey, please—"

"No, you two keep playing in the garbage. I've got things to do."

Nick watched as she stalked back into the house. "Oh, brother."

"I'll go talk to her."

He slumped down on the ground and leaned against the trash cans. "She has every right to be angry. I can't keep up with anything. There's no telling what I'll lose next, possibly my mind."

"Look around," I said. "You're surrounded by forest. Two expensive pieces of jewelry are missing from your house. I think you have burglars. It would be very easy for someone to sneak in through the woods and steal from your house. Get a good security system and stop blaming yourself."

That was Nick's pep talk. Next, I went into the house to try to cheer Pamela. I found her pacing her kitchen.

"I'm not very happy about this, David."

"I can tell."

"I'm beginning to believe Nick has a serious problem, one that needs therapy."

"I don't think it's that bad."

She stopped pacing and leaned against the counter, arms folded. "I thought once we were married and he'd settled down, this problem would go away, but now I'm thinking he needs professional help. He needs constant supervision."

I was beginning to see why Pamela had married this guy. He was husband and child all in one convenient package. Did I see Kary that way? Loving wife and sweet innocent child, a replacement for—I didn't allow that thought to go any further.

"Before you call in the guys in white coats, will you give me a chance to find the watch? As I told Nick, you're out here in the woods, no alarm system, no close neighbors. Valuable jewelry is missing. I think it's burglars."

"I think it's Nick."

"Then you don't need me."

She looked down at the floor. I saw her lower lip tremble and was immediately chagrined.

"Hey, I'm sorry. That sounded a little harsh."

She looked at me, tears brimming. "No, I do need you, David. I'm so worried about him. Whatever it costs, please prove it's burglars, or aliens, or whatever. I don't want it to be Nick."

"Me, either."

Nick and I took another walk around the house. He gave me a complete description of the watch. I said I'd check with him later and left. My cell phone rang just as I got into my car. It was Melanie Gentry.

"Any luck?" Her voice was eager.

"Sort of," I said. "Mr. Lassiter does have a notebook. I had a friend play through the songs. The tunes are copies of the ones in the book you gave me. No new ones, I'm afraid."

"Do you have it?"

I would have been suspicious even without Camden's warning. "No, Lassiter wants to hang onto it. It has some of his music in it, too."

I could almost see her beaming. "It could be very helpful in establishing exactly when she wrote some of the songs. Perhaps it could prove that she came up with the tunes, not Ashford."

"Or it could prove she didn't."

"I want to see it. As soon as you have it, call me."

I closed my phone and sat for a while. Something didn't make sense. Neither John Ashford nor Laura Gentry were famous enough to merit such intensity.

◇◇◇

The first Saturday afternoon of the Falling Leaves Festival is not the time to be walking downtown, but I managed to swim upstream against the tide of ambling tourists to Fairbanks and Blum. People were three deep at the booth, checking out the merchandise. Apparently, Tommy had brought enough chains. The shelves and display cases were full, and plenty of money was exchanging hands. This hadn't improved Annie Blum's disposition. She still looked like a witch whose Halloween had been canceled.

Tommy handed a package to a man, took his money, and thanked him. He turned to me. "Can I help you?"

"Just a little information, please. You know anyone who deals in heart-shaped lockets?"

"What kind you looking for?"

I described Pamela's necklace. He shook his head. Annie gave me a sour look.

"Told you he wouldn't be much help."

"Just shut up," Tommy said.

"You said I could take a break. That was half an hour ago."

"So go. What's keeping you?"

She gestured to the crowd. "You think you can handle this by yourself? I've got to keep an eye on things. Didn't that policeman tell us to be on the lookout? No telling how many thieves are in this crowd."

Tommy turned to her in exasperation. "Why the hell do you even come to the festival?" he asked, which was exactly what I was wondering. "You never have any fun, and you drag me down. Why don't you go home?"

"I don't trust you. You could tell me you made five thousand when really it was six. I do half the work. I want half the money. I'm staying here to keep you honest."

"You're staying here to drive me crazy." He turned back to me. "Sorry, Mister, I don't know anything about heart-shaped lockets."

Annie was busy with a customer. I lowered my voice. "You've got yourself an ornery partner there."

"Yeah, the only reason I put up with her is because she's a great designer. Before we teamed up, my stuff was going nowhere. Now people can't get enough of it. Trouble is, she can't put the links together like I can. It's one of those—what do you call it? Symbolic relationships?"

"Symbiotic, maybe."

"Huh? Yeah, that's it. Like those fish who live in those poisonous plants under the sea. I'm the fish. She's the poisonous plant."

I thanked him for his time and started the struggle back up the street. I almost ran into the solid square bulk of Jordan Finley.

"Excuse me, Mister Policeman. I'm lost."

Jordan's sharp blue eyes were hidden behind his sunglasses, but I could guess his expression. "The town dump is five miles straight ahead."

"Are you the cop warning everyone about pickpockets?"

"That's my job, that and keeping the Low Rock element sober."

Low Rock is a community just over the state line known for its moonshiners. Low Rockers love the festival. They see it as an occasion to put on their shoes and come to town. "I thought I saw America's Most Toothless wandering around."

Jordan's blank sunglasses surveyed the crowd. "What are you doing here, Randall?"

"I had a hankering for a corn dog."

We stepped back for a woman pushing a stroller. Two babies rode inside while a third child clung to her skirt. Their faces were smeared with chocolate ice cream. Balloons bobbed from their wrists. A harried-looking father followed, carrying a fourth child and a plastic bag full of stuffed animals. For a moment, I envisioned Kary as the mother, Donnie trailing obediently behind.

"You on a case or just slumming?"

"Trying to locate a missing locket, a missing watch, and some missing songs—oh, and Camden's possessed by the spirit of the dead songwriter."

Jordan's blank stare swung my way. "I don't recall him having too much trouble until you moved in."

"Oh, yeah, I'm a lightning rod for the paranormal." I prepared myself for a lecture from Jordan about my work habits, my choice of clients, and general endangerment of the tenants of 302 Grace.

He surprised me. "You need my help with anything, let me know, Randall. I'm on duty till eight."

"Thanks. That's the best offer I've had all week."

"What's this about some missing songs and a dead songwriter?"

"Don't worry. He's been dead for a long time."

"And he just popped in to say hello?"

"There's some question about the authorship of his songs."

Jordan readjusted his sunglasses. "Wouldn't have anything to do with Albert Bennett, would it?"

"Maybe."

Jordan lowered the sunglasses to give me the full intensity of his gaze.

Time to steer the conversation in another direction. "Have you had any problems in the Greenleaf Forest area? I think my client's house has been broken into twice."

"Has your client reported this to the police?"

"I'm going to find out what happened."

Jordan's snort was just this side of sarcastic. "Tell him to buy himself a good burglar alarm system." A scuffle near the corn dog stand caught his attention. "Hey! None of that. You boys move along."

As he went to separate the teenagers, I wedged myself through the crowd and down the street to Lily's booth, which fortunately had a crowd. Lily saw me and waved.

"We've sold twenty crystals!"

"That's great." I moved to one side so she could help her next customer, a wispy-looking woman with a bow in her hair. I really think sixty is too old to be wearing hair bows, but I wasn't going to point this out. "Where are your helpers?"

"Margery went back to my house for more crystals, and Clark got too hot. He's used to being indoors."

Hiding out from those pesky aliens. "Need a hand?"

"Gosh, yes, if you've got time."

It wasn't hard to hand people crystals and make sure nobody carried one off. If anyone asked me a question, I made up an answer. "Yes, the blue has good soothing rays. No, if you're Aquarius, you ought to stick to amethyst. The best one for healing properties? Rose quartz cures all."

Lily was too busy with her end of the table to pay attention to me. After a while, we had a lull in the action. We plopped in the folding chairs.

Lily carefully folded the money into her cash box. "We're doing extremely well, David. Thanks so much for your help."

"No problem."

"Did you find out anything about the missing locket?"

"No. That's okay. I've got plenty of other things to think about."

"I really want to help. Maybe the crystals can tell us." She took some spears and made a circle. "The yellow ones often point toward the truth."

I let her play with her rocks. "Well, see what they say about Albert Bennett."

She looked up. "Susie Bennett's great uncle? That was so sad."

"You know a member of his family?"

"Susie comes to my herb drying class."

"Where does she live? Do you think she'd talk to me?"

"I don't see why not. She lives on Brookbank Avenue near the drugstore."

I gave her a hug. "Lily, you amaze me."

She looked startled and blushed. "It's the crystals."

I didn't care what it was. I was just happy to have a lead.

◇◇◇

After fighting my way through the crowds to the Fury, I drove the backstreets to get to Brookbank Avenue. Susie Bennett lived in a modest brick house with a landscaped yard and a big pot of yellow chrysanthemums on the front porch. She was a trim woman with short graying hair and blue eyes that looked me up and down and decided I was worth talking to.

"Ms. Bennett, I'm David Randall. I'd first like to offer my sympathies."

"Thank you. Albert Bennett and I weren't close, but it was still a shock. What can I do for you?"

"I'm a private investigator, and I'm working on another case that may be connected to your great uncle's murder. I understand his notebook of musical notation was the only thing taken and it was left behind?"

"Yes," she said. "I don't know anything about music, but apparently, somebody thought this notebook was important. It belonged to Albert's father, Horatio. I never knew him. He lived in New York City for most of his life. The police said it was some experimental thing. I can't see how it would be valuable, except to other musicians."

"Can you tell me exactly what happened?"

She bent down to pluck the dead leaves off the chrysanthemum. "Albert must have surprised the thief. He was struck over the head, and when he fell, he hit the corner of a table." She straightened and tossed the dead leaves behind a bush. She dusted her hands. "He was a very wealthy man, not that I'll ever see any of it. He always had cash and jewelry in the house, but nothing else was taken. Whoever broke in was after that notebook. Your guess is as good as mine why anybody would want a notebook full of scribblings no one else can read."

Kind of like the notebook I had—almost. "Were there any witnesses? Any clues at all?"

"No."

"Ms. Bennett, would you mind if I had a look in your uncle's house?"

"I don't mind, but I don't have a key. I guess you could ask the police."

◇◇◇

Jordan had given me strict orders to keep out of Albert Bennett's house. Nothing was said, however, about walking around the outside. I kept away from the yellow tape and cautiously made my way around the large stone house. Huge bushes made a barrier between Bennett's house and the neighbor's. A series of broken branches and scattered twigs suggested the intruder had made his escape through these bushes, but as I walked along, I noticed several rents where someone might have pushed through. Had the police checked every one? Maybe the neighborhood kids liked to play in these bushes. Maybe there was more than one way through.

I was halfway around the back of the barrier when I found another likely-looking escape route. Ignoring the scratchy branches, I parted the leaves, pushed through, and found myself in a wooded area. The ground was covered with fallen leaves. No sense trying to find footprints, and I was pretty sure the police would've given this a thorough going over, so I walked on a little further. Just past the woods was another neighborhood, and right there, surrounded by a chain link fence, was a playground.

Another playground. Great. And since it was Saturday afternoon, there were kids all over it.

I took a deep breath and pushed away any memories of playing with Lindsey. I was on a case. I was going to solve a mystery. I could try all I liked, but I couldn't spend the rest of my life avoiding children. They weren't supposed to talk to strangers anyway.

Most of the kids were playing basketball with some teenagers and completely ignored me. The smaller children were on the swings, screaming about who could go the highest, and on the sliding board, screaming about whose turn it was. I strolled around to the sidewalk trying not to look creepy. Trash had collected along the bottom of the fence, and the wind had blown scraps of plastic and paper into the links. Strange marks on one curl of paper caught my attention. I pulled the paper free and straightened it out. I saw the little wormy tracks Horatio Bennett considered music and the words "Tranquil Breeze." This must be a piece of the missing pages torn from Bennett's notebook. I looked around, hoping to find more. A tiny round object looked up from the trash—and when I say looked up, that's exactly what it did. I reached down and picked up the small plastic eye. The little black bead rolled around in the clear plastic shell. Well, with all these kids here, this eye must have fallen off one of their toys. But I had the feeling I'd seen something like this before.

I put the paper and the little eye in my pocket. The kids were still screaming at each other, but a few had stopped swinging and were regarding me suspiciously. I gave them a friendly wave and walked back the way I'd come. In the safety of the Fury, I took out the toy eye and examined it. Now I remembered where I'd seen little plastic eyes like this.

On Melanie Gentry's sweater.

Chapter Seventeen
"The Lovers' Quarrel"

I thought I'd had enough drama and excitement for one day, but when I got home, I found the Psychic Service Network van parked out front. A cameraman and a sound technician stood at the open back of the van, talking and looking bored. Camden and Ellin were going at it from opposite ends of the dining room table. I wasn't surprised that the topic of choice for the day was our old dead pal Ashford. Camden had the back of a chair in a white-knuckle grip.

"What does he say? What does he do?"

Ellin hesitated. "He's just more...forceful."

"And you like that? I thought you always told me you didn't care for the Cro-Magnon stuff."

"I don't. I'm trying to explain. You asked me how he was different, and I'm telling you. He just takes over. He's pushy, obnoxious, demanding—"

"Exciting. You like this guy, don't you?"

"No! I hate him." She actually sounded sincere for a moment. Then Ellin the Producer took over. "But I can't deny I find this whole experience fascinating. You would, too, if you could remember any of it. Despite his faults, Ashford is an interesting man, and I think he's the victim here."

"You think Laura destroyed his career."

"I think there are two sides to every story. He deserves to be heard."

"I deserve to be heard, too." He let go of the chair and came to her. "I'm losing whole chunks of my life while this interloper makes time with my woman. Or is that too prehistoric a concept for you, 'my woman'? No, wait, I forgot, you like that kind of forceful talk."

"Cam. Stop it."

"It doesn't sound like I have much choice."

"I can't believe you're jealous of a ghost."

He gave her a searching look. "Don't you want me to be?" His voice was much quieter. "I'm jealous of anyone, dead or alive, who wants to spend time with you. Don't you know that?"

Why couldn't she say she loved him? She's the hardest woman I've ever known, and I've known some boulders. Silence stretched until she finally spoke.

"There's no need to be jealous. I want Ashford to resolve his problems and leave. Why don't you let him come on the show? He'd reach a huge audience, and someone might be able to help him."

Wrong answer. Something along the lines of "I love you, don't worry, we'll work this out," might have been nice. Way too much to ask.

Another long pause. "It's not a question of 'let,'" Camden said. "I don't have any control over him."

"Tell Randall to keep out of this," she said. "Ashford can tell his story and then he'd leave. That's what you want, isn't it?"

"Yes."

"You can't tell me Randall isn't using this experience for his own gain. Doesn't he talk to Ashford, get clues about this case of his?"

Camden had decided to go stubborn on her. "I suppose so. I don't remember."

"Of course he does. He's right here in the house. If Ashford is helping him solve this case, then he can certainly come on the show."

Camden had had enough. "Okay. Fine. I'm not even involved. Ashford's just using me so he can walk around. You and Randall do what you want."

He went out to the porch, passing me without a glance. I wandered into the dining room, figuring Ellin would attack, and she did.

"What do you mean by sneaking up like that? I'll bet you heard everything."

"I sure did. I overhear all your conversations." I went to the fridge for a cola. "One of these days, you're going to push too hard."

She followed me. "It's none of your business. This possession thing with Ashford is bizarre. It's scary having Cam like this."

"Yeah, I'll bet it's a real turn-on."

"Damn it, Randall! That's not what I meant."

"Oh, yes, it is. All of a sudden, Camden's in charge. He makes the moves, starts the action. You've got yourself a real macho man."

"And I told Cam I don't like that. I like him the way he is. He has this absurd idea I'm enamored of Ashford. My God, Ashford's dead! He's been dead for years! Cam must be crazy."

"He is. He's crazy to love a woman who doesn't love him." Wait a minute. That didn't sound right. Isn't that what I've been doing?

Ellin's jaw dropped. "Doesn't love him? Of course I love him! I always have."

"You sure have weird ways of showing it."

"Stay out of it."

"Was Ashford just here? Didn't you get what you wanted?"

"No, he wasn't here. The crew and I have been waiting around all day."

"Then maybe he doesn't want to talk to you."

"Well, I certainly don't want to talk to you." She stalked out.

I went to the front porch. Camden was sitting on the porch swing. We watched as the men got into the van, Ellin got into her car, and both vehicles drove away. He gave me a weary look. "Don't say anything."

I took a seat in one of the rocking chairs. "Isn't it about time you found a new girlfriend?"

"Maybe I should go to the community college with Kary and take Caveman 101."

"Can you reach Ashford in any way? Can you recall anything of his visits?"

"No. Are you any closer to solving this case?"

"I'm happy to say I have some clues. Have a look at this." I handed him the little plastic eye. "I found this in the woods behind Bennett's house."

"It's an eye."

"Yep. Just like the ones on Melanie's farm animal sweater."

He held it a few moments longer. "Yes, it is." He handed the eye back to me. "Why would Melanie be in the woods behind Bennett's house?"

"Here's something else." I took out the piece of paper. "Torn from Bennett's notebook, if I'm not mistaken. Those are his goofy little marks."

Camden read the title. "'Tranquil Breeze.'"

"Must have been a song he was writing. You remember you warned me about giving Lassiter's notebook to Melanie or to anyone else?"

"Yes, but I don't know why."

"I don't know why anyone would want either notebook, but if Melanie's after Bennett's, too, there must be some connection."

"You think Melanie's the culprit?"

"I don't know." I sat brooding on the eye for a while until Camden spoke.

"You didn't scare Kary off. She's just confused."

"Been confiding in you, too, huh?"

"No, I managed to get a few impressions. I haven't been picking up very much lately, thanks to Ashford."

"Coming back from Lassiter's, I had to say something." I looked out across the yard. "I know exactly how Ashford felt about Laura. She was younger than he was, too. Of course, back then, it wasn't such a big deal." I glanced at him. "What do you mean by confused? I can tell she has feelings for me."

"I'm sure she does."

"What makes her think Donnie's a better choice? Is it the age difference?"

"She just needs some time."

"Yeah, by the time she figures things out, she'll be pregnant with Donnie, Junior."

He stopped swinging and gave me one of his looks. "No."

He said this so seriously, I had to take a moment before saying anything else. "No, she won't get married, or no, she won't get pregnant?"

"I'll let Kary tell you that, when and if she's ready."

"So there is a chance?" I leaned forward for a better look into his eyes. "This isn't Ashford jerking me around, is it?"

"No, this is me jerking you around." I gave his shoulder a punch and he grinned. "Randall, I can't see things too clearly right now, but yes, there is a chance."

"And there's a chance she'll marry Donnie."

"At least your competition is alive."

A roar of dual exhausts shook more leaves from the trees, and Rufus' Bigfoot truck pulled up in the drive. Rufus hopped out and hurried around to open the door for Angie. The truck sighed in relief as she exited.

"Well, somebody got lucky," I remarked to Camden before the happy couple were in earshot.

I wasn't sure both of them could fit up the front steps, but they did.

Rufus took off his cap to scratch his scraggly hair. "Owe you an apology, Randall."

"What for?"

"This morning, that son of a bitch Ashford called me a pea-brained hick and a rural moron. I can see why you wanted to pop him one."

I indicated Camden. "And you see why I can't."

"Sorry, Rufe," Camden said.

Rufus offered Angie a rocking chair, but she wisely decided she wouldn't fit and chose the porch steps. He sat down beside her. "We gotta get rid of that bastard, Cam. You need an exorcism or something. Doesn't that girlfriend of yours know how to do that?"

"No," he said. "In fact, she likes Ashford."

Rufus rolled his eyes at me. "This is too weird."

"This kind of thing happen often around here?" Angie wanted to know.

"More than we like," I said.

Rufus ground one large fist into his palm. "Maybe I could smack him out."

"I wish you could." Camden changed the subject. "How are things coming along for the festival?"

"We're about ready," Rufus said. "Buddy's got a pile of carvings done, and Angie said she'd help man the booth. You want to spell somebody a few hours?"

"Sure, if it doesn't interfere with Ashford's schedule."

Rufus turned to me. "How 'bout you, Randall?"

"Let me get this case solved first."

"Is that what it's going to take to get rid of Ashford?"

"I hope so."

"What have you got so far?"

"A notebook of old songs and a plastic eyeball."

Kary was next to arrive wearing a slim corduroy skirt and print blouse, her arms full of books, her blonde hair swinging free.

"Looks like a house meeting," she said with a smile. "Angie, I brought those patterns."

"Great." Angie heaved herself up. "Let's spread everything out on the dining room table and see what we've got."

"Patterns?" Rufus said.

"Dress patterns," Kary said. "Angie said she'd help modify one of my pageant gowns."

Rufus looked at his ladylove with growing respect. "You sew, too?"

"Hey, when you're my size, you have to. I'll make you a shirt some time, big boy." She ambled into the house, and Kary followed, avoiding eye contact with me.

Damn. I knew I shouldn't have declared myself. Now she was going to be nervous around me. Camden tried to be encouraging. "Don't worry. She'll help you."

Rufus smirked. "Randall needs a gown modified, too?"

"He needs a favor from Kary," Camden said.

"That ain't all he needs."

"A favor," Camden said, as if he'd just thought of something. "I've got to get those crystals back to Lily. Where are they?"

"You already did that," I said.

"Are you sure? I'd better check."

Camden went inside. Rufus watched him go, his low brow furrowed. "Not like him to forget."

"He hasn't been himself." It occurred to me that Rufus, with his vast knowledge of Parkland family trees, might have a clue about Camden's. "You know anything about his family?"

Rufus dug into the back pocket of his jeans for a round can of chewing tobacco. "Nope. Never says nothing about them."

"Thought you might have heard something."

"He grew up in some boys' home, that's all I know." He scooped out a wad and stuffed it in his mouth. "Who's asking?"

"Something Lily said to me the other day. Her Tarot cards tell her Camden's going through an identity crisis."

Rufus spoke around the bulge in his cheek. "She got that right."

"I don't think she meant possession."

"Well, hell, ask him. Ask her."

Camden came back, looking confused. "You were right."

"And they were all safe. No demon crystal from hell."

Rufus and I exchanged a glance. "Come on," Rufus said. "Buddy brought a new supply of pumpkins you need to see. They're out back."

While Rufus and Camden checked out the pumpkins, I wandered in to watch the girls' sewing club. Kary's white evening gown lay across the table, bits of light brown tissue pinned here and there. Angie, her mouth full of pins, moved the tissue and frowned and moved it again while Kary watched, occasionally consulting a book of dress designs. They were deeply involved in this task, so I had the opportunity to study Kary and plan my next move.

I wouldn't declare myself any more. I wouldn't even hint at it. I'd just ask for a favor, remind her of her promise to tape the songs for Lassiter.

Angie removed the last pin from her mouth. "This is going to work. Won't take me long."

"Thanks, Angie," Kary said. "I really appreciate it."

She shrugged one massive shoulder. "It'll give me something to do while I'm between jobs." She sat down at the table and picked up the scissors.

"Kary, if you've got time, would you record a few numbers for Mister Lassiter?"

Relief crossed her face. Did she think I was going to proclaim my undying love in front of Angie? Well, no telling what she thought I'd do. "All right."

I sat down in the blue armchair in the island and recorded the songs as she played. After a while, all the tunes ran together. I was getting sick and tired of all this minor stuff. I was going to have to get a boxed set of Sousa marches for an antidote.

But the songs had a different effect on our unwanted house-guest, Ashford. Kary was halfway through "Two Hearts Singing" when Ashford came in, followed by a wide-eyed Rufus.

"He just slipped in," he said to me.

"Yeah, I can tell."

Ashford went to the piano and stood there, transfixed. Then he began to sing.

Early one morning
Heard my heart singing,
Heard your heart singing,
Answering my own.
Come let me love you,

Come be my lady,
Come to my arms, love,
Here is your home.

The sad, sweet melody sounded even better when Camden's voice sang the words. Angie stopped sewing. Rufus looked from me to Camden.

"Damn, that's pretty."

When Kary came to the end, Ashford said, "Play it again, if you please, young lady." I'd never heard him speak so politely.

Kary hadn't had the pleasure of meeting Ashford, so she assumed it was Camden. She started the song again. This time, Ashford listened and then came to me, his eyes bright and hard.

"This is my music, Randall. It came from my soul. You have to see that. This Melanie Gentry does not have any claim to it."

Kary stared at him. "Cam? What are you talking about?"

Ashford swung around. "I am not Cam, young lady. I am John Burrows Ashford. This music you play so beautifully was written by me and stolen, along with my heart. I loved a young woman much like yourself. She wrote some music, but not this song. A few little tunes. She showed promise, but she was undisciplined. And now her unscrupulous relative schemes to defile my name."

Heavy stuff, but Kary was not distracted. "What are you doing in Cam?"

"I took the only channel available."

"Well, you're not going to stay there!"

"It's okay," I said. "He's leaving, right, Ashford?"

Of course he decided to be difficult. "Why should I? Isn't anyone interested in my side of this?"

"I am," Angie said. "This sure beats the hell out of any tabloid TV I've seen lately." She slumped into a chair in the island while Kary remained perched on the piano bench, her eyes on Camden. Rufus filled the doorway.

Ashford surveyed his audience and found it satisfactory. He glanced at me for the go-ahead, and I shrugged. "They're all yours."

"Very well." He took a lecturer's stance and launched into everything I already knew so far. Rufus, Angie, and Kary hung on his every word.

I hated him. The more Ashford popped in, the less Camden was in control. This guy was the worst sponge of all. But I couldn't do anything about it, unless I wanted to channel somebody bigger and meaner who could beat the crap out of him on another astral plane.

He told about loving Laura more than life itself and about her accident the night of the storm, about taking his own life, and about Melanie Gentry's dastardly plans to discredit him.

"So there's some sort of proof you're looking for," Rufus said, once again confounding me by catching on so quickly.

"Yes," Ashford said. "It's sad but true I must have tangible proof of my own work. My letters contain none of my original notation, as Randall has seen." He looked around. "Don't you see? The music is mine. That's why I'm here. You must find proof."

For the moment, it was hard to ignore Ashford's appeal, especially when he was using Camden's face. "It would help if you knew what this proof looks like," I said. "A letter? A piece of music? Someone still alive who knew you? Lassiter is my best lead, and all he had was this notebook of his own tunes and some of Laura's."

"And mine," Ashford said. "The man had no right to copy 'Two Hearts Singing.'"

"He was just using the tunes as examples." I was tired of the way Ashford took offense as easily as he took Camden's breath. "I'm going to return the book tomorrow. I'll ask him some more questions."

"I shall come with you."

"No, you shall not. You want Lassiter to think I'm crazy, bringing along somebody who thinks he's John Ashford?"

Ashford indicated the group with a sweep of his hand. "They understand!"

"Rufus and Kary live here. This kind of stuff's old hat to them, and Angie's got an open mind. You won't find this kind of reception out in the real world. That's why you couldn't be on television. If you don't do this my way, you'll never find out the truth. And I think we've had enough of you for now, so beat it."

He scowled. "Your manners are barbaric."

"I work hard at it. Go on. Get out."

Another scowl, and then Camden's features went slack. This time, he didn't just stand in a daze. His eyes rolled up and he collapsed. The four of us almost bumped heads trying to reach him. Rufus got there first. He picked Camden up and put him on the sofa. In a few minutes, his eyes opened.

"Ashford again," I said. "He bored us all rigid with his tale of woe. You remember anything?"

"Oh, my God. Again?" He pushed his hair out of his eyes. "No, not a thing."

Angie leaned her meaty forearms over the sofa. I waited for it to tip over. "Seems to me this Ashford is getting stronger. What's his game?"

"He says he'll leave once the case is solved." But I was beginning to have my doubts. Ashford could have a pretty good life, using Camden's body, stealing Camden's girl. What if he decided not to go?

Camden slowly sat up and looked at the circle of concerned faces. "Any suggestions?"

"I've got a few more leads to follow," I said. "I'm doing the best I can."

The evening only got worse. Once we were sure Camden was okay, Kary modeled her evening gown for us, and it took all my resolve not to run screaming into the night with her across my shoulder. She and Rufus and Angie went out to the movies. Camden, still dazed from his latest close encounter, went upstairs. After a while, I could hear him singing something called "The Lovers' Quarrel," which I found more than appropriate. That left me with Ashford's biography, Lassiter's notebook, and a bad case of the blues.

I looked around my office, wondering if somehow I'd gotten into a rogue time machine somebody left lying around the house. Hadn't I just been sitting here, staring at my computer screen? Was I any further along with anything? Was there any connection between Bennett's notebook and Lassiter's and this murder in Washington? Was I trying to make a case out of nothing?

And still no reply from Denise Baker Number Four. I tried her number again. Still not home or possibly not picking up. Maybe I'd scared her off. Maybe she thought I was crazy. Maybe I'd have better luck with Denise Number Six.

I'd just closed my phone when it rang. Hoping it was Denise, I was surprised to see the caller ID said, "Ellin Belton." Good grief, what did she want? I prepared myself for another lecture, but her voice was calm.

"Randall, I'd like to talk to you. I've been thinking about what you said."

"I was a little harsh, sorry.'

"No, I mean when you said one of these days I'm going to push too hard. You probably don't believe me, but I have Cam's best interests at heart."

I didn't believe her, but I said, "Okay."

"I know he loves that big old white elephant of a house. I'm just trying to help him make some more money. Are you planning to pay rent? I know most of those people living there don't contribute a dime."

"I'm not staying. This is just temporary until I can find an apartment and an office." Every time I said this, I felt I was fighting a losing battle to convince myself. "But if by some chance I decided to stay, I'd pay my fair share." It occurred to me she might know something that could help me. "Do you know Melanie Gentry or Byron Ashford?"

"I don't know Melanie, but I've seen Byron at the club."

"The club?"

"The Parkland Country Club."

I didn't know Camden was dating a society gal. "Know anything about him?"

"He's very arrogant, very careless with his money, likes to gamble. I hear he's in a bit of financial trouble. His private jet and his house in Washington are both up for sale."

"Washington as in D.C.?"

"Yes."

"You wouldn't happen to know if he was in Washington this week?"

"I don't know. I could ask Mother. She hears everything that goes on at the club."

"Would you do that? It could be important."

There was a moment of silence as if she was debating whether or not to help me. "If you solve your case, you're moving out, right?"

"Right." That was my plan, anyway.

"Then I'm going to help you any way I can."

Chapter Eighteen
"The Fortune Teller"

The next morning when I came down to the kitchen, Kary was fixing coffee and toast. Her hair was tangled, and she was wearing her overlarge white terrycloth robe.

"Hi," she said. "Want some toast?"

"Yes, thanks." I was glad I had pulled on a clean tee shirt and shorts instead of wandering downstairs in my pajama shorts. I poured myself a cup of coffee. As I sat down on one of the stools, I noticed several fat textbooks on the counter: *Elements of Education, Curriculum Development, Science and Society.* When I thumbed through the education book, what I thought was a bookmark turned out to be a brochure with "Adoption: Is It Right For You?" on the front, surrounded by pictures of smiling children. Kary was busy at the toaster, so before she turned around to me, I quickly shoved the brochure back into the book.

She handed me two pieces of toast on a plate. "You want butter? Jelly?"

"Both, please." Her robe had slipped down over one perfect shoulder. She passed the butter dish and handed me a jar of strawberry jelly. She got her toast and sat down across from me at the counter. For a moment, I imagined we were married and sharing a tender breakfast moment. Unfortunately, the light from the little diamond ring kept stabbing me in the eye.

Kary readjusted her robe, a serious gaze in her big brown eyes. She looked as if she hadn't had much sleep.

"David, about that incident yesterday. I've seen Cam have some strong visions, but nothing like that. It was almost as if he couldn't control this spirit. John Ashford said you had to find proof he wrote his music. Can you do that? Then will he go away? He's dead, isn't he?"

"Yes, and I wish he'd stayed dead, but something stirred him up. I think it's this new documentary and the sudden interest in American folk music, plus Ashford thinks he's a big name like Stephen Foster and wants more screen time. Don't worry. I'll get rid of him."

"I want to help."

"Check all your sources and references for any connection between him and Ashford."

"All right." She started to spread butter on her toast and set her knife down. She pushed her plate aside. "I know Cam's receptive to spirits, but usually he's himself and just tells people what they say. Have you ever seen him taken over like this?"

"No, this is a new one on me."

"How did you meet? I don't think he ever told me."

We were both roaring drunk down at the Crow Bar. Camden was up on a table singing something operatic and trying not to be psychic, and I was trying to drown myself in grief. Neither of us was successful. "Oh, we met at a bar downtown. Just struck up a conversation. How about you?"

"We met at Cam's church. They don't demand anything of you. If you want to sing, okay. If you don't, okay. If you want to take Communion, that's fine. If you don't, you aren't condemned. Maybe you don't really believe. Maybe you just need a quiet place to sit and think. You're still welcome. You're not shunned or kicked out or—sorry. I didn't mean to get so carried away."

I would have given anything to brush away the sudden stray tear that rolled down her cheek. "Sounds like you knew what you needed and found it."

Kary blotted her face with her napkin. "Cam knew." She reached for her coffee cup. "If we work together, we can help Cam get rid of John Ashford."

I'd stopped listening after "if we work together," but tuned in for the last part.

"That's a good idea."

She took a sip of coffee and seemed to be back in control. "You're easy to talk to, David. Maybe you shouldn't have given up that bartending dream."

"I inherited my dad's Tell Me All Face."

"Would you pass me another napkin, please?"

The napkins were on the other side of the stack of textbooks. Underneath the textbooks was a garish-looking newspaper. At first, I thought it was the *National Inquirer*. "Are you studying tabloids, too?"

"Oh, that's the Psychic Service newspaper. Ellin must have left it here."

On the front, the headline blared: "Crystal Psychics—Your Chance to Shine." Inside, there were listings for dozens of psychics and advisors, some specializing in lost objects, some in numerology, some in relationships. There were soul searchers, ghost busters, spiritual ministers, past life researchers, even animal psychics. I turned to the back where an ad promised love, happiness, and success if you called the special psychic hotline.

"I should throw it away," Kary said. "Cam doesn't work for the service anymore."

I turned through the rest of the paper. Glowing testimonials from satisfied customers. Lucky numbers to call for celebrity forecasts. The monthly horoscope. A quiz to test your psychic ability. "He just worked on the real cases, though, right? Like the missing girl he found in the drainpipe."

Kary shuddered. "I can't imagine what that must have been like."

Squeals and giggles sounded from the front of the house. I closed the paper. "Ol' Fred sounds cheerful this morning."

My remark made Kary laugh. "That's Rufus' niece. She likes to play on the porch swing."

I felt my smile freeze on my face. "Great. Is she going to be here all day?"

"Just till Sunday School." She got up. "I'll go see if she'd like some cereal or something."

I made my escape to the backyard. I took the *US Psychic World News and Report* and sat in one of the blue-and-white striped lounge chairs under the trees. I was absorbed in a woman's gushing story of how she'd found true love and won the lottery, thanks to the Service, when I became aware I was being watched. I slowly lowered the paper. My heart gave a thud. There stood Rufus' niece, a little girl with long blonde hair tied back in a ponytail. She was wearing a pink outfit, tiny gold earrings shaped like teddy bears, and "Beauty and the Beast" sneakers. She was absolutely perfect.

"Go away," I said.

She regarded me thoughtfully and then decided I wasn't worth the effort. She skipped back to the house, ponytail swinging gracefully. My throat ached, wanting to call her back.

I sat still for a long time, the words of the psychic newspaper blurring. Damn. Damn! Wasn't I ever going to get over it?

After a while, Camden came out. "She's gone," he said quietly.

"About time." I did a double take. He had on a dark gray suit, a white shirt with thin gray stripes, gray socks, dark shoes, a burgundy tie, and his hair was actually combed. "What's the occasion?"

"Church. Can you give me a ride?"

I had forgotten it was Sunday. "Yeah, sure."

"We're all going. Why don't you come along?"

"I haven't finished reading this intriguing little tabloid."

"Kary needs a ride, too."

I looked over my shoulder. Kary waved from the kitchen door. She had put on a royal blue dress that made her hair look even more like spun gold.

"Does she sing in the choir, too?" She certainly looked like an angel.

"No."

"So we could share a pew?"

"Yep."

"Give me five minutes."

I put on my suit and tie, and we went to Victory Holiness Church.

Kary and I sat about four pews from the back next to an elderly Korean couple and two dark-skinned teenage girls who whispered congratulations to Kary over her engagement. She introduced me to the people around us and handed me a hymnbook. I looked around at the stained glass windows with names and dates underneath, indicating the church members who had donated each window. My feet sank into thick-deep red carpet. Two tall candlesticks and four collection plates sat on a long table at the front. Above the alter shone a larger stained glass window depicting angels in flight and light coming from the clouds in long streamers of gold. I could hear the hum of air conditioning, but some people used paper fans to keep cool.

The church filled up and the choir filed in, rows of smiling men and women in red robes, including Camden on the end of the first row. After the first hymn and several Bible readings, the choir stood. I noticed they didn't use any music, and instead of an organ, a small gray-haired black woman came around to a piano, flexed her little fingers, and charged in.

The choir began with a deep rich hum, and then Camden's clear tenor took off with the melody. He would sing a line, and the choir would respond. It was uplifting. That's the only word I could think of to describe it. I'd never heard the song. It was all about standing on the solid rock and needing a safe place and all that kind of thing. In some places, the congregation sang along. The song swooped up to a clear high note that rang long after the song ended. The choir sat down as several people said, "Amen!" right out loud. One of the choir ladies reached over and patted Camden's knee. His hair was back in his eyes. He loosened his tie and turned his attention to the minister.

"Thank you, choir, for that splendid number," the minister said. "A fitting beginning to our revival week. Now, if everyone would turn in your Bibles to Psalm Thirty-Four."

I managed to make it through the rest of the service. I hadn't been to church in a while, and the last time had been for something I never want to think about again. The song had stirred up unwanted emotions and by the time we sang the last hymn, I was pretty edgy. The beautiful little church, the emotion-filled anthem, the angels in the golden clouds, all the talk about revival and renewal—I just couldn't take it.

I waited out by the Fury until Camden waded through the appreciative crowd. I saw Kary talking with a group of excited women, oohing and ahhing over her hand, so I figured we'd be here a while. No doubt they were discussing every little detail of her impending wedding.

Like me, Camden had taken off his jacket and rolled up his shirtsleeves. It was a particularly warm day.

"Sounded good," I said as he walked up.

"Thanks."

I opened the car door. "Get in, and I'll crank up the air."

The car was beginning to get out of the blast furnace stage when Camden said, "My offer still stands."

"And I've told you I don't want to know. Don't start with me."

"I think you'd feel better."

"Don't tell me how to feel." I kept my eyes on the little church and the group of brightly dressed women, but I could tell he was giving me one of those power stares.

"How long are you going to carry this around?"

"As long as I want, okay?" I said. "Back off."

He didn't say anything for a long while. I thought he was going to drop the subject. Then he said, "Lindsey has something to say to you."

Hearing her name made me grip the steering wheel. "Damn it, Camden."

"You need to hear it."

I wasn't sure I could unclench my teeth. "No."

Another long look from Camden. I put my head down on the steering wheel and steadily pushed her image from my mind. With a creak the back doors opened, letting in a rush of hot air and Kary, who apologized for keeping us.

"You didn't fall asleep, did you, David?"

I straightened, keeping my gaze forward. "I'm wide awake," I said. "Let's go home."

◇◇◇

At the house, we had a quiet lunch. Afterwards, Kary sat down in the island with her laptop to start her research, Camden went upstairs to take a nap, and I went to work.

Time to quit brooding. I wanted to find Pamela's locket and Nick's watch and get that out of the way so I could concentrate on Laura and Ashford. These couples were getting annoying.

I met Lily on the porch, wearing what looked like a bridesmaid's dress of light blue with a little half jacket and a fisherman's hat. Her hair poked out like a dandelion gone to seed. She had another box of crystals.

"Sorry, Lily, Camden's taking a nap. You want to leave those with me?"

She handed me the box. "All right. I thought of someone else you might ask about lockets. Mama Irene. She's very good with the Tarot."

"Tarot cards, you mean?"

"Plus she makes jewelry. She might have a lead for you."

"Do you have her address?"

Following Lily's directions, I found Mama Irene's house, a very normal-looking white split-level. A stunning young woman answered the door, her black hair a cloud of smoky curls, her mouth a perfect pout. She was wearing a satiny purple blouse and black slacks.

I didn't think it was possible, but I asked anyway. "Uh, Mama Irene?"

"No, I'm Ivy," she said. "Mama's not here. Did you want a reading?"

"No, thanks. When will she be back?"

Ivy blinked her big dark eyes. "Oh, please, come in. I need the practice. I'll do you for free."

How could I resist such an offer? "I really don't believe in fortune-telling."

"Oh, that's okay. Come in."

I expected the inside of the house to be dark and smoky, all gypsy caravan, with beaded curtains and weird dried things hanging from the ceiling, but it was Early American, a cheerful orange and brown. The only difference was a small round table covered with a red velvet cloth in the middle of the living room. Ivy pulled two large cushions from a chair and put them on the floor.

"Have a seat."

She sat down on the other cushion and took out a pack of large pink cards. She started to shuffle the cards and paused. "I don't even know your name."

"David Randall."

She focused on me like a camera lens. "Okay, David, we need to choose a significator for you. I'm thinking the King of Swords."

"Fine by me."

She searched the deck for a picture of a dark serious-looking king holding a large silver sword. She put the card on the table.

"David, I want you to shuffle the cards three times, all the while thinking of the question you want answered."

After I shuffled the cards, Ivy had me cut them into three piles. Then she stacked them back up, laid six of them in a cross-shaped pattern and four more in a line to the right of the pattern. She was practically bouncing on her cushion.

"This is so exciting. I hardly ever get a chance to try this out on anyone."

"Glad I stopped by."

"Okay, are you ready?"

"Yes, ma'am."

"Remember, sometimes you have to interpret what the cards are telling you. It isn't always clear at first." She picked up the first card. "This covers him, the general atmosphere of the question asked. Four of Pentacles. One possessive of material things, inheritance, gifts."

I hadn't really thought of a question. I'd just been humoring her, but the locket and watch were gifts, all right. Maybe these little pieces of colored paper were going to tell me something, after all.

Ivy picked up the second card. "This crosses him, for good or evil. The Queen of Swords, a sad woman."

Laura. Or possibly Melanie. Or Ellin.

"This crowns him. Ace of Rods, a time of beginning, marriage, birth, enterprise, creation. This is below him: Knight of Rods, reversed. Conflict, division in emotional or business life. This is behind him: Ace of Pentacles, reversed, the evil side of wealth. This is before him: The Hanged Man."

"That doesn't look too good."

"It isn't a bad card," she said. "It means spirituality, self-sacrifice."

I could think only of losing Kary. If that wasn't self-sacrifice, and if I didn't feel like hanging myself, then I didn't know what else it could be.

Ivy moved to the line of four cards and turned over the first one. It showed a man carrying seven big sticks. "This card represents your attitude. The Seven of Rods: ultimate victor, courage, persistence."

"You bet."

She turned over the second card. "This card is the environment surrounding the question. Page of Rods, reversed. Hmmm, bad news, indecision, instability."

Got that one, all right.

"Now to your hopes and fears." The third card showed an odd-looking man in fancy robes. "The Hierophant. This means a spiritual nature and a marriage or alliance of some kind. Is there someone special in your life? This is a very good card."

"Let's see what the last one says."

She turned over card number four. "This is the outcome: Six of Swords. A journey by water. Action toward resolution of difficulties." She sat back, looking pleased with herself. "A very good reading. Did it answer your question?"

"Let's see. If I get past the bad woman and carry some big sticks across the water, I'll be able to marry the girl of my dreams. Otherwise, I have to hang myself."

For a moment, Ivy looked exactly like Lily, that same big-eyed look of disbelief, but then she smiled. "Well, everything is open to interpretation, but I'd say the outcome is going to be pretty good." She pointed to the Seven of Rods. "You've got the courage and persistence to see it through."

"I still don't know where the missing watch is."

"Oh, but you'll find it." She stretched her fingers. "I didn't have to look in the book once. Want a drink?"

"Sure."

She went into the kitchen. I looked at the brightly-colored pictures spread out on the red cloth. Journey by water, my ass. Where was the mysterious dark-haired stranger? The promise of long life?

Ivy came back carrying a tray with two glasses of lemonade and some oddly shaped cookies. "Mama Irene made these. I know they look funny, but they taste good. Do you like peanut butter?"

"My favorite." I took a bite. "Very good."

She sat down on her cushion. "So you've lost your watch? That's too bad."

"I'm looking for a watch and a locket."

Ivy frowned at the cards. "Was that your question?"

"Sort of."

"I can't see any pattern here for lost objects."

"Maybe they fell in the lake." At her frown, I pointed to the last card. "Journey by water."

"Oh, that's for you."

"A cruise in my future?"

"It's possible." She chewed thoughtfully on that luscious lower lip. "I haven't seen that card come up very often."

"You did a very good job. Sure I don't owe you anything?"

"Oh, no. I've been studying with Mama Irene for about six months now, and I really haven't had the chance to read many

strangers. I've already gone through all my friends and family—
those who'd let me, that is. Some people just aren't believers, no
matter how many times the answer stares them right in the face."

I was staring right into her lovely little face and almost choked
on my cookie.

Ivy.

She pounded me on the back. "Take a drink, quick."

I gulped some lemonade and caught my breath. "I think I
know where the watch is."

"Well, of course you do. I gave you a very good reading."

"Better than you know."

Chapter Nineteen
"Death and the Lady"

I drove to the Vincent house, parked the Fury, and started my search around the house. Pamela had asked Nick to pull the ivy out of her flowerbed, and he'd done a thorough job. The beds were clean and ready to plant. So where had he tossed the unwanted ivy? I found a tangle of leaves and vines near the edge of the forest and after rooting through, saw a gleam of silver, and pulled out the watch.

When I got back to the house, Nick was on the porch. "I saw your car."

I held up the watch. "And it's still ticking."

The relief that swept over his face surprised me. I hadn't realized how deeply the loss of the watch had disturbed him.

"You found it!"

I handed it to him. "It was in the discarded ivy."

"I never thought of that. When I was pulling at all the vines, it must have slipped off." He put his hand over his eyes the way I'd seen Camden do to clear his vision. "Thank God."

Pamela came out onto the porch. "What's all the excitement?"

"David found my watch."

"How wonderful! Where was it?"

Nick put the watch on. "In the pile of ivy I pulled out of your flowerbed. I don't know why I didn't think to look there."

Pamela beamed at me. "David, how can I thank you?"

"No thanks yet," I said. "I haven't found your locket."

Pamela shook her head. "Don't worry about my locket. Finding Nick's watch means a great deal more to me. What gave you the idea to look in the ivy?"

"Oh, I had a Tarot reading. Led me right to the watch."

She laughed. "I don't believe it."

"My reader was a lovely young woman named Ivy."

"Ivy! Well, aren't you clever?"

I could've basked in Pamela's smile all day, but I had other mysteries to solve. She wrote me a check, and she and Nick thanked me again. I said good-by and got into the Fury.

◇◇◇

Next, I planned to interview some of Laura's old acquaintances at the Shady Oaks Rest Home, stop by Lassiter's to give him the notebook and recording, and then head back to the college to see what else Tate Thomas could tell me.

That's what I planned. That's not what happened.

Shady Oaks was a typical rest home, a long, low brick building surrounded by a fence. A few of the residents were sitting in rocking chairs on the front porch. One smiled and waved as I went in.

The woman at the desk looked up from her computer. "May I help you?"

"I'm David Randall. I called earlier about visiting a Mrs. Amelia Barnes and Mrs. Modene Fiddler."

She checked a list on her calendar. "They're in the parlor. Just go straight. It's the first room on your left."

"Thanks."

The parlor was a sunny room with lots of comfortable chairs. A TV blared a talk show from one corner; two men dozed over a checker game in another. Faced with about a dozen elderly women, all of whom stared at me avidly, I cleared my throat.

"Mrs. Barnes and Mrs. Fiddler?"

A spry-looking woman in a flowered dress beckoned. "Over here, dear. I'm Amelia Barnes." She pointed to a wizened little woman in a wheelchair next to her. "This here's Modene Fiddler." She gave the wheelchair a kick. "Modene! That man's here about Laura Gentry."

Modene gave a start and opened tiny blue eyes as clear as the October sky. "Hello, Sweetie."

I pulled a chair over and sat down. "I'm glad to meet you both. Thanks for seeing me."

"Oh, no. We should thank you for letting us see you," Amelia Barnes said. "You are one handsome man."

Modene put one tiny claw on my knee. "I could go for you."

Amelia Barnes took Modene's hand off my knee. "What do you need to know?"

"Anything you can tell me about Laura Gentry and John Burrows Ashford."

"I never knew John Ashford, but Laura and I went to school together. She was a mighty pretty girl, but way too flighty for most of the boys."

"Do you know if she wrote music? I'm trying to find proof that she's the author of some folk songs."

"She used to be a good friend. Then she met Ashford and he was all she ever wanted to talk about. I found that tiresome."

I felt Modene's little hand creep back onto my knee. I gave it a pat and she beamed.

"We're a very musical family, too," she said. "You should talk to my sister, Lodene."

"Is she here?"

"Oh, my, no, she lives at home. You go out past the old Hendricks place—"

"For heaven's sake, Modene, he don't know the old Hendricks place."

"Well, it's a big white house with a pig out front pulling a wheelbarrow."

"That makes even less sense."

"I didn't put it there. The people that bought the house must think it's pretty. I don't know how they got it to pull a wheelbarrow."

Amelia sighed. "How many times do I have to tell you? It's not a real pig."

I tried to get the conversation back on track. "Mrs. Fiddler, would your sister know anything about Laura Gentry's music?"

"Wouldn't hurt to ask her."

"Mrs. Barnes, did Laura ever talk to you about Ashford's songs? Did she ever show you any of the music?"

"No, lord, all she wanted to talk about was how grand he was and wasn't she lucky to have snagged such a man. Never said a word to me about songs. Of course, we all knew Ashford wrote songs. He thought he was something, he did."

"What do you know about her death?"

"Fell in the river and drowned. Poor thing. I think Ashford pushed her. He was probably tired of her by then. He fancied himself quite the ladies' man."

"But there isn't any real proof he had anything to do with her death?"

She sighed again and seemed to sink back. "That was a long time ago."

Modene Fiddler's blue eyes shone like little jewels. "Turn right at the second mailbox, the one that's setting crookwards. Go past True Vine Baptist Church. It's the gray house setting back from the road. Lodene will know. Or ask Robert."

"Robert's been dead for twenty-five years," Amelia said.

"Then why'd he come see me last Sunday?"

"That was your nephew."

A smiling young woman in a pink smock came and announced lunchtime. I thanked Amelia Barnes and Modene Fiddler.

Modene held onto my arm. "Give me a kiss."

I kissed her soft wrinkled cheek, and she laughed.

"You're a devil," she said.

Following Modene's directions, I drove out into the country-side past some truly ugly mobile homes. I found the pig pulling the wheelbarrow, a remarkably grotesque work of yard art. I passed True Vine Baptist and found Lodene Fiddler's house. Expecting a tilted shack with major appliances rusting on the front porch, I was surprised to drive up to a small neat house framed by flower gardens. A short furry dog barked excitedly as I went up the porch steps, but was too timid to approach. A woman in her seventies opened the door. She wasn't wizened yet, but she was going to be. Her eyes were the same October sky blue.

"Yes?"

"Mrs. Lodene Fiddler? My name's David Randall. I was just speaking with your sister Modene at Shady Oaks. She said you might be able to help me."

"Help you with what?"

"I'm trying to find out all I can about Laura Gentry and John Burrows Ashford."

"What for?"

"Laura's great-granddaughter hired me to find out if Laura wrote any of the songs in *Patchwork Melodies*."

"Why should that matter now?"

"There's a great deal of money involved."

Lodene Fiddler grimaced. "Ain't that always the way? None of it coming to me, I'll bet."

"I don't think so."

"Well, I don't know nothing that could help you, so if you'll excuse me."

She started to close the door when I heard an odd metallic plonking sound, like someone hammering on piano strings.

"That's a dulcimer, isn't it?"

"Evelene's practicing. Told her it was a waste of time. Everybody's all booked for the festival."

"I know someone who's looking for a dulcimer player."

She scowled at me. "God's truth?"

"Yes, ma'am."

She opened the door. "Well, come in and talk to her. See if she's interested."

Evelene Fiddler was a surprisingly punk young woman with spiky pink hair, a nose ring, a tattered yellow tee shirt hanging high over baggy jeans, and a slash of magenta lipstick. Her dark eyes, glazed with some shiny green stuff, gave me the once-over. "Who's this?"

Lodene said, "This here's Mister Randall, come asking about the Gentry family. Says he knows a fella needs a dulcimer player."

Evelene's sullen demeanor changed. "Really? What's the name of the group? Would they let me sit in? I know all the standards and can fake the rest."

I used my cell phone to call Buddy. He was delighted by my news. "Lemme talk to her."

I handed the phone to Evelene. Her tone was respectful. "Yes, sir. Yes, I know that one. I can come practice whenever you say. Okay, great, thanks." She handed the phone back to me. "He says I can come over today at five."

"Well, all right, then," Lodene said.

"Thanks, Mister Randall." Evelene returned to beating on the dulcimer with renewed vigor.

"I'll see you out." As we walked to the front door, Lodene said, "I appreciate that. Evelene's been really down ever since her group broke up. Seems her boyfriend had other ideas and other girls. This'll cheer her up."

"Glad I could help out."

She paused at the door. "About Laura Gentry. My great-uncle Robert saw what happened to her. Says he never got over it. Says she just jumped in the river and was swept away. There was no way he could've saved her, but he ran along the riverbank, hoping he could do something. Found her later downstream, all white and cold, he said, her hair spread out like a fan, her eyes staring wide open. He'd tell us about it and tears would start down his cheeks. Must have been a dreadful sight."

"Was John Ashford there?"

"No. Robert says she was out walking by herself."

Evelene was playing a minor tune now, plaintive and slow. The notes fell like soft drops of water.

"He went to speak to her, but never got the chance. He said he wished he could've said something to make her stop, but you can't stop someone when they're bound to die, now, can you?"

"I don't think you can."

"Ashford died soon afterwards. Robert says some people said it was of a broken heart, but Robert always claimed the man had no heart to break. Never shed a tear for poor Laura, just went right on."

"People grieve in different ways."

She gave me a sharp glance. "Know something about that, do you? Let me tell you, my Elwin's been gone these ten years, and doesn't a day go by I don't weep for him. Don't guess I'll ever run out of tears. People tell me I'll get over it. Maybe I don't want to get over it. Maybe it's the only thing that reminds me I'm human." Abruptly she reared back and called, "Evelene! Play something else. I'm tired of that sad song."

The dulcimer leaped into a lively run of notes. Lodene listened for a while and then looked back at me. "That's better."

People get over it. Maybe I don't want to get over it. Maybe it's the only thing that reminds me I'm human.

I sat in the Fury for a while, thinking about what Lodene Fiddler had said. I'd run out of tears a long time ago, but there was no way I'd ever get over losing Lindsey. What's the point of having people in your life when you know you're going to lose them? No matter how I felt about Kary, was any sort of relationship worth the pain?

Or was all this just my twisted way of punishing myself for not being able to find my daughter when she needed me the most?

The image leaped to my mind before I could stop it: the car upside down, a mass of jagged metal. Scrambling up the hillside, screaming her name, unable to see past the flames and rolls of black smoke—

My hands shook as I started the car. Reliving the accident would not solve anything. Concentrate on this case, I told myself. Maybe this time you can do something right.

Chapter Twenty
"Oh! Susanna"

When I drove up Lassiter's street, I saw yellow police tape around his house and a crowd of gawking neighbors. I parked the Fury a good block away and then wandered up to join the gawkers.

"What happened here?"

A round little woman with a face like a potato shook her head. "Police found Mister Lassiter about an hour ago. Said he'd been attacked and the house torn to pieces."

I peered around the crowd, trying to see into the house. From here, I could see a windstorm of damaged *National Geographics*, gaudy yellow covers strewn about like petals. "Do they have any suspects?"

Another woman, larger and more animated, spoke up, "Damn teenagers, that's what it was! Vandals! Drug heads! Imagine attacking a poor old man."

"Wasn't no kids," a man said. "Police said it was one burglar."

"You don't know," another argued.

Potato Woman kept shaking her head. "Everybody round here knows Mister Lassiter didn't have no money or valuables. Whoever did this did it just to be mean."

"Well, they'll know what mean is if he dies," the large woman said. "They'll put them under the jail."

"Has there been this kind of trouble in your neighborhood before?" I asked.

"No, never," someone else said. "We look after each other round here. I'll bet this was just some crazy kids looking for trouble."

Potato Woman seemed to realize I was not from round here. "Who are you? One of them reporters?"

"No, I'm a friend of Lassiter's. Which hospital did they take him to?"

"Mercy on Sixth."

I thanked her, made a few more comments of a general and sympathetic nature, and slipped away. I got into my car and looked at the faded notebook.

Damn.

I found Mercy Hospital, went inside, and inquired about Lassiter. Bad news. He'd died from head injuries fifteen minutes after they brought him in.

◇◇◇

I knew I wouldn't be able to get anywhere near Lassiter's house. I'd have to try tomorrow. I drove back to Grace Street. I'd gotten so used to turning off of Food Row and into the neighborhood I almost forgot 302 was not my home.

But it could be, I reminded myself.

Kary was sitting on the porch reading one of her large textbooks and making notes. She smiled as I came up the walk. "Did you take the recording to Mr. Lassiter? What did he say? I hope he liked it."

He never got the chance to hear it. I hated to have to tell her. "He had an accident, Kary. I'm sorry to tell you he's dead."

"Oh, no." Her eyes filled with tears. She set her book aside. "What happened?"

"I'm not sure, but I think someone broke into his house looking for his notebook."

"That poor old man! Do you think it was the same person who killed Albert Bennett?"

"I think there's definitely a connection."

"Oh, my God."

I gave her my handkerchief. "I'll find out who did this."

Her voice was muffled as she wiped her face. "You'd better. He was the nicest old fellow. Who'd want to kill him?"

"I know Ashford and Bennett came along many years after Stephen Foster, but everybody kept a notebook, and that's what this killer is after."

She took a deep breath and got control. "Then maybe what I found out will help. Stephen Foster died in 1864. Ashford was born in 1884 or 1885, so of course, he would've been familiar with Foster's work. Everyone was. Horatio Bennett, though, was also born in 1843."

I did the math. "So he was twenty-one when Foster died."

"Which means they could've met, if Horatio was ever in New York. Foster was in Cincinnati from 1846 until 1850 as a bookkeeper, then he married and moved to Allegheny and also spent a lot of time in New York City."

Susie Bennett had told me Horatio had lived in New York. "Kary, it's entirely possible they could've met. Now, could some musical work of Foster's gotten into his notebook? Or into Ashford's? It must not have been in Bennett's, because the killer left the notebook behind. And there isn't anything by Foster in the notebook Lassiter loaned to us."

"Do you still have it?"

I got the notebook out of the trunk and brought it to her. She turned the pages carefully, inspecting each one.

"Maybe somebody just thinks there's a piece by Foster in Lassiter's notebook," I said. "Isn't everything by Foster accounted for?"

Kary smoothed the next page. "Well, this is what I found out. Even back in the 1800s, music was pirated. Singers would take songs to publishers and say they had written them. 'Oh! Susanna,' for instance, had as many as eighteen pirated editions. Copyright laws were not what they are today, and often Foster sold the rights to his songs and others made the real profits, or he just gave his works to publishers. But here's the interesting part, David. According to present knowledge, there are only three copies of the first edition of 'Oh! Susanna.'"

"According to present knowledge. Which means, as far as they know."

"That's right. Another copy would be a priceless piece of music."

Something people might kill for? Melanie had acted surprised to hear Lassiter had a notebook when she was the one who told me he had information. According to Ellin, Byron Ashford had money troubles. Would he have knocked off a Smithsonian director and Harmon Lassiter, trying to find something to solve his financial problems?

"David, there's something here." Kary's slim fingers tugged at the last few pages in the notebook. "It's stuck, but I think I can get it out without tearing it." She pulled gently at the fragile paper. "Oh, my goodness."

I looked over her shoulder. The music looked completely different from Lassiter's and from Ashford's. "What is it? Tell me it's by Stephen Foster. There are examples of his work on the web, right? Let's look it up."

We took the notebook into the office and checked the music with some online examples of Foster's. They looked the same.

"Is this 'Oh! Susanna'?" I asked Kary.

"It's part of it." She poured over the piece of paper. "And look at the date: February 25, 1848." She shook her head in amazement. "It looks like one of the earliest editions. If it's authentic, then this must be what everyone's after."

"Okay. Now what do we do with it?"

"I guess it should go to Mr. Lassiter's family, if he has any."

"I'll check." I planned to go back to Oakville, anyway and look in Lassiter's house.

"You don't want to give it to Melanie, do you?"

"She says she's only interested in making sure Laura Gentry gets credit and is mentioned in the documentary. She never said anything about Stephen Foster." But she seemed awfully eager to get her hands on the notebook. And what was an eye from her sweater doing in the woods behind Albert Bennett's house?

That reminded me of something else. I took the little scrap of paper out of my pocket. "I found this near Bennett's house. Any idea what 'Tranquil Breeze' might mean? Is that a song by Foster?"

"No," she said. "Maybe it's a song by Bennett or Ashford. I could find out."

"That would be great, thanks."

She carefully pulled the Foster piece out of the notebook, agreeing with me that until I decided what to do with it, the music should be kept somewhere safe and separate.

She went to the bookshelf in the living room and pulled out the "D" volume of the old set of encyclopedias. "The piano bench is a little too obvious. Why don't we put it in here?"

"'D' for—?"

"For Foster's last little piece of song. 'Dear hearts and gentle friends.'"

"That'll work."

She slid the music into the encyclopedia, her hand lingering for a moment on the worn cover, her expression pensive. A victory hug was in order, but I hesitated.

"Are you sure you want to keep working on this?"

"Finding a lost piece of music by Stephen Foster should have been an exciting event, but Mr. Lassiter was killed and so was Albert Bennett."

"It's upsetting, but—"

Her eyes sparkled. "I'm not upset. I'm angry. I don't want anyone else to die, certainly not over a piece of worn-out paper."

"We'll find the murderer. Where's the rest of the gang?"

"Fred's in the park. Rufus and Angie went somewhere together, and Cam's still asleep."

I'd seen a package of hamburger in the refrigerator. "How about if I grill some burgers for supper?"

By the time I'd cleaned the grill and had the burgers frying, Rufus and Angie had returned, Fred had wandered in from the park, and Camden was awake. Everyone except Fred was impressed by my culinary skill. I explained that, after two failed marriages, I'd better know how to cook.

Angie brought a plate out to the grill. "You can put the burgers on here, Randall."

"Thank you." I plopped the first finished burgers onto the plate.

She shooed a few stray flies away from the burgers. "You'll have to share all your recipes."

I raised my spatula. "Let me warn you. I can tell when I'm being made sport of."

Her smile made her tiny eyes almost disappear. "I didn't realize you were so sensitive."

"I have many layers."

"Like a big old cake? I believe it."

"That entitles you to the cheeseburger of your choice."

We decided to picnic in the backyard, so Rufus set up more lawn chairs. Ellin came in just as we were sitting down to eat. Kary and Fred looked alarmed, as if they expected her to grab a fork and start stabbing people. Camden indicated a chair beside him.

"Hi, Ellie. Join us for dinner?"

"No, thank you. If I might speak to you for a moment, please? In private?"

Camden excused himself. We watched them go with varying levels of apprehension.

Kary's eyes were wide. "She doesn't look too happy, does she?"

"Does she ever look happy?" I asked.

Fred stopped eating long enough to speak for us all, even though his mouth was full: "That woman gives me the willies."

We got real quiet. We could hear Ellin's voice—hell, I think all of Parkland could hear Ellin's voice—but we couldn't make out any words. We heard pauses where Camden must have answered, or tried to.

"What in the world does she want this time?" Kary said. "I wish she'd do her own psychic thing and leave Cam alone."

We listened. Now it was too quiet out there.

"Do you suppose she's killed him?" I asked.

"Wouldn't be surprised," Rufus said.

"I'll go see."

I walked through the island and peered out the front door. Ellin's car was gone, and Camden stood on the porch, looking out across the yard. The screen door squeaked when I opened it, but he didn't turn around.

"I think the next saucer's due at eight fourteen," I said.

He pushed his hair out of his eyes. "If it shows any sign of stopping I'm hopping on board. Maybe women on other planets are easier to understand."

"Don't count on it."

"Sometimes I wonder," he began, and then stopped.

"Wonder what?"

He shook his head. "Nothing. Thanks for cooking supper. We'll put you on the list."

"The list?"

"We take turns. I usually make lasagna, and Kary makes a mean tuna casserole."

"Don't start with any plans for me. This is just temporary, remember? Oh, and come in the house for a second. I need to show you something."

We went to the bookcase, and I showed him the scrap of music tucked into the encyclopedia. The minute he touched the paper, his eyes went wide.

"It's real, isn't it?" I asked.

"Where did you find it?"

"In Lassiter's notebook. Kary and I figure Horatio Bennett might have met Stephen Foster when they were both living in New York."

"Then how did it get in Lassiter's notebook?"

"Who knows? That was a long time ago. Ashford might have hidden it there, or Laura. Foster was famous in their day, too."

He touched the paper again. His eyes glazed over. I wondered if he was seeing Stephen Foster sitting at a desk writing this song, or maybe standing at a window, the tune forming in his head. "This could be worth a fortune."

"Worth killing over. Lassiter's dead and his house trashed. Someone was looking for this."

Camden put the music back in its hiding place. "This is why Ashford didn't want anyone to have Lassiter's notebook."

"I'm wondering if that warning includes Tate Thomas. His secretary told me Thomas was excited about finding something. Now, what if he suspected this connection between Bennett and Ashford and Foster and encouraged Melanie and Byron, too, to hunt for this notebook?"

"Why not hire someone like yourself to find it for him?"

"And why not ask his colleague, Albert? Something's going on here, and until I figure it out, the best place for this little piece of music is volume 'D,' and the best place for the notebook is in the trunk of my car."

◇◇◇

That night as I stretched out on my bed, I thought: I told Camden this was temporary, but I'm still here. I enjoyed sitting on the porch watching the birds. I enjoyed cooking for everyone. It was as if I had my life back. Almost.

Outside, the remaining oak leaves rustled softly. I drifted off to sleep. Then I realized the rustling sound wasn't the leaves. It was the rustle of a dress, of lace. She wasn't very distinct, but I would have known that white lacy dress and those long brown curls anywhere. She was standing in my doorway. As she opened her mouth to speak, I jerked myself awake.

"No!"

Heart pounding, I made myself look where she'd been standing. There was nothing there. Of course there was nothing there.

"There's nothing there," I said aloud, but that other part of me asked, What did she want? What was she trying to tell you?

Shut up! I told that inner voice. There's nothing there.

I finally convinced myself and went back to sleep. I forced myself not to dream, and, as usual, it worked.

Chapter Twenty-one
"A Breeze From the Hills"

Monday morning, I wanted to get back to Oakville. Maybe things had settled and I could have a look around. As luck would have it, Lassiter's street was quiet and the houses on either side of his looked empty. I parked the Fury around the corner and walked back, taking the side driveway and coming around behind the ancient garage. The wind tossed leaves and more pieces of *National Geographic* in the small backyard, a whirl of shredded yellow covers, brown tape, and faded address labels. The policeman who stepped out onto the back stoop almost saw me, but I ducked back behind the garage. I caught my elbow on a rough board and stifled a curse. I hadn't seen a police car. Probably waiting to see if the criminal returned to the scene of the crime. Not the place I needed to be.

The policeman went inside. I cautiously made my way back to the Fury and drove to the nearest gas station to think about my next move. My phone rang. It was Kary.

"David, I found out that Ashford and Bennett met in Oakville. I found a reference in one of the old newspaper accounts of the Bennett System. Bennett invited several musicians and composers to his mountain retreat in the hopes of selling them on his system. According to the report, Ashford attended this meeting. The report doesn't say what he thought of it, though. That would've been interesting."

"Thanks," I said. "Do you know where this retreat was?"

"Let's see." There was a pause while she checked her source. "Here it is. Oh, my. Well, this answers your question. It was called Tranquil Breeze."

All this time I thought "Tranquil Breeze" was the name of a song.

"Tranquil Breeze? You're sure?"

"Yes, but that was years ago, David. It might not be there anymore."

I used my phone's direction application to look up Tranquil Breeze. I found a Mountain Breeze and a Friendly Breezes Trail, but no Tranquil Breeze.

I bought a sandwich and a Coke and headed up to Mountain Breeze. Mountain Breeze was an upscale development of huge cabins perched on the hillside, each with a spectacular view of the mountains and valleys. The owners had given their homes names like "Heaven on Earth" and "Our Home in the Sky." I found a man pulling mail from his mailbox and asked about Tranquil Breeze.

"This is a new development," he said. "Nothing was up here till about two years ago. You might try the old road that goes up to Glen Valley."

"Is that Friendly Breezes Trail?"

"Yeah, that's what they're calling it now."

Friendly Breezes Trail wound around and about until it seemed to meet itself. The few houses I saw were half hidden in the trees, or so old and moldy I couldn't imagine anyone living inside. About halfway up, I came to a roadside stand. I pulled over and parked. I bought an apple and asked the elderly woman at the cash register about Tranquil Breeze.

She wiped her hands on her apron. "Now there's a name I haven't heard in a long time."

"I'm looking for the Bennett place."

"Yes, there were some Bennetts living there."

"This would've been around the late Twenties, early Thirties."

"That's about the time my family moved here."

"Did you know John Ashford or Laura Gentry?"

To my surprise, she blushed. "Lord, yes, everyone knew John Ashford."

"What can you tell me about him?"

"Well, now, I personally didn't know him. I knew who he was. His songs were mighty popular around here."

"So it's possible he could've stayed with Bennett when he came to town?"

"I imagine so. He was always wanting to talk about his songs and showing people how he wrote them, like he was some sort of special music teacher. Some folks hung on his every word, especially that Gentry girl. She thought she could write songs, too, but they was never any good."

"I heard there was a tragedy involving Laura Gentry."

"Jumped in the river and drowned herself."

"And Ashford?"

"Don't know what happened to him. This Bennett fellow, now, his place burned down round about '45, '46. Never was rebuilt."

"So the house was a meeting place for local musicians?"

"I suppose you could say that. According to what I've heard, there was some fancy parties there. Ashford always liked to surround himself with pretty women. They'd come from all over just to meet him."

I'll bet Laura loved that. "Thanks. I appreciate the information. Has anyone else been asking about Tranquil Breeze?"

"Well, come to think of it, there was a couple come by. Some lady and her boyfriend. I guess that's who it was. They argued like they was married."

"Do you remember what they looked like? They might have been friends of mine."

She thought a moment. "They was fairly ordinary. He wasn't a friendly fellow, that's all I can say about him. The woman, now, she was a bit nicer. Had on one of them sweaters with little animals on it. Always did like those."

Melanie Gentry. "Were they in a red Honda?"

"No, some fancy car. Real sporty."

Had Byron Ashford been with her? "And they wanted to know where the Bennett place was?"

"Just like you. And just like you, I told them it had burnt down. They looked right disappointed. Still wanted to know where it was."

"I'd like to know, too," I said. "I'm studying the history of this region, and I'm always interested in the little offbeat stories."

"Well, you just continue up this road till you come to a cross-roads. Turn left and go about half a mile. You'll see a driveway, but that's all that's left. Might be a few bricks or boards. I ain't been out there in years."

An RV pulled up and five overweight tourists in shorts and baseball caps got out. I thanked the woman and got back into the Fury. I drove to the crossroads and turned left. It took me a few tries to find the driveway half-hidden by trees and vines. Someone's tires had pushed down the grass and broken the small branches that had fallen in the driveway. I rounded a slight curve and came upon the vine-covered ruins of what had once been a large cabin. I got out and had a look. More tire tracks showed where a car had turned around. Another set of tracks had dried in a low place in the drive, a set with distinctively wide tread. Not the kind of tires on a Honda. The kind you'd find on a sports car, say for instance, on a Corvette like the one parked beside Byron Ashford's house.

If the couple the woman talked to were indeed Melanie and Byron, what made those two decide to take a road trip together? How did they know about Tranquil Breeze, and what did they expect to find here?

The woman at the road side stand and her talk of parties at Tranquil Breeze gave me an idea how the copy of "Oh! Suzanna" might have found its way into Lassiter's notebook. Lassiter had told me his mother knew both Ashford and Laura Gentry and that she had been to "some kind of party" at Ashford's house, which could have been Tranquil Breeze. Lassiter also recalled

Laura playing his mother's piano, playing the tunes in his notebook. What if Ashford had given Lassiter's mother "Oh! Suzanna"? Ashford was scornful of Foster's work. He might have decided to give it away. Or Laura might have realized the song's worth and hidden it, not in *Patchwork Melodies*, but in her friend's notebook where no one would think to look.

◇◇◇

Angie met me at the door. "Whew. He's been Ashford all morning. That is one ornery rascal."

"All day?"

"And you got a visitor in your office."

I had recognized Melanie's red Honda in the driveway. "She hasn't met Ashford, has she?"

"I been doing my best to keep them apart, but you know how Ashford is."

I reached my office in time to hear Ashford declare in his best Pompous Ass voice, "So here is the young woman who would smear my good name."

When Angie went to the door, Ashford must have used the opportunity to enter my office and approach Melanie Gentry. He had his back to me, so I could see Melanie's startled face.

"Your good name? I don't even know you."

Ashford immediately began his sad story. "Not in this body, no, how could you? But I assure you I am John Burrows Ashford, and as for what transpired between myself and your great-grandmother, you were not there! How dare you presume to know anything about our relationship? I loved Laura Gentry with all my heart. I never harmed her. You cannot know the depth of my feelings for her."

Melanie glanced at me, her eyes narrowed to suspicious slits. "What is going on? What is all this?"

I decided to attack it head-on. "This is the spirit of John Ashford. He's decided to park in Camden for the day. Anything you'd like to ask him?"

"If this is your idea of a joke, it's a pretty sick one." She moved away from him. "No, there's nothing I'd like to ask him, alive or dead, but there's plenty I'd like to ask you."

"Camden—I mean, Ashford, will you leave? This is private business."

He stood, arms folded. "I'll not go until this young woman apologizes for the slanderous tales she has perpetrated about me."

Melanie clutched her pocketbook like a shield. "Tell your insane friend to get out."

"Ashford."

"I'll not budge."

"If this sort of thing continues, I'll take my business elsewhere."

I couldn't afford to lose a paying client and someone who might be involved in all the events surrounding the notebook. "Ashford, we'll settle this later, I promise."

He tossed his head. "I demand an apology."

"Melanie," I said, "just tell him you're sorry so he'll leave, please."

"I refuse to play your crazy game. What are you trying to prove? Why should I apologize to a total stranger?"

I don't know how long they would have stood there, glaring at each other, if Angie hadn't reached in and pulled Ashford out of the room. He had time for one startled "urk!" before he was gone. I shut the door.

"I'm very sorry. Camden is susceptible to spirits and some-times he gets carried away." I didn't have time to explain in detail, and anyway, she didn't care.

She made a great show of sitting down and fussing with her skirt and her hair. She wasn't wearing the animal sweater. I wondered if it was at the cleaners getting its eyes restored. "After all that, I hope you have some good news for me about the notebook. Did you find it?"

"I have a pretty good idea where it is." In the trunk of my car.

She'd forgotten all about Ashford's demands. "You've done an excellent job. I really can't tell you what this means to me."

"Well, give it a shot. What exactly does it mean to you?"

For a brief moment, she looked annoyed, as if having to explain things again to a cretin such as myself was beneath her. Then she smiled. "It means my great-grandmother will get the credit she deserves. It means the new documentary can set the record straight. It's part of history."

I didn't tell her my theory of history: it's all wrong. Just like you, Ms. Gentry, I suspected. "Just credit and glory. Nothing else?"

"That's enough for me."

"Sure there's not some money involved somewhere?"

She made a dismissive gesture. "I want Laura's good name to be restored, that's all."

She had to know. Why else would she want the notebook? Did she want the notebook badly enough to break into a house and knock an old man on the head?

Was Melanie Gentry capable of murder?

I hadn't thought so at first, but after seeing the anger in her eyes when confronted with Ashford, I was beginning to wonder just how far this woman would go to get what she wanted.

"What if the information in the notebook proves Ashford wrote the songs?" I asked her.

"Then that's it, I suppose. I will have done all I could."

She'd told me when we first met she knew nothing about Albert Bennett. "Have you been up to the mountains lately to see where Ashford and Laura lived?"

"No."

"Albert Bennett's great-grandfather Horatio knew Ashford. He had a cabin in the mountains called Tranquil Breeze. Did you know about that?"

"No. What does this have to do with anything?"

"Mister Bennett may have had something to help support your claim."

"This is the man who was killed? Didn't the murderer leave his notebook behind?"

"Yes. I'm surprised you haven't asked to see it."

"The police say it's just scribbles and they have to keep it as evidence. I can't see how that would help me, at all. I'm only interested in Lassiter's notebook. As soon as you find it, you let me know." She got up. "I'll talk to you tomorrow."

I saw her to the door and watched her drive away. Maybe she truly wanted Laura Gentry to take her rightful place in history. Maybe I was a harem dancer in a previous life.

Wait a minute. Was that Ellin's car in the driveway?

I had only a moment to process this, when damned if I didn't hear Ellin and Angie getting into it. My first clue that Ellin was using her voice only dogs can hear. The remaining oak leaves were falling rapidly.

Ellin had confronted Angie at the dining room table. Angie, placid as ever, cut some cloth into a large blouse shape.

"Well, hell, blondie, if I wasn't so crazy about Rufe, I'd be all over the little guy, and I mean all over. What's your problem? I'm surprised that boutique babe hasn't carved her initials in him already."

I hadn't seen Ellin speechless. I enjoyed the sight for five seconds. Then she said, "This is none of your business, you interfering cow!"

Angie gave one of her glacial shrugs. "You don't want him, fine by me. I know lots of girls who'd be thrilled to have such a nice guy."

Ellin was scandalized. "Of course I want him! I love him. I always have. Doesn't anyone in this stupid house see that?"

Angie lobbed her next bomb. "Seems to me you like him better when he's Ashford."

"Ashford is a pig!"

"But a mighty sexy pig, now, isn't he?"

I never thought Ellin Belton would ever actually be glad to see me, but she glanced in my direction and gave a frantic signal. "Randall, get over here and tell this woman the truth! Tell this woman how much I love Cam!"

"I have a better idea," I said. "*You* tell Camden how much you love him."

As before, she got this odd expression on her face and closed up shop. "I don't know why I bothered with you," she said. "Or you," she added to Angie. "Neither one of you has the slightest idea how I feel."

"Neither does Camden." I turned to Angie. "What did you do with him?"

"I tossed him in his room."

"Go on up," I told Ellin. "Whoever's up there will be glad to see you."

"I came to see you."

"Me?"

She went past me, heading toward the office. "Could we talk in your office?"

I followed, amazed. "What do you want?"

"You asked me to find out if Byron Ashford was in Washington this week. Mother said he was. She has society friends up there, and they saw him at a fund-raiser at the Smithsonian."

So Byron hadn't been in the Bahamas as his answering machine reported, but conveniently at the Smithsonian where he could easily slip away from a party. "Thanks. That's actually very helpful news." But I knew this wasn't the only reason she was here. She could've just as easily called me with the information. "And?"

"And Robertson still wants to meet Cam. Have you talked to him?"

She should be halfway up the stairs to comfort Camden or enjoy Ashford's manly presence, but apparently, the position at the Psychic Service Network came above all things.

"I thought you two had already thrashed this out."

"And I thought you were going to help me convince him."

"Look," I said, "why don't you go upstairs and talk to him? I know you want this spooky possession thing to happen on camera, but it's not doing Camden any good. I want Ashford to get out and stay out. Then maybe Camden will take part in the documentary—as himself." I wanted to add, wouldn't that be enough for you? But I had an idea nothing would be enough for Ellin Belton.

"I really wanted to go with the Spiritualism angle," she said. "It would be ratings dynamite. Robertson's in town for another two days, and then he's going to another location."

"Well, go up and see what Camden says."

She glanced at her watch. "I've got to get back to the studio. I don't have time to argue with him again, and I don't really want to. If he doesn't want to help me, then that's the way it is."

"I don't think it's a question of wanting to help you. He's not in control. Ashford is. You have to decide which one you really want."

She gave me an icy stare and left without another word.

Chapter Twenty-two
"The Cruel Mother"

I went up to the third floor to Camden's bedroom. It was a large open room. Light filtered in through pale sheer draperies looped off-handedly over wooden curtain rods. Except for the ornate light fixtures and elaborate molding around the ceiling, which must have been original, there was a stack of books on the floor, an old wingback chair, a bureau with clawed feet, and a telescope pointed out the back window. Camden was sitting on the edge of his bed, his head down in his hands. I knocked on the open door.

He didn't look up. "Come in."

"You missed a great catfight." I sat down in the chair.

"How long have I been gone?"

"Angie says all day."

He raised his head. "Ashford's getting stronger. He's not going to leave."

"Yes, he is. I've got the answer. Lassiter's notebook."

"He's not going to leave. Even if you have the proof he needs, he's not going back to wherever he came from."

"He has to. Kick him out. Make him leave."

There was a pause. Camden looked away. "Maybe I don't want to."

I sat up in the chair. "What? What are you talking about? You want to be John Ashford? I don't believe it."

He didn't meet my eyes. "At least he knows who he is."

I got up and walked around so he had to look at me. "That's Ashford talking, not you. He's going right back to hell where he belongs. You think I'm going to let that self-righteous jackass stay? You think anybody who knows you would choose Ashford? You think Kary would like that? Rufus? Fred? What about Ellin?"

"I think she'd be happy with Ashford."

"I think you're an idiot." I was rewarded with a glint of anger in his eyes. "Ashford's working on you from the inside. He even bragged about it to me. If you let him take over, then you're a bigger pushover than I thought."

"I don't know what Ashford's doing," he said. "I haven't been here for days! You tell me what I'm supposed to do."

"Well, you're not supposed to give up." I leaned against the bureau. "Lassiter's dead. Someone trashed his house. I don't have to be psychic to know what they were looking for. Why did you say not to let Melanie Gentry have the notebook?"

"I don't know. It was one of the few things that came to me when I was myself."

"Well, I've got it now. Is the same thug going to come after me?"

"All I can see are two hearts singing."

"Yeah, we've been there already. It's the name of Ashford's pet song."

"It's something else." He pushed back his hair. "It's all mixed up with the past, the future—I don't know. How reliable can I be with Ashford popping in whenever he feels like it? I just know Melanie Gentry shouldn't get her hands on it."

"Okay. She won't."

There was another pause, longer and grayer than the first.

Camden got up and headed toward his bathroom. "I told Buddy I'd help him with his festival display."

"You don't want to be John Ashford."

He stopped. I didn't think he was going to answer me, but finally he did. "No. But I'm not sure who I want to be."

I went downstairs. I called the airport and got the first flight out of Parkland to Richmond. Just to be on the safe side, I took the notebook with me.

◇◇◇

The flight to Richmond took a little less than an hour. Then I spent another hour and a half in the rental car, looking for the right address. I expected some small faded welfare mother, not this sleek suburban mom, complete with minivan, golden lab puppy, and three teenaged kids. Denise Baker Rice was trim, her dark hair short and curly. Her eyes were dark. Her features were regular, unremarkable. There was nothing of Camden about her, not in expression or gesture.

She glanced at me. "Yes?"

"Mrs. Rice, my name is David Randall. I'm a private investigator, and I need your help. Would you mind answering a few questions?"

The puppy barked and wiggled on his leash. She gave the end of the leash to the oldest girl, who was deep in conversation with her sister and barely noticed me. "Sara, would you take Sunshine to the backyard, please, and help Allie with the groceries?"

Sara gave one of those deep exasperated sighs the young are famous for, but she agreed to the unreasonable demands. She took a bag of groceries, Allie took a bag, and the youngest girl grabbed the six pack of Cokes and trailed after. Denise Rice shut the van door and gave me a searching look.

"What's this all about?"

I took a chance. "It's about your son. Your first one."

She stared at me for so long I thought she wasn't going to answer. I thought, I've got the wrong woman. But then she cleared her throat. "Look, I was barely sixteen. I couldn't keep him. It was the only choice I had."

"I'm not here to pass judgment. I'm not even an intermediary. Camden doesn't know I've been looking for you."

"How the hell did you find me? I thought all those records were sealed." Her voice trembled slightly. "Camden? Is that his name?"

I reached into my pocket. I'd brought a snapshot along. "That's the name he goes by. That's him in the middle. The pretty blonde is a good friend, Kary, and the big guy is Rufus. He has a house in Parkland. We all live there."

I could tell she didn't want to look at the picture, but her curiosity was too strong. "Oh, my God," she said softly. She took the picture from my hand. "He looks just like Martin." She left me for a few minutes, drifting back into memory. Then she said, "Perhaps you'd better come inside."

Inside was a typical suburban home: ranch-style furniture, lots of browns and reds and yellows, and big windows displaying a fenced-in backyard where the youngest child raced in circles with the puppy. The groceries had been deposited on the counter separating the living room from a big shiny kitchen loaded with the latest appliances. Denise Rice walked to the stairway that led to the upstairs and listened a moment, as if to assure herself the other children were busy and wouldn't interrupt. She motioned me to the living room sofa and took a seat opposite me in a recliner.

"So, Mister Randall, you found me. Now what?"

"That's entirely up to you. Camden needs to know a little something about you and his father."

She looked at the picture again. "He's all right, then. He's healthy. He has a nice home. What does he do for a living?"

"He works in a clothing store, and he helps people out. He's clairvoyant and damn good. Are you psychic? Is Camden's father?"

"You're not going to tell me that's how you found me."

"No, nothing spooky. Just the Internet."

A wry smile curved her mouth. "After all this time. Why now? What does he want? What do you want?" She paused. I waited. "I'm not some cruel, heartless mother, Mister Randall. I'm very glad he's alive and has good friends like you and this pretty woman. But that part of my life is behind me. I can't see that it would do either of us any good to meet now. We're complete strangers." Still, her gaze strayed to the photo.

"It would help him to know who you are. A little background, a little history. Do you have anything I could take back? A memento, perhaps? A baby shoe?"

"No. Nothing. I told you, I was sixteen and scared to death. I didn't even see him after he was born." Another glance at the picture. "He's very handsome."

"There's another girl in his life. Her name's Ellin. I'm pretty sure he wants to marry her."

"Good. He's getting on with his life, then." She gave me a worried look. "Unless there's something you haven't told me. This doesn't involve bone marrow or a kidney, does it?"

I imagined her reaction if I told her about Ashford. "No, Camden just needs to know about his real family." Which, counting Daisy and Denise's girls, includes four half-sisters. Wait till I sprung this on him.

"There isn't anything to tell."

"What about his father?"

"A crazy fling, that's all. I had no idea I could become pregnant the first time I had sex. Brilliant, huh?"

"His name?"

"I met him at a party. He was the most beautiful man I'd ever seen. When it was all over, he left. He said his name was Martin, and that's all I ever knew." She touched Camden's picture. "He's right there, Mister Randall. You're looking at him." She laughed a slight laugh. "I don't believe he has a single feature of mine, does he?"

"You're his mother," I said quietly.

She got up and left the picture on the coffee table, as if to distance herself from any part of Camden. She stood by the window and watched her daughter and the puppy roll on the ground, chewing on each other. "Thank you for the information. I'd be lying if I said I never wondered about him. I'm glad he's doing well. But if he doesn't know you're here, then it seems to me he isn't interested in opening a relationship. That's fine with me. It would be difficult explaining things to my children."

"I think he might be interested in speaking with you."

She shook her head. "That part of my life is over."

I got up and wandered around the room. Denise Rice had dismissed me, but I wasn't ready to go. There had to be something here I could use. I walked over to the piano in the corner and looked through the array of vocal scores stacked on the bench.

"The kids musical?"

"What?" She turned to face me. It was obvious from her expression she thought I'd gone.

"Your kids. Do they have musical talent?"

"Sara tries, but she has a hard time with it. I can't get the other two interested."

Several framed documents hung above the piano. Closer inspection revealed they were awards and degrees in music, all in her name. There was also a picture of Denise Rice and other women in a choral group and a framed copy of a newspaper article, a good review of her debut at one of the Houston theaters as Mabel in *The Pirates of Penzance*. "A clear and true soprano," the reviewer had written, "with a warm, inviting tone."

"Mrs. Rice." When I had her full attention, I said, "Your son has a fine tenor voice. He loves to sing." I pointed to the review. "This description fits his voice. Clear and true."

Her expression changed. "He's a singer?"

"Church choir, choral societies, birthdays, weddings, in the shower, whatever. All the time."

"All the time." Her voice was wistful.

"Drives us crazy. It means everything to him. I'm sure if he ever had the chance, he'd like to thank you for that."

She nodded, her eyes slowly filling with tears.

"I've taken up enough of your time," I said. "I'll leave my number, if that's okay. No pressure. No expectations. I won't bother you again, I promise." I left my card on the piano and the photo on the coffee table. As I started out, she said,

"Michael."

I turned, puzzled.

"Michael," she said. "That's what I wanted to call him. It was my father's name."

"Thank you. He'll be glad to know." It wasn't much, but I hoped to hell it would be enough.

Chapter Twenty-three
"The Unwilling Bride"

I couldn't get a flight home until early Tuesday morning. By the time I got back to the house, Camden was downtown at the festival with Buddy, Angie, and Rufus. I expected Kary to be with them, but she was home, sitting in the porch swing, hemming her pageant gown.

"Ms. Gentry stopped by about sixteen times," she said. "I told her I didn't know where you'd gone, but it must have been important. She said it better have something to do with her case."

"Thanks. I didn't mean for her to bother you."

Kary snipped a piece of thread. "She didn't bother me. She just kept getting more and more annoyed. She went into your office and I asked her what she was looking for. She said you still had her great-grandmother's letters, so she grabbed them off your desk and left."

The notebook was still locked in the trunk of the Fury. Seemed a good place to leave it. I took a shower and put on some clean clothes. I got a Coke out of the fridge for me and brought a diet soda out to Kary.

She thanked me. "I hope your trip was successful."

"I hope so, too," I said. "I found Camden's mother."

She set her gown aside. "Are you serious? What did she say? What does she look like? Does she want to see Cam?"

"She'd rather not see him."

Kary's happiness faded. "Oh. Well. I guess I can identify with that."

"She's very nice, has a family, a husband, a new life. She doesn't look like him at all, but she's a musician, a singer. Camden must have inherited his voice from her. I took a picture along, and she says Camden looks just like his father, but she couldn't tell me anything about him."

"You were hoping to have good news for him, weren't you?"

"It may be enough to help him the next time Ashford's on board. That's what I'm counting on." I took a drink. "He doesn't know I did this."

"You want to keep it a secret?"

"If I had better news, no. But wait and let me tell him when the time's right."

"He's never said anything about his parents," she said. "We have this sort of pact. I don't mention mine, and he doesn't mention his."

"You don't have a pact with me," I said. "I'd like to know why you live here."

For a moment, I thought I'd gone too far, but Kary was in an unusually pensive mood. She took a sip of her soda and put the can on the porch rail. "I told you I didn't want to be a part of the Ingram Bible Hour. That isn't the whole story. When I was seventeen, I got pregnant. It was a mistake, of course. It was really stupid, but my boyfriend and I were curious and I was rebelling against all those rules. My parents as you can imagine were horrified. Their religion doesn't believe in abortion, and neither do I. But they were mainly concerned about how having an unwed mother would affect their ratings, so I left. They said, okay, that's it, good-by."

My throat began to ache. "So you had the baby?"

"I lost her when she was six months old. That's when Cam took me in. I'd been staying with a girlfriend. I was really sick and upset about the baby for a long time."

If only I'd been here. "I'm sure you were."

"My family wouldn't have anything to do with me, and I felt that God had given up on me, too. Do you know what that's like, David, to spend your whole life being told that God will take care of you and you're special and nothing bad can happen and then there's nothing? Nothing. There's no answer when you pray. There's no solace. All those happy little hymns and songs. Empty. Meaningless."

My throat was so tight, all I could do was nod.

"It took me about three years to come out of depression. Music helped. Sometimes I'd play for hours. I don't know what Cam told his tenants, but no one ever complained, not even Fred. I'd lost my scholarship, so I started taking a class or two at the community college, and eventually, I decided to come back to life." Her voice became softer. "But the worst part is, I can't have any more children."

"Neither can I." When she looked at me in surprise, I realized I'd said this aloud. Well, she had just told me her most private story. It was only fair that I tell her mine. "I had a little girl once. Lindsey. When she was eight years old, she and I were in a car accident."

In my mind, I saw the car roll over and burst into flames. I saw the dark hillside, the faces of rescue workers, the black plumes of smoke. I saw my hands, cut and bloody from clawing through the brush and burning metal. I didn't see Lindsey. I couldn't find her.

"I couldn't find her." Once the words were out, I wanted to scream them, scream and cry and tear things apart. But I was calmed by the depth of sympathy in Kary's brown eyes. She didn't say, "You did all you could," or "That's too much to carry around," or "If it was an accident, you can't blame yourself." She just reached over and put her hand on mine.

"I named my little girl Elizabeth. That's my middle name. I was going to call her Beth."

"Lindsey was Lindsey Marie."

"A lovely name." We sat in silence for a few moments. Kary straightened the lace trim on her gown. "Once I have a good job, I'm going to adopt a baby. Donnie's not sure he likes that idea. The thing is, he knew about my situation before we started dating. Now he's asking me to forget or at least postpone my plans. But I really want a family, David. I always thought I could adopt some children no one else wanted and give them a good home, the way Cam did for me."

Adoption: Is It Right For You? Whatever you want, I started to say. We'll adopt fifty children, a hundred. No, how could I face having another child, even a child with Kary?

I couldn't talk about this anymore. I managed to clear the emotion from my throat. "If you've got a plan for your life, and he's not on board, maybe he's not the one."

And maybe I'm not the one, either.

◇◇◇

I headed back to the college. Luckily for me, Thomas was in.

"But someone's with him just now," the secretary said. "She'll be just a minute, I'm sure."

"She?"

"Ms. Gentry. She stopped by to give him some reports."

"What exactly does Ms. Gentry do at the college?"

"She's an administrative assistant. She does all the kinds of things I do, only she has an office."

"Does she stop by a lot?"

"Recently, she's been by more often. I imagine they're discussing the budget." She picked up a stack of papers. "I have to go make some copies. Just go on in after she leaves. That'll be okay."

I thanked her and waited until she was gone before approaching the closed door to listen. I could hear voices raised in argument. Thomas' voice sounded desperate.

"How in the hell could you be so stupid? Couldn't you have waited to find out?"

Melanie's voice was shrill. "Stupid! I don't think I'm the stupid one here. If you're not careful, I'm going straight to the police."

Immediately, he calmed down. I could hardly hear his next words. "All right, all right. The main problem is the notebook wasn't there. Are you sure Randall doesn't have it?"

Melanie was calmer, too. "He told me Lassiter wanted to hang onto it because it had some of his music. I never touched the old man. He wouldn't let me into his house."

"Well, somebody touched him."

"Byron, of course."

"What would he be doing there?"

"The same thing he was doing at the Smithsonian." She gave a brief laugh. "I've got the goods on him, too, so whatever anyone finds belongs to me."

"You have no idea of the value, the historical importance—"

"I don't care," she said. "I want my money."

The secretary returned, so I had to move away from the door and pretend I was up stretching.

"They're still in there?" she said. "Sorry about that. You want to come back tomorrow?"

I didn't want Melanie to see me. "Let me give you my cell phone number. I think I'll go get a cup of coffee, and you can call when Thomas is ready to see me."

I made sure I was out of sight and waited in one of the little courtyards beside the building until the secretary called with the all clear. As a precaution, I waited a few more minutes and then went in.

Tate Thomas was visibly upset, his face pale, his hands trembling as he wiped his forehead with a handkerchief. He motioned me to a seat. "You'll have to excuse me, Mr. Randall. I think I'm coming down with a cold."

"This will just take a second." I plopped the notebook on his desk.

Talk about an instant cure. He immediately leaned forward and gasped in surprise. "Is this Lassiter's?"

I nodded.

His eyes gleamed. "Have you shown this to Melanie Gentry?"

"No, just you."

He opened the notebook and looked at Lassiter's tiny notes. He turned a few pages. "Copies of songs, some original works. Not very original, but some game attempts at capturing the essence." He went through the notebook page by page. "I recognize some of Laura Gentry's work. Copied, of course. And here are a few of Ashford's. Lots of inferior tunes by Lassiter, some familiar tunes by Gentry and Ashford, and the original notation for 'Two Hearts Singing,' perhaps Ashford's most famous song, written here by Ashford himself. Let me just make sure."

Thomas reached across to his crowded bookshelf and pulled down a large volume. "I believe there's an example of his handwriting in here, a photocopy of a speech he gave to a musical society."

The handwriting in the speech matched exactly.

"In your opinion, could this notebook prove Ashford is the author of 'Two Hearts Singing'?"

"I would say so, yes."

"Is there any proof in this notebook that Laura Gentry wrote any of the songs in *Patchwork Melodies*?"

"No, if anything, it proves she had very little to do with the collection."

Bad news for Melanie, but good news for Camden. Ashford was going to have to vacate the premises. "Is it worth anything?"

"Maybe to a collector of folk music." He kept searching through the pages. "Is this all? I mean, he didn't have another notebook?"

"This is it. Were you looking for something else?"

He couldn't keep the disappointment from his voice. "Well, there's always the chance there might be an unpublished gem hidden somewhere." I saw his expression change as he found the place in the cover where Kary had removed "Oh! Susanna," but he didn't say anything. Kary had borrowed some special glue from the college media center and repaired the cover. "Mr. Randall, this is a remarkable find. May I ask what you plan to do with it?"

"Well, since it proves Ashford is the real composer of *Patchwork Melodies*, I doubt Melanie Gentry will want to it. I thought about Lassiter's family, but he doesn't have any." At the mention of Lassiter's name, Thomas winced. "Yesterday in Oakville, someone killed Harmon Lassiter. I think they were looking for this notebook."

"Yes, I heard something about that. That's dreadful news."

"And I'm sure you also heard about the murder at the Smithsonian."

"Yes, indeed. A horrible thing."

"Someone killed Horatio's son, Albert Bennett, over a notebook, too. What do you think they're looking for?"

"I'm sure I have no idea," he said. "However, if you'd care to leave Lassiter's notebook with me, I could check it over more thoroughly. Perhaps there's something that's been overlooked." He paused as if coming up with an idea. "Kendal Robertson might like to examine it while he's in town. He's an expert. He might find something I didn't."

"Thanks, but I'd better keep it," I said.

I could tell Thomas did not want to let go of the notebook. "Really, Mr. Randall, it's no problem. I assure you I'll keep it safe."

"Yes, but will you be safe? Three people have been murdered. I don't want you to be the fourth."

He swallowed hard and handed the notebook to me. "I understand. Perhaps, when this is all cleared up, you can bring it back."

"I'll be glad to."

"I assume you'll be calling Melanie Gentry?"

"Yes."

Thomas looked defeated. "Very well."

I was going to call Melanie, but first, I wanted to talk to Byron Ashford, and I wanted to have a look at his tires.

◇◇◇

I'd hoped to get a look at the Corvette before Byron saw me, but he met me at his front door. "What's this all about?"

"Just thought I'd check by and see if you'd changed your mind about working with Melanie Gentry."

"Why should I?"

"You haven't had any contact with her?"

"No."

I didn't think he was going to let me in, but he grudgingly stepped aside. We went into the living room. He didn't offer me a seat.

"I can only spare a few minutes, Mr. Randall. I've got several errands to run. Have you found any proof that Laura wrote anything?"

"Not really."

"So you've just been asking around?"

"Yeah." He was lying, so I joined in. "Nothing so far."

He relaxed somewhat and then jumped all in. "You haven't come across a very old notebook that belongs to some old guy in Oakville named Lassiter, have you? I think some of my great-grandfather's original handwritten notation is in that book. If Melanie Gentry gets her hands on it, she'll destroy it."

"Why would she do that?"

"Because she's a nut. I wish I had it. It would settle this non-sense about authorship once and for all. You haven't unearthed it, have you? The old geezer says he won't sell it to an Ashford."

"You've talked to him recently?"

"No, some time ago. He said it contained just his songs, but you never know."

If, as Melanie intimated, Byron killed Lassiter for the note-book, it wasn't in Lassiter's house. Now Byron was fishing for clues to its whereabouts.

"I'll talk to Melanie," I said. "Maybe I can find out something about this notebook. Why didn't you mention it before?"

"You're working for Melanie Gentry. Why should I help?"

"But if I find this notebook, you want it."

"Damn right I do."

"You haven't been out to the mountains lately, have you? Maybe take the Corvette for a spin?"

He frowned as if I'd said something in a foreign language. "What?"

"Your great-grandfather used to visit a fellow musician at his mountain home, Tranquil Breeze. Thought you might have been curious to see it."

His eyes narrowed. "No. I've never heard of any place like that."

"Just asking. You have a terrific car, by the way."

As I'd hoped, he was so proud of the Corvette, he didn't mind showing it off. While he bragged about aluminum cylinder heads and compression ratios, I wandered around the car, making admiring noises. Unfortunately, the tires were clean, with no convenient pieces of dried mud that could be compared with the dirt at the cabin, but I could bet money the tread matched what I'd seen at Tranquil Breeze.

I opened the driver's door. "Don't suppose you'd let me take her for a spin?"

"No way I'm letting you drive this car."

"I'll sit and dream, then."

He laughed. "You'll never be able to afford one of these, that's for sure."

I slid behind the wheel and pretended to admire the interior, all the while hoping to spot some clue he'd been at Lassiter's house. But except for some white shirts and a pair of tan slacks folded neatly on the passenger's seat, Byron kept his treasured car spotless.

I wanted a closer look at these clothes. "Where's the hood release? I'd like to see the engine."

For a few moments while the hood was up, I glanced through the clothes. No blood stains. No rips or tears. Nothing in the pockets of the slacks. But down in the cuff of one leg, I felt a very thin slip of paper. I curled the paper in my hand as I exited the car. I spent another twenty minutes learning more about Corvette engines than I ever wanted to know. After thanking Byron for his time, I drove to the nearest gas station and examined my treasure. Well, I'd been having pretty good luck with little pieces of paper. This one was no exception. It was a mailing label from a magazine, and not just any magazine. A *National Geographic* magazine, mailed to Harmon Lassiter, 1045 Evenway Avenue, Oakville, NC.

I put the label in the Fury's glove compartment. Now what? Take the label to Jordan? Confront Byron? I decided to bag it and save it. It might come in handy.

Chapter Twenty-four
"The Sinful Maiden"

I kept hoping Ashford would get tired and bored and leave on his own, but he still put in appearances. This time I was ready for him. I looked through the house for Camden and couldn't find him. Then I knew he was Ashford when I found him in my car, frowning at the controls and testing the steering wheel. Camden doesn't drive.

I leaned in the open window. "Ashford, what the hell are you doing?"

He glared at me. "Learning how to operate your automobile. It's a bit more complicated than my machine, but not beyond the scope of my understanding."

"And why do you need my automobile?"

"I intend to go to my great-grandson and tell him the truth."

"I got your truth. Get out of the car."

Reluctantly, he followed me to the porch. I handed him the notebook. "Here's your proof, now scram."

He turned the pages, his face pensive. "Yes, this is my writing. This is the original version of 'Two Hearts Singing.'" He looked up from his reading. "I want to see Byron."

"No," I said. "That's impossible. He'll never believe you're his great-grandfather."

"Are you planning to give Byron this notebook? Will he turn it over to the proper authorities? How can I be sure this won't fall into the wrong hands?"

"It's in my hands. I'm the good guy, remember? I'll take care of everything. You get out of Camden like you said you would."

I didn't like the look Ashford had in Camden's eyes, that cold calculating glitter. "I wish to speak to my great-grandson. I want to be sure this information is in the hands of an Ashford. Then I'll go."

Byron Ashford would never believe the spirit of his dark domineering relative was in a fair slight man who favored sloppy clothes. "No. You keep adding demands, and this notebook's confetti. You wanted proof. Here's the proof. Now get lost. I want to talk to Camden."

In a moment, Camden's face relaxed. "I'm here."

"It's about time." I put the notebook back in the trunk of the Fury and slammed it shut. I came back to the porch. "Are you going back to the festival today?"

"In a little while."

"Okay. I've just about solved this case, so that should be the last of Ashford. The songs are his." He nodded. "You all right?" He looked odd, but then, Ashford bouncing in and out couldn't have been comfortable. "Come inside and get a Pop-Tart. As soon as I talk to Melanie, I'll give you a lift downtown."

"Okay," he said.

I went into the office to call Melanie Gentry, but first, I sat down at my desk to think.

Melanie Gentry and Byron Ashford. Each one wanted the notebook, but couldn't get it. Suppose they knew about the connection to Stephen Foster and the possibility of another copy of the first edition of "Oh! Susanna." Suppose they were working together, and this feud of theirs was all for show. Suppose they said, Bennett's notebook didn't have what we wanted. Lassiter won't give his notebook to either of us. Let's get someone else to find the notebook for us. Even if they hated each other, they still might work together to achieve a common goal, especially if it involved a large sum of money, just like Tommy and Annie with their jewelry booth.

But there was someone else in this equation, someone who might not have needed money, but needed a big discovery to save his job: Tate Thomas. Being a music expert, he must have known about a possible copy of "Oh! Susanna." When Melanie Gentry came to him with her complaints about Ashford, he must have known the connection to Bennett and then to Foster. Find the notebooks, he would've told her. Hire someone who'll have no idea of their worth. If there's anything by Foster, let me have the discovery, and you can have any money a collector might pay. But Byron Ashford wanted in, too. He had debts to pay. So Byron took his private jet to Washington and was playing in the old sheet music when he was surprised by a director and had to kill him. Then he went after Lassiter.

Did Thomas know these people were on a murderous spree? Or had he planned the whole thing?

No, wait. There was something else. I overheard Melanie say she had the goods on Byron, and then she said, "too." She said, "If you're not careful, I'm going straight to the police." When she was in the woods, what if she saw the murderer leave Albert Bennett's house and was now blackmailing this person? And who would that be? Why not Bennett's old colleague, Tate Thomas? Thomas desperately needed a discovery to save his job and to assure him a place in the documentary. What if his old buddy refused to show him Horatio's notebook, and Thomas took it by force?

Time to find out.

Melanie Gentry answered the phone on the second ring. "Mister Randall, I hope you have good news for me."

"That depends," I said. "I hope you have a few answers for me. Did you know Harmon Lassiter had been murdered?"

I heard her suck in her breath. Pretty dramatic and possibly rehearsed. She knew Lassiter was dead. "Murdered?"

"I'm wondering if someone was after his notebook."

Another gasp. "You're not suggesting—"

"I'm just thinking out loud."

She immediately gave up Byron. "Byron Ashford would do anything to keep me from getting that notebook. You need to talk to him."

"I will."

"What about the notebook? You still have it, don't you? Is it safe? Where is it?"

Now, how did she know I had it? Thomas must have called her right after I left. "It's safe. I'm sorry, but it proves Ashford wrote the songs, not Laura."

Silence. Then she said, "Oh. Well, I'd still like to see it."

"I'd be glad for you to see it, but I think it ought to go to Lassiter's family."

Another long silence. "I suppose that's best. Where is it now?"

I knew Melanie and Byron were working together. Did I want either one of them to ransack 302 Grace or show up on the doorstep with murderous intent? "Why don't we meet at the college?" I said. Nice safe neutral territory. I'll call Jordan and have him standing by. "Thomas' office? Say, in about an hour?"

She agreed. The minute she hung up, I heard a noise. A car noise. Had someone driven up? I looked out my window. No, someone had driven out. The Fury was gone.

God! I leaped up and ran outside. Damn it to hell! I should have realized something was up when Ashford gave in too easily. The sneaky bastard had pretended to be Camden, had taken my spare key off the kitchen board, and was speeding toward Byron Ashford's with the notebook in the trunk.

Don't panic, I told myself. He doesn't know the way to Byron's, does he? He'll have to stop and ask someone. There's a chance I can still catch him.

Catch him with what? Everyone else was at the festival. I took out my phone to call a cab when Ellin drove up. Perfect!

"Lend me your car!"

"I will not," she said. "What the hell is this?"

"Ashford's run off with Camden. He's heading for Byron's. Move over!"

"No! You get in."

I ran around and hopped in the passenger's seat. No telling what Byron Ashford would think when Camden burst in.

Ellin gripped the steering wheel. "This is just great. I thought about what you said and came back to talk to him. Why weren't you watching him?"

"I thought Camden was back." She started down Willow. "Don't go this way. You'll run into all the festival traffic."

"Don't tell me how to drive. I'm going to cross over Food Row at the bakery and take the service road."

"That'll take too long."

"Well, I'm not going through town."

"You can cut across the Super Food parking lot and get to Twenty-Four."

"That's illegal!"

"Damn it, will you quit arguing? There's no telling what Byron will do."

We argued all the way to Lesser Lake. We parked and got out at Byron Ashford's house where the front door was open. Not a good sign. I entered cautiously, keeping Ellin behind me.

"Ashford? Anybody home?"

Silence. Then a moaning sound.

I followed the sound to the living room and found Byron Ashford trying to sit up. He clutched his head and groaned. "Double-crossing bitch."

I helped him sit up. "Where is she? Was anyone with her?"

He winced. Blood seeped through his fingers. "Some crazy little guy waving a notebook and saying something about being my great-grandfather."

"Where are they?"

He tried to focus. "The pier, I think. What the hell's going on?"

"I'll tell you later. See what you can do to help him," I told Ellin, who was peering around me. "But don't let him leave. Call Jordan."

I ran out to the pier. Melanie Gentry was untying the rope that held the speedboat to a piling. I didn't see Camden. Good God, had she already tossed him overboard?

"Hi," I said.

She turned, startled. I don't know how I could have ever thought this woman was attractive. She gave me a look Medusa would have envied. I strolled a little closer and caught a glimpse of Camden's limp body lying in the boat.

Now Melanie's expression was smug. "You had the notebook all along, didn't you?" She gestured toward Camden. "He got it out of your car to show Byron, and now it's mine."

"Okay, so you have the notebook. Find what you were looking for?"

"No, but I'm sure it's in there."

"Would 'it' be a little number called 'Oh! Susanna'?"

Her smug look vanished. "How do you know about that?"

"Because I have it. Did you have to kill two people to get it?"

This didn't rattle her. "I haven't killed anyone."

"But you know who did."

"Maybe I do."

"Well, I do, too." I moved closer. "You work at the college. You knew Thomas and Albert Bennett were acquainted, might have even heard them arguing. People get touchy about important discoveries over there, don't they? Thomas thought there was something in Albert's father's notebook, but when Albert refused to let him look at it, I think there was an altercation. I think you saw Thomas kill Albert. The notebook didn't have what he wanted, so he left it on the lawn."

"I had nothing to do with that."

"Well, you left a couple of clues behind. For one thing, your pig is missing an eye."

She gaped at me. I pointed to her sweater. "That one right there. I found it in the bushes at Albert Bennett's house. You were waiting for Thomas, weren't you? You saw what happened and now you're blackmailing him."

"That's ridiculous."

"Then why did you tell him, 'If you're not careful, I'm going straight to the police'?"

She didn't answer.

"All this noise about hating Byron Ashford. Why did you go with him to Tranquil Breeze? Didn't know it had burned down, did you? Did you go with him to Lassiter's house, too?"

"You should be talking to Byron Ashford, not accusing me."

"Fine. Let me get Camden out of your way, and you can come with me. The police would love to hear your side of this story."

Her expression hardened. "Oh, no. I'm getting rid of Ashford."

"That's going to be a little difficult. He's dead."

"No, no, he's come back. He drowned Laura, and I'm going to drown him. Byron and Thomas will go to jail, and the notebook will belong to me."

"It's useless. It's just Ashford's work."

"I don't believe you." She got into the boat and started the motor. Camden hadn't moved. I could see blood in his pale hair and more blood on one of the oars.

I tried to reason with Melanie. "Listen to me. That's not Ashford and you know it. You can't kill an innocent man, not over some stupid morbid folk songs! Give it up!"

"The notebook's mine!"

"Okay, okay! You can have it. Just back away. Let me take Camden with me, and you can have anything you want." Including an all-expense paid trip to the loony bin.

She shook her head and gunned the motor. As the boat dug into the water and zoomed away from the pier, I ran and made a flying leap. I missed the boat, but grabbed hold of the rope and hung on. When she looked back and saw me doing my ski-less act, I thought she'd speed up to get rid of me, but the boat spluttered to a stop. As I swam for the boat, I saw that Camden had recovered and yanked out the key. She was grappling with him, trying to wrench the key from his hands. He managed to pull her arm behind her, and the boat rocked violently as she tried to shake him off.

I reached the boat and heaved myself over the side just as she elbowed Camden in the stomach and he went down with a groan. Melanie flung herself at me, fingernails out like talons.

My heavy wet clothes slowed me down, but the tilting slippery deck saved me from being shredded by her claws. I fell with a thud and crashed into the side of the boat. Just as I slid to the other side, I felt the rope tug around my neck. Melanie's insane anger gave her a strength I would not have believed. I tried to wedge my fingers under the rope, thinking the next slide across the deck would be my last, when Camden jumped on Melanie's back and both of them fell backward. Melanie took advantage of this to roll him overboard. He immediately sank, then struggled to the surface, gasping. From somewhere on the shore, I heard Ellin shriek.

"Cam!"

I jumped down into the dark water. Above me, the boat roared to life. I managed to snag Camden's arm before the water churned in a furious storm of bubbles, and I realized Melanie was going to do her best to run us over.

Minnesota is the Land of Ten Thousand Lakes, and I've been in most of them, a strong swimmer enjoying the water, although this water was damn cold. Camden's never even been in a wading pool, much less dark icy Lesser Lake. I knew he wouldn't like it, but the only way to avoid getting minced was to go deeper. I grasped the soggy folds of his shirt and yanked him down as the boat zigzagged above us. Then I hauled him up to the surface for a quick breath.

"Take it easy. I've got you. We have to go back under."

He was panicked and exhausted, but the boat was heading right for us. I plunged back under, tugging Camden with me. By now, I was exhausted, too. How many more passes would Melanie attempt? The next time we surfaced, however, she must have decided we could drown on our own. The boat careened around the corner, leaving a series of waves that jostled and slapped at us. Camden didn't crawl on top of me the way drowning victims often do. He passed out, which made it easier to haul him in. It was a long way to the shore where Ellin jumped up and down, still shrieking, but I made it. She kicked off her shoes and waded into the shallows to help drag Camden up onto the grass where I pushed on his chest and she breathed in his mouth until he coughed up a couple of gallons and decided to live.

I sat back, trembling. Melanie Gentry had disappeared around the corner of the lake. Ellin cradled Camden in her lap, stroking his forehead and making odd little croaking sounds. It took me a moment to realize she was crying.

"It's okay," I said. "He's going to be all right."

It wouldn't have surprised me if she'd said, "But what about my show?" She didn't. She held him tighter and started hiccupping.

I staggered to my feet, my clothes clinging to me like cold wet plastic wrap. "Come on. We need to get inside."

With one stop to rest, I was able to carry Camden up to Byron's house. I put him on the sofa while Ellin hunted for some blankets. She tossed me one, and I tied it around my shoulders. It was brown and very warm. I hoped it was expensive. Then I helped Ellin peel of Camden's wet shirt. His head was still bleeding from where Melanie had smacked him with the oar.

"Too bad he's not awake," I said as she struggled with his pants. "He'd be thrilled."

She was still snorting up tears. "Shut up."

"You've never seen him naked, have you? You should be thrilled, too."

Her eyes blazed. "Damn you, Randall. This isn't funny."

No, but it was a whole lot better than the pale sobbing Ellin. I had her back up to speed, so I backed off. Byron Ashford was conscious, but he was a pale green color. Ellin had already called nine-one-one, covered him up, and put a cushion under his feet.

I dried myself with the blanket. "Okay, Byron, now's the time to tell your story. Make it quick."

He managed a glare. "I don't have to say anything to you."

I turned to Ellin. "I'm going after Melanie. Did you call Jordan?"

"He's on his way. Going after her? With what?"

"The Fury."

"But she could be across the state line by now."

"Ellin, Lesser Lake's not that big. She's going to have to pull up at the marina, and guess how many people are there today on festival weekend?"

Ellin's smile was grim and satisfied. "About a thousand."

"At least." I ran out.

Sure enough, the Lesser Lake Marina was crammed with boats of all sizes, the parking lot full of trucks, cars, RVs, and campers. I left the Fury on the side of the highway and searched, ignoring the curious stares at my wet, wrinkled clothes. Unless she'd had the foresight to leave a vehicle here, Melanie would have to park Byron's boat and steal a car to make her getaway. Otherwise, she'd have to turn around and go back to his house, where she'd run right into Jordan and/or Ellin, and she'd never make it out alive.

I scanned the crowd and the array of boats, but didn't see her. Sailboats skimmed the water. Pontoon boats drifted, music and laughter echoing across the lake. Off to one side, children splashed in paddleboats. I walked out on one of the piers. All the slips were filled. Had she managed to get here first, find a parking place, and get away?

Then Byron's boat came around the corner, slowly and carefully, as if Melanie were looking for a place to pull in without calling any attention to herself. I ducked down behind the boats and waited until she was closer.

Journey by water, the Tarot cards had said, and I wanted to prove those little pieces of cardboard right. The minute two kids exited their paddleboat, I jumped in, scooted down in the seat, and paddled for Byron Ashford's speedboat. As I'd hoped, there was enough noise and action going on that Melanie ignored a rogue paddleboat as she searched for a landing spot.

By the time I heaved myself into the speedboat, she had time for only one howl of outrage. Then she grabbed a pole with a nasty-looking hook on the end and swung at my head. With no one at the controls, the boat teetered precariously, sprays of water splashing up onto the deck. I dodged Melanie's frantic swings until one caught me on the shoulder, and the hook snagged my shirt. As I fought for balance on the slippery surface, I clutched the hook and gave the pole a quick shove back, catching Melanie in the chest. With a furious cry, she landed on her rear and slid into the steering column. Eight ball in the side pocket. I threw the pole overboard and snatched the notebook from the deck.

Breathing hard, Melanie scrambled to her feet. She looked around for another weapon and found the oar. She held it up like a batter prepared to smack the winning homerun. "Give that back!"

The boat continued to rock and drift away from the dock. I felt like a lumberjack trying to balance on a log, but I managed to hold the notebook high. "You don't deserve it."

"Give it to me!"

As she swung furiously, I ducked under the oar and tried to snag her foot, but my feet slid out from under me. She brought the oar down with a crash, narrowly missing my head. I rolled over, regained my balance, and dangled the notebook over the edge of the boat.

She halted, panting. "You wouldn't dare!"

"Try me."

She threw down the oar and jumped for the notebook, but the rocking boat and her uneven footing caused her to seriously miscalculate the distance. She sailed by me and windmilled over the side. I tossed the notebook down on the deck, turned off the motor, leaned over, and reached for her.

"Melanie! Give me your hand."

She sank, came up gasping, her hair slicked over her face. "No."

"This is stupid. Come on."

She went down and splashed up again. "No. You're right. I don't deserve it. I did everything wrong. I'm going to drown, just like Laura."

She wanted to make a grand gesture, but this crazy woman had tried to kill me and Camden, and I'd had enough of her theatrics. I jumped in and dragged her out. Why should she get out the easy way when she'd caused me so much trouble?

She sat and sobbed in a puddle as I drove the speedboat to the dock where a crowd had gathered to watch the drama, including two policemen. I happily mentioned Jordan's name and handed a drenched Melanie over to them.

"And could you guys follow me? There's someone else who may need a ride."

◇◇◇

When I came back to Byron's den, Jordan and the paramedics were there. They'd checked Camden and said he was all right. Byron had a concussion, but he still loudly demanded to call his lawyer.

Once again, I wrapped myself up, shivering, and tried to get warm. Ellin had Camden bundled up in blankets and was sitting by him, drying his hair with a hair dryer set on low.

"Did you catch that crazy woman, Randall?"

"Yes, I did, just as the cards foretold."

When the other policemen walked in with Melanie, Byron tried to lunge for her.

"There she is! That's the woman who attacked me!"

She was shaking from cold and anger. "This was all your idea!"

The paramedics had to hold him down. "My idea! You're crazy!"

"Let's work together, you said. Let's share the money, you said. Did I tell you to kill people?"

"I'm not taking the blame for this!"

Tommy Fairbanks and Annie Blum could've taken lessons. Jordan stood listening, his mouth quirked in a wry smile.

"I never told you to kill anyone, Byron."

"I didn't kill anyone!"

"Ashford knew all about it. He knew you killed Albert Bennett and Harmon Lassiter."

Byron lay back, fists clenched. "That is not my great-grand-father, you delusional idiot. Can't you see this was all a trick? Shut up! Nobody has any proof of anything."

"Oh, I don't know about that," I said.

Jordan glanced at me. "Care to enlighten us?"

"I found an address label from one of Lassiter's magazines in Byron's pants."

Byron stared. "What the hell are you talking about?"

"Right before you took those clothes to the cleaners. I'm guessing that was one of those errands you had to run, just to make sure there weren't any traces of your visit to Oakdale. But those little labels were flying everywhere, weren't they, especially if Lassiter was fighting for his life. You probably had to scrape them off your shoes, clean them out of your car. But you missed one."

Jordan's eyes narrowed. "Do you actually have this label, Randall?"

"I bagged it for you. His fingerprints might be on it, but I'm guessing you can find more evidence at Lassiter's house, if you don't mind checking through all the magazines."

Gray-faced, Byron Ashford looked from my face to Jordan's. "I want my lawyer."

Jordan motioned to the officers. "Take Mister Ashford in and make sure he's all right. Let him call his lawyer. I'll be by to talk with both of them later. And take Ms. Gentry in, too."

Still arguing, Byron and Melanie were escorted out by the policemen. Jordan turned to me. "I'll want to talk to you, too."

"There's someone else you need to talk to first."

◇◇◇

This time I ignored the secretary and went right on in to Thomas' office. He looked up from the papers on his desk. His eyes widened at the sight of Jordan.

"Mr. Randall? What's this?"

"I think you know. It has to do with 'Oh! Susanna' and a certain notebook."

For a moment, he brightened. "It was actually in that notebook? You found it?"

"There's a piece of it, yes."

Then he sat back. His shoulders slumped. "How did you find out?"

"Here's what I think happened. You can fill in the blanks. When Melanie Gentry approached you about finding proof Laura wrote the songs in *Patchwork Melodies*, you started thinking about Ashford and Horatio Bennett and the possible connection to Stephen Foster. I think you made a deal with Melanie. Find the notebook and I'll make sure you get your proof. Just bring the notebook to me. But Albert Bennett's notebook didn't have what you wanted, so Melanie hired me. You knew Lassiter's family had known Ashford's, and that he had a notebook, but he refused to let Melanie or Bryon see it. You figured, correctly, that he might lend it to a third uninterested party. You're a music scholar, so you knew Horatio had lived in New York the same time as Foster, so Foster's music could be in that notebook, and you desperately needed some kind of major find to save your job and your reputation. The PBS documentary was going to be your way to fame and fortune."

Thomas put his hand over his eyes and stayed silent.

"You quarreled with Albert, didn't you? Maybe pushed him? Didn't mean to kill him. But Melanie saw what happened. She threatened to go to the police unless you shared any money you might get from the sale of 'Oh! Susanna'—if it was in the notebook."

"I knew it was." Thomas' voice trembled. "It had to be."

"Was all this worth it?"

He kept his head down. "I didn't mean to push him that hard."

"Mr. Thomas, you don't have to say anything else." Jordan read him the rest of his rights.

Chapter Twenty-Five
"Two Hearts Singing"

When I got back, Ellin was furious. "What was she trying to do? This isn't Ashford. It's Cam."

"Glad you can tell the difference." Byron had all sorts of electronic gadgets in his kitchen, including a fancy coffeemaker. I brought one cup to Ellin, who set it on the table. I sat down in a chair, my hands around the other cup. "How's he doing?"

"I don't think he got too cold," she said. "He's breathing all right, and I didn't see any other injuries."

I leaned back in the chair. I was finally getting warm, myself. Thank God for mild October weather. If Melanie had dunked us in January, we'd be popsicles by now.

"The paramedics said he'll be okay. He was awake a while ago and knew what day it was."

"We'll camp here for a while, then."

She was uncertain. "Randall, take a good look and tell me what's going on. Is Ashford back?"

I peered into Camden's eyes and saw what she was talking about: he wasn't there. "I don't know what's happened. Camden? Are you in there? Ashford, for God's sake, let go."

But Ashford wasn't there, either. Something had gone wrong. Maybe the shock of the water, or the constant leeching of his personality, or Ashford's realization that Laura's great-granddaughter could be capable of such violence. Camden seemed lost in some distant limbo land.

Ellin grasped his hand. "Cam? Come back. Come on now, don't do this."

But she wasn't getting through. I hoped to God it had something to do with his sense of identity, because I was going in with the only ammunition I had.

"Camden," I said. "I know you're in there. Listen to me. I've got important news. I found your mother. Her name is Denise. She lives in Richmond."

No reaction. Better step up the pace.

"She's about forty-five, real attractive, dark curly hair and dark eyes. She says you look exactly like your father. His name is Martin. She's married, so you've got three half-sisters. Well, actually, you've got four, because there's a woman named Daisy in Bell City who wants to see you. And get this: your mom's a singer like you. Must be where you got your voice."

Nothing. Well, maybe I was on the wrong channel. I closed my eyes, concentrated, and repeated everything mentally. Then I added what I hoped would be the trump card. *I found out something else. Your name isn't John. It's Michael. That's what your real mother named you. So Michael, damn it, listen to me! You aren't Ashford. You don't need him. You aren't John. You're Michael.*

When I opened my eyes, Ellin was staring at me. "What were you doing?" Her voice was fierce.

"It's a little something we do now and then."

This took a few minutes to register. Then the heat went up a thousand degrees. "Are you trying to tell me you're psychic?"

"I'm not telling you anything. Sometimes when Camden sends a message, I pick it up."

"You're lying. You're just saying this to provoke me."

"Everything I say provokes you. This is the truth. Camden and I have a link, an open channel, a two-way brain connection, whatever you want to call it, and I was hoping to get through to him."

"I don't believe this."

"Sad but true."

She shook her head in despair. "You, of all people!"

"Yes, me. I'm not too happy about it, either, but if it'll help Camden, I'll try it, so if you'll excuse me—"

"Oh, no you don't." She'd reached her limit. We were about to witness an explosion. "You and the rest of the world may be psychic as hell, but you can't do *this*."

She took Camden in her arms and gave him a long passionate kiss. Then another. Then a couple more. It must have been the first time she really gave in to her feelings for him, and Camden began to respond with equal fervor. It was like watching two semis loaded with dynamite crash head-on inside a volcano. Impressive.

"You're right," I said, though she was beyond hearing. "I can't do that. I'll only take friendship so far."

Neither of them heard me. Ellin had her hands in Camden's hair and he had a firm grip around her waist and they were kissing over and around every place they could reach and a few they couldn't. When they came up for air, they looked glazed and happy.

"Don't mind me," I waved. "Carry on."

◇◇◇

Since he wasn't using the house, we spent the night at Byron's. I found a very comfortable bedroom down the hall, and the kids slept on the sofa, although from all the noises, I don't think they slept much. In the morning, I found them all rolled up together, Ellin on top, sound asleep. Camden woke when I shuffled in with more coffee.

"What the hell happened?" he wanted to know. "I was sinking in cold black water, and then—" he indicated Ellin asleep in his arms "—this. Not that I'm complaining."

"Melanie Gentry decided she'd had enough of Ashford."

"Is Ellie okay?"

"Overwhelmed by your manly physique."

"Damn." He sighed. "A golden opportunity to impress her, and I've been in a freezing lake."

"I don't think that was a problem."

For the first time, Camden realized he and Ellin were pajama-less. Ellin murmured contentedly and snuggled closer. He stroked her hair. "That part wasn't a dream?"

"We should all have such dreams."

Ellin opened her eyes and gazed up at him with truly sickening adoration. "I love you so much."

Camden and I were both struck dumb. He recovered first. They were fairly well occupied for the next twenty minutes. I made some waffles and watched TV in the kitchen. Then it was time to head for home.

Camden slept in the car. Ellin used this opportunity to attack. "You didn't really find Cam's mother, did you?"

"Of course I did," I said. "You think I made all that up? Camden knows the truth when he hears it, and it pulled him back from wherever he was."

"Oh, so now you're going to take all the credit, is that it?"

"You think a couple of sloppy kisses did the trick? Think again, Miss Sex Machine."

We argued all the way home. I enjoyed it. She was still chewing me out when I parked the car and kept on even when Camden got out and went into the house. I'm sure almost drowning wasn't nearly as bad as having to listen to the two of us.

"All that crap about having a link between your brains! You were just trying to goad me."

I finally gave up trying to convince her. I doubt I'd made any difference, anyway. If she wanted to believe all that high-powered lip action sucked him back from the abyss, who was I to argue?

"Okay, okay, so I'm lying. Maybe you needed a little push to declare yourself. Don't I at least get credit for that?"

"I was going to, anyway."

"Well, you sure took your time."

She got out of the car and slammed the door, sending the birds from the feeder in a flurry of wings—and in that instant, I knew what had happened to Pamela Vincent's locket.

◇◇◇

Pamela met me at the front door of her house. A new gold heart-shaped locket rested in the hollow of her creamy throat.

"You sounded so mysterious over the phone, David. What's going on?"

"I've figured it out," I said. "Can we take a walk?"

We crossed the back lawn and walked a short way into the surrounding woods until I heard the crows. It had been a while since I climbed a tree, but the nest wasn't very high. Amid the jumble of leaves, feathers, string, and a foil wrapper from a stick of gum, there was a gold heart-shaped locket. I handed it down to Pamela. She gave a cry of delight.

"How did you know?"

I hopped down and brushed off my clothes. "Well, my guess is one of the crows peeked in and decided he liked that shiny object. The screen was off, so all he had to do was reach in the open window and pick it up. He couldn't have flown far. The locket's too heavy."

We walked back across the lawn. "Nick will be so pleased," she said. "And relieved."

"Can't blame this one on him."

She put the locket around her neck and fastened the clasp. "Now I have two hearts." Her beautiful face glowed. "But this is my favorite. Thank you so much."

"You're welcome."

She rearranged the chains of the two necklaces. "*Two Hearts Entwined.* That would make a nice title, wouldn't it? Or *Two Hearts Forever.*"

"*Two Hearts Singing.*"

"Why, that's lovely."

"It's not original."

"It makes a nice story." She smiled, her hand over the two hearts. "A story with a happy ending."

At least one of these stories had a happy ending.

"What if I find the answer and you don't like it?" I'd asked Melanie Gentry. She'd ended up under water and into jail.

"Do you have anything of Camden's?" I'd asked Denise Wellborn.

"That part of my life is over," she'd replied.

And "Is that what you want?" I'd asked Kary when Donnie offered her a ring and a new life, a life far away from the holier-than-thou parents she still loved?

Kary, repairing the lace on her gown, slowly stitching her life back together. "Once I get a good job, I'm going to adopt a baby. I really want a family."

How could this be a happy ending for me?

◇◇◇

Camden was pretty well blissed out. I found him on the porch swing the next morning, working his way through a carton of Bryer's All Natural Vanilla and humming something cheerful. I sat down in a rocking chair and told him to hand it over.

"I've got an idea about that copy of 'Oh! Susanna,'" I said. "Why not let Ellin present it to Kendal Robertson? That'll make them both happy. All these murders connected with the folk songs will give that documentary an exciting edge and maybe some extra screen time for Ellin."

"That's a great idea. Thanks."

"Just trying to keep the peace."

"Is it still in its hiding place?"

"Still in volume 'D.'"

"'Dear hearts and gentle friends.'"

"That's the one."

We ate in silence for a while, and then he said, "She doesn't want to see me, does she?"

I knew he wasn't talking about Ellin. He was talking about his mother. I handed the carton back to him. "For what it's worth, she kept your picture."

"My picture?"

"I took that one of you and Kary and Rufus on the porch."

"Hope it shows my good side."

"She said you looked exactly like your father."

"Martin," he said, as if trying out the word.

"That's what she said. I'll keep looking, if you want me to."

He didn't jump on this offer, but he didn't say no, either. "I don't know about that. My mother was just a one-night stand for him."

"Maybe not. You'll have to hear his side of the story."

He stayed quiet for a while and then said, "She didn't give me up because she didn't want me."

"No. She was very young. She knew she couldn't take care of you."

He gazed off into the distance. I wondered if he was able to see the past, too, the young Denise struggling to make this difficult decision, the tiny baby bundled up and brought to the Green Valley Home, maybe one last kiss, one last touch of the baby's hand. "But she cared enough to name me." He came back to the present. "I think we'll meet someday."

I recalled his mother's wistful expression when I told her about Camden's voice. "That's a real possibility."

"And I have four sisters?"

"Three little ones and one big one."

"Daisy."

"She'd like to see you. I can take you to Bell City whenever you're ready."

His slight smile turned into a grin. "Thanks, Dave."

I returned the grin. "My pleasure, Mike."

Then he became serious. "Randall, I'm not going to say everything will be all right, that you can forget your tragedy and get on with your life as if nothing ever happened. I only want to tell you one thing."

"All right." I faced him and those all-knowing eyes. "One thing."

"Try to remember your dream tonight."

My laugh didn't quite work. "Oh, this is good. Now you can predict what people will be dreaming. You're scaring me."

"You've been dreaming it for a long time, but you refuse to see it. Just this once, let go."

"Fine. I'll let go. That doesn't mean I'll dream anything."

"Yes, you will."

"How can you be so damn sure?"

His eyes were clearer than I'd ever seen them. "Because I'm going to make sure it reaches you."

◇◇◇

That night, I had a dream.

There was Lindsey in her Sunday dress, the white one with the ruffles and lace, long white ribbons in her brown curls. She was standing in a field of wildflowers, soft white light glowing around her. Just beyond the field was a playground. I could see other children on the swings and going down the sliding board.

She shook her finger. "Now why didn't you listen to Cam? I have something to tell you. I've been trying and trying."

Because I didn't want to hear it, I answered, but now I do.

My voice didn't actually come out in the dream, but she heard me.

She smiled that sweet innocent smile I thought I'd never see again. "That's good."

What did you want to tell me? I asked, although I knew now in my heart what she was going to say. How could I have been so mistaken? How could I have denied myself this for so long? She was my baby, my daughter. I knew what was coming, and I wanted to hear it.

"There was nothing you could've done, Daddy. It was an accident."

If only I could live that day over. But I broke a promise, Lindsey. I promised to look after you.

"No, you didn't. Look."

The scene appeared, faint and distorted. I saw the car flip and crash. I saw the hillside, thick with smoke. I saw myself frantically searching. Then I saw that same soft white light flow over the wreckage and the vision rippled until I was gazing into Lindsey's eyes. Then she told me something I didn't know.

"You couldn't find me because I was already gone, see? I was in the light."

In the light.

A light that folded around her and carried her to the safety of this place filled with flowers and the laughter of children. A light that radiated from her like the glow of a little star and filled me with a growing sense of peace.

"You would have kept that promise if you could."

Yes. Yes, I would have.

"You did your best, Daddy. I'm all right."

But will I be all right? I miss you so much.

She blew me a kiss. "You'll see me again. I won't be far away."

She waved and skipped across the field toward the playground. The light around her became too bright for me to see.

The dream faded. Lindsey had forgiven me.

I had to find a way to forgive myself.

◇◇◇

It was still a few days till Halloween, but the next evening, we put candles in Buddy's jack o'lanterns and had them grinning out into the night. The neighbors had theirs ready, too, so the whole street gleamed with jagged faces. Rufus, Buddy, Velmer, and Evelene had stopped by for a few minutes with the exciting news that Evelene's dulcimer playing had been just the right touch for the Nasal Frogs, and they'd been invited to play for the Falling Leaves All-Night Pig Picking, the premiere event of the festival.

They were in a hurry, but Evelene ran up the porch steps to give me a kiss on the cheek. "Thanks! This is the best thing that's ever happened to me."

The best thing that's ever happened to me. I'm making other people happy.

Kary had been very quiet all day. Several times I'd caught her looking at me, her expression unreadable. A short while ago, she'd gone out with Donnie for a serious discussion, she'd said. Choosing a date, I thought. Picking out china patterns.

I sat on the porch, listening to Camden sing "Two Hearts Singing" as he washed the supper dishes. I wondered how love could be so screwy. He loved Ellin. God knows why. And I loved Kary enough to let her go.

Early this morning,
Heard my heart singing,
Heard your heart singing,
Answering my own.

A strange car pulled up in the drive. When I saw Kary get out, something jumped in my chest. She waved good-by to the driver and stood for a while, watching the car until it was out of sight. She came up the walk and stopped when she saw me.

"Hi, David."

The little diamond ring was gone.

Come let me love you,
Come be my lady,
Come to my arms, love,
Here is your home.

I could hardly hear her over the singing in my heart. She smiled up at me, her blonde hair shining the jack o'lantern light. I held out my hand. I found my voice.

"Come in," I said.

To receive a free catalog of Poisoned Pen Press titles, please contact us in one of the following ways:

Phone: 1-800-421-3976
Facsimile: 1-480-949-1707
Email: info@poisonedpenpress.com
Website: www.poisonedpenpress.com

Poisoned Pen Press
6962 E. First Ave. Ste. 103
Scottsdale, AZ 85251